High Tide at Harvest Moon

By: Taryn Blackthorne

High Tide at Harvest Moon

Copyright © 2016

Taryn Blackthorne

www.tarynblackthorne.com

Cover design by Erica Petit Illustration

http://andromnesia.com

Blackthorne
Publishing

Published by Blackthorne Publishing

ISBN: (ebook) 978-0-9949382-1-3 (print) 978-0-9949382-0-6

PUBLISHER'S NOTE

This is a work of fiction. Names, characters, places, and incidents are either the product of the author's imagination or are used fictitiously, and any resemblance to actual persons, living or dead, business establishments, events, or locales is entirely coincidental.

This book is dedicated to who have the strength, dedication and perseverance to become what they dream.

Dream well.

Author's Note

Acadia University is a university in Wolfville, Nova Scotia, Canada. It is known world-wide for its long history and high academic standards. Though I am a graduate of its Arts and Education programs, I am not affiliated with the University in any way, and any inaccuracies are entirely my own. Although Acadia's teaching and hiring practices have changed over the years, I have altered some details of University policies to suit the needs of my plot.

Acknowledgements

Every writer I know will tell you, without help and support, there's no way a book can be completed. This book is no different. I would first and foremost like to thank my parents, who's support and love are indispensable. My brother, Rutger, deserves mention for scribbling questions on my notes and walking away. It was maddening and necessary for these characters to find their road home. My editors, Donna Alward and Nancy Cassidy, for their love, support, butt kicks when I hid in my cave and gentle hand movements when talking me off the ledge of 'I-can't-do-this' during pep talks. Without them, this book would still be hidden in a notebook in the bottom of my desk. Finally, a shout out to my writer peeps, Michelle Helliwell, Nicola R. White, Kelly Boyce, Julia Phillips Smith, and everyone else in RWAC. Your friendship, advice and write ins have been instrumental. And you all share my tea addiction. Bless you.

CHAPTER ONE

The guy in Lexi Coolen's front seat smelled like the inside of a rum barrel. She grimaced at her roommate, Tiffany, slouched in the back of her car. Tiff didn't smell much better.

Acadia students filled Harbourside Street this Friday night. Well, Lexi amended as she glanced at the dashboard clock, Saturday morning. She was grumpy. And the crowds were giving her a headache. Didn't these people have work? Then again, Lexi was a grad student, not a freshman. One with a few years of real-world work under her belt as well. Tiffany's call had dragged her out of bed.

Tiffany belched and the interior of Lexi's old Camry now smelled of sour hops. Ugh. Welcome to the weekend in a university town. Ah well, at least this boyfriend had called Lexi for a ride. Lexi considered how to explain—again—the no-overnight guests at her home rule when Tiffany solved the problem for her.

"Can you take Kerr home, too? Please, Lexi?" Tiffany begged. At least that's what Lexi thought she said. The slurring made it difficult to tell. Lexi grimaced at Kerr, the town tomcat. She didn't know him personally, just *of* him. Her best friend Hannah had mentioned his reputation several times. She wrinkled her nose. Kerr MacDonald had a penchant for loving and leaving half the frosh population in town. Dumping him out onto the sidewalk sounded like a good idea, but she doubted Tiff would let her. Her gut clenched at the thought of being in a vehicle that long with the man. She tapped the steering wheel. She had two firm rules for her life: no strange men in enclosed areas, and no swearing. She looked at the sleeping form on her front seat. Vulnerable. Snoring. *Crud knuckles.*

"Fine. Where does he live?" Maybe she could get away with dropping him off close to his place. She chewed her lip. If he was drunk enough to be out of it, taking him home might be OK.

Kerr roused from his stupor long enough to look over at Lexi, managed to shake his head once, then landed his noggin back with a thud against the window. "Ladies first."

How gentlemanly. Probably making sure his "woman" was where she was supposed to be. She frowned. That wasn't fair. She didn't really know him. She might find him disreputable, but the women he wooed weekly must find something attractive about him. He couldn't be all bad, could he? He'd called for a ride for Tiffany, hadn't he?

Lexi scowled, annoyed at her own train of thought. She didn't want to think good thoughts about Kerr MacDonald. He'd yelled into the phone, made her fall on the floor as she fought the sheets, half awake, just so he wouldn't have to pay cab fare. She had to be the only woman he'd met whom he'd got *out* of bed. Not that she wanted to get into bed with him. Or anyone else. She was too busy for that sort of thing right now.

"Yeah. Me first. I'm a lady." Tiffany flicked her long blonde hair out of her eyes and slapped Lexi on the back, or she tried. Then reeled. Blanched.

Please don't throw up in my little car.

This was ridiculous. They hadn't even moved off the street yet. Tiffany was the worst roommate she'd ever had. Kerr was Tiffany's problem. Let Tiffany deal with him.

"Oh no. There is only going to be one trip. I'm not taking him by myself, are you nuts?"

"Aww, Lexi," Kerr rolled his head over to look at her and smiled. It was a lady killer grin, meant to weaken knees and drop coed panties. The fact that the man wearing the smile was pushing thirty and her roommate was nineteen didn't seem to bother anyone else. So why did it bother her? At least her annoyance with Kerr gave her immunity to his charms. She rolled her eyes at his attempts to bewitch her. Seriously? Seduction must be his default setting.

She inched the car forward to avoid the swaying and weaving students making their way to the coffee shop on the corner of Main and Harbourside. Honestly? She wasn't even his type. She wasn't tall and willowy like Tiffany. Not that she was short. She just sort of blended in. Except for her boobs, which she cursed every day for being too big. They didn't seem to match the rest of her. She wore her hair long enough to cover them, except tonight she had one auburn braid down her back. She always thought her hair gave her skin some color, but pulled back and combined with her black tank top she'd slept in, she no doubt looked doubly pale.

Then there were her eyes. Not lovely blue, or striking green, but a simple, homespun sort of brown. Not very cute when you put the whole package together. Not that she'd ever had aspirations as a runway model, but being prettier might have made her life a little easier. Someone belched. She frowned at her front seat passenger. Kerr waggled his eyebrows at her and she snorted.

Put aside the fact she didn't like him, there were other things that made taking him to his place a bad idea. Like the fact that the guy outweighed her by about 100 pounds of pure muscle. She wouldn't be able to lift him out of the car. Were there stairs at his place? No way she'd get him up stairs. Neighbors? Would she be seen? She had one master's degree already and was up for an associate professorship. She really didn't want to be put on Kerr's list of recent conquests.

The town busy-bodies were after dirt on her. Their leader, Mrs. Faye, had taken a keen and instant dislike of her when Lexi, having been asked for her honest opinion of the woman's yappy little dog, had given it. Lexi refused to explain why she hated any kind of canine jaws snapping at her to Mrs. Faye, even if the Pomeranian fuzz ball could only reach her ankles. That was a secret she couldn't share with anyone, not if she wanted to live. Reveal it and she put a death sentence on both their heads. She wouldn't put a stranger's life in danger like that. Even one as disagreeable as Mrs. Faye. The results were she had to work doubly hard at keeping her nose and reputation clean.

Kerr lifted his right hand and put it over his heart.

"I promise to be a good boy. Unless you want me to be bad, Professor. And see me after class?" He snorted at his own joke and then he suddenly paled. Lexi froze. *Please don't* you *be sick.* She willed his bile back down his throat and not over her or the front seat. Tiffany-puke was bad enough. She might lose it at Kerr-puke. His eyes flashed and he closed them tightly for a moment. Then two. Lexi tensed, ready for anything. He seemed to settle his predicament and relaxed again. She let out a tiny whoosh of relief.

"Teaching Assistant, and it's to help pay for my degree, you drunkard. Aw, heavens above, you stink. Sit back, I'll get you both to our house, then we'll have to see. OK, Tiffany?"

But Tiffany snored loudly in the back. Lexi sighed. Finally, they'd made it onto Main Street and away from the foot traffic the Wolf's Den Tavern generated over the weekend. The girl was young. Lexi rolled down the windows, unwilling to admit she'd never understood the appeal of getting stupid drunk, even when she'd been nineteen. That had been twelve years and a lifetime ago. Every once in a while she'd hear the voices of the past in her nightmares.

Her head ached from the fumes, her cuts burned.

"Take a drink, you little bitch. Maybe we won't bleed you."

A bottle pushed against her lips, liquid searing a throat raw from screaming. Laughter in the darkness while she sputtered, followed by silence as they readied them-selves. Then it began again. First breath against her skin, then teeth. The punctures sterilized with more vodka.

She shuddered. Back then she'd been stuck in a violent, pain-filled world where nothing made sense, least of all the people closest to her. She'd take this night over any one of those in a heartbeat.

Lexi shook Tiffany awake once they were in the driveway. Even though nobody had thrown up on the trip, she wasn't in a mood to be gentle. It didn't help that everyone but her slumbered. The town cop at the checkpoint by Highland Avenue had waved her through, laughing at her cargo. She didn't recognize the officer's last name, which she hoped meant the man didn't have any connection with Mrs. Faye, but she'd still bet she'd hear about it when she went to get her hair cut next week. Wolfville was a strange place. Every small town had gossips like Mrs. Faye, but there seemed to be great gaps, whole swallows of town that weren't talked about, as if by some mutual agreement. Like pockets of silence in a full room, certain people, places and events just weren't discussed. Lexi shook her head. She'd tried to discern a pattern, so far without any luck. Probably some sort of reaction to being a university town.

With Tiffany now making movement in a positive direction, she walked around the car to work on waking her other passenger. She might have been gentler with him, but only because she was fearful of reprisals. He was already bigger. She didn't want him meaner.

She needn't have worried. Kerr's snore sounded like a snarl, it was so loud, and he woke himself up with it, blinked accusingly at her before settling back to sleep again. Her porch light flickered, and Lexi glanced at the house. Tiffany stumbled at the first step, staggered sideways, and crushed Lexi's prize rosebush. She stifled a sigh. She'd worked all summer on her walkway flower garden, after working all last year on putting in the walkway, porch swing, fixing the deck and the myriad of other house improvements she'd done by herself.

Tiffany giggled at her bleeding hand. Lexi had never seen her so drunk before. She decided to deal with one problem at a time. Just before she reached her, Tiffany fell hard on the stone. Lifting her was difficult. Tiffany's tiny frame was suddenly tantamount to a freight train. Lexi bit her cheek to keep from growling in frustration, thankful the moon was full so she didn't trip on the welcome mat or her potted petunias. She managed to stumble and drag Tiffany into the house, up the refurbished staircase to Tiffany's bathroom where she set the girl up in the tub with a pillow behind her head. Upright and in a place that was easy to clean up. Perfect. Which left the toned and hulking Kerr growling away in her car.

Lexi was tempted to just leave him there till morning. But if he ralphed in her front seat, it was hard to say if she would ever get the smell out. And it was her car, fudge it all. She wasn't just going to give it up. It wasn't much to look at, but it was hers. She stood, hands on hips, debating. He could spend the night on the porch without too much trouble. It wasn't that cold out, despite being the last week of September. She pulled at her lip. Blankets. She'd pile blankets all over him. Did she have enough? Probably not. She frowned. OK, he was a stranger to her, but Tiffany slept with him. Maybe he could stay on the couch. She could lock her bedroom door.

"Kerr? Kerr?" she tapped his face and his fist came dangerously close to her nose, followed by a guttural snarl. Well, that decided things. She wasn't leaving him in her car and he wasn't coming inside her house. She'd have to suck it up and drive him home. Maybe familiar surroundings would get him out of the car where she couldn't.

"Kerr, where do you live? What's your address?"

Kerr groaned and doubled over. She sucked in a breath and wrenched the door open. Tugging on his much larger frame, she managed to get his head over the pavement, not between his legs. His massive hand grabbed her wrist and squeezed. She felt bones grind together and yelped. Kerr groaned again, long and low, like a dog whining. Stupid man. It was his own fault. Still, he was hurting. Lexi hated to see anyone hurting. She rubbed his back with her free hand and brushed her fingers through his silky black hair. With a gentle voice, she whispered to him.

"Kerr, let me take you home. I need to take you home."

Kerr shivered and moaned before answering in a deeper than normal voice, "Not home. Too close. Too close." He whined again.

"Where? Where's too close? Here? You don't want to stay here with us?" Lexi wasn't crazy about giving up the second bathroom in the house, the one she'd claimed. She was not putting him in a bed to throw up all over the place. Another muscle spasm crawled over his frame. His hand squeezed again. If he didn't let go of her wrist she might have no choice. Not to mention, she might not have a wrist in the morning. Willy Wonka on a wombat, his fingers were strong. She tried to extricate herself. Kerr shook his head.

"Alpha," he whispered.

Lexi's blood froze. No. Impossible. She'd left that life. "What?" she croaked.

"Alpha. Please." Kerr finally raised his head. His normally blue eyes were yellow, completely yellow save for the pupil. No whites. Kerr wasn't human, he was a Shifter. And he was shifting.

**

Kerr focused on breathing as he looked up at Lexi. Jocky Grieve had developed a whiskey that would affect Shifters. It held a ridiculous amount of alcohol to cover the taste of the herbal mixture he'd concocted. Shifter metabolisms were super-fast and the herbs slowed it down enough to let the booze hit. It was toxic to humans in larger doses, but it worked. Kerr could drink till he was drunk, smile at the pretty little females the local university attracted. Weave a few steps with them on the dance floor, let them pet him. It fed his wolf's need for touch. Not much conversation was required of a drunk dance, was there? A few kisses, pull 'em in close and nuzzle their ears or neck, sometimes he even got lucky. No morning smooches and a quick getaway were the key. Otherwise you had girls expecting something.

Perfect, right? Well, there was a downside. The biggest drawback to the whole thing was mooncall could hit, hard, and pull you under much faster. Jocky and the rest of the non-human staff had booked the full moon off. Most of the Pack would be at Forbes's already. He'd intended to go out just before moon rise, but Tiffany had let herself into his town apartment. She was a regular dance partner, in and out of the sheets. She'd wanted to play. He'd let her. Afterward, he'd fallen asleep so she'd been poking around his place and uncovered some old photographs of Kerr's brother. And Kerr's brother had had his arm around Clara Rose...

To distract her—and himself—from the discovery, he'd suggested going out to the Wolf's Den. He'd meant to stop after one drink, but she'd kept asking him about the pictures and he kept ordering more drinks to put her off. Pretty soon, he'd lost all sense of time and now he was in trouble. More to the point, two innocent women were in danger. He'd never allow another innocent to be harmed. The monster riding around in him stretched and strained. Another spasm hit him and he closed his eyes as pain crawled over his frame. He had to get loose. Get away. But he was barely holding back the change.

CHAPTER TWO

"Son of a Siberian Sap Sucker!" Lexi cursed and smashed the dash. At least that was her version of swearing. Did the same job without hurting anyone. She'd had the other words hurled at her often enough that she refused to use them against another human being. Some words cut deeper than knives. And they could never be unsaid.

She had enough knife scars that she could compare the two with authority.

Lexi had managed to get Kerr tucked back into the car, lock up her house, and was currently on the highway. She hit the dash again before rummaging in her purse one-handed for her cell.

"Lexieeeeeeeee…" Kerr had curled in on himself, trying to fight off the shift. He rocked back and forth.

"I know, buddy. I know. I'm trying to get you someplace outside of town. If all else fails we can stop on the side of the road. Hang on." Lexi fist-pumped the air when she found the dang phone. She hit speed dial on the number she'd been dodging for months.

"Lexi… You… Danger… I'm going to… Danger," Kerr gasped, trying to warn her. That was sweet. And too freaking late.

"Full moon. You're about to turn furry, fangy and feed on anything that moves? Got it. Now shut up and concentrate on keeping it together." Lexi worked on keeping her heart rate controlled and her panic at bay. Fear stink right now was not a good idea.

"There's another F you forgot," Kerr managed. Her lips quirked, despite her irritation with the Neanderthal. If he could make quips he was forcing it back. She prayed it would give her enough time. The other line kept ringing and ringing. It was the full moon everywhere. But they were four hours behind. It wasn't even dark there. Please, please answer. Beside her, bones snapped and Kerr grunted at the sudden pain. His fingers had claws now.

"Lexi. Your mother is currently with your stepfather." Wessel was her stepfather's second and his voice oozed disapproval through the speaker. She set the phone in its holder and put her hand on Kerr's forehead. She stroked his hair and he seemed to like it, so she kept doing it.

"Tell them to stop screwing and get her on the phone then, Wessel. I need her."

"You'll not take that tone with me, you little bitch." Wessel had never taken her rejection of Mum well.

Kerr barked a warning at the speaker, and then growled. His eyes danced back and forth from human blue to Shifter yellow.

"Lexi?" Wessel's tone had gone hunter-cold.

"Get. My. Mother," she ground out. There was a long pause on the other end and Kerr turned his body to her. He pulled her free hand between his legs. It wasn't sexual, Lexi knew. He was trying to get as much touch as he could to anchor himself. He was practically crawling up her shoulder. Good thing she'd buckled him in.

"Lexi, honey?" Her mother's voice was deceptively sweet, a sure sign she was angry or wanted something, but it had the desired Kerr-reaction, who crooned at the Alpha female's picture on her phone's display. Kerr's eyes settled on blue, though Lexi had the disturbing impression it was his beast that stared out at her, not Kerr. He put his cheek against her bicep.

"Mum. I need the location of the local Alpha and an invite. I've got one of his Pack who's about to go all mooncall in the front seat of my car."

"As a human, that's incredibly irresponsible of you, Lexi."

"No kidding."

The disapproval in her tone stung, as did the reminder of her status in her mother's eyes. Human. Just human. Kerr picked up on her momentary distress and rumbled a warning. Lexi eyed her phone, worried he'd smash it before she could get him to the safety of the Pack. Silence from the phone for over a minute increased her stress. Had she lost the connection?

"Mum?"

"I'm here. Are you touching him?"

"He's got my hand between his legs."

"Well, there's hope for you yet."

"Mum! His pants are on and so are mine."

"How disappointing."

Good old Mum. If she wasn't going to become a Shifter, the least Lexi could do was date one, in Mum's opinion. She doubted her black tank top and fuzzy PJ bottoms were a turn on for the guy. Especially when he was dating a nineteen-year-old. Kerr's tongue darted out and slid up the inside of her elbow. She shivered and squeaked, mostly from terror. Mostly.

"Mum, I'm heading west, outside of Wolfville, on the 101. Focus?"

"Your father is making a call."

"Stepfather. Not my real father. Remember?" She gritted her teeth again. Kerr stopped his explorations of her arm to give her mother another warning growl.

"Is he touching in any other way?" Her mother, wisely, decided to fight that fight another day.

Lexi sighed with momentary relief. Kerr resumed. "He's licking the inside of my arm."

Lexi's mother made a few *ooh* and *ahh* sounds for a minute. Kerr didn't even pause.

"Any change?"

"Nope. Is he trying to find the tastiest spot?"

"No," Kerr said. Then leaned as close as he could get to her ear. "Mine."

Oh sugar-shot salvation. "Mum?"

Her mother's delighted laugh burst out of the speaker and filled the confines of the car.

"Mum!"

"Don't bark at me, young lady. You called here, not the other way around."

"So hang up the phone and refuse to help me. I'm sure Wessel is begging you to do just that and let's face it, you're really good at bailing. I'll deal with the lusty homicidal Shifter on my own. Not like I haven't cleaned up other people's messes before."

"Don't you dare—"

There was a bit of a commotion as the phone was wrestled from her mother. Kerr roared a challenge into her dash at something her mother said but she missed. The car swerved from his sudden motion and her flinching. Lucky for them both he'd released her arm to scream at the phone. It took both hands to right their course. She prayed there weren't any RCMP around to see. Any male of authority except his Alpha would be seen as a threat and that would not turn out well. Lexi counted the seconds, but the rear view stayed clear. Her ears took longer to stop ringing, and by time they had, her mother's mate's voice filled the space, murmuring nonsense as he tried to calm Kerr's snarls.

"Sunny, I'm here now," Lexi told her stepfather.

"Do you have to get your mother all riled up?"

Right. All her fault again. Her mother was such an angel. "What do you want me to say? You know we can't talk to each other since…"

"Apologize to her?"

He had to be joking. "Sunny."

"I know, I know. You two agreed to disagree that you've done anything wrong."

"Sunny!" The yell slipped out. You didn't yell at the Alpha. You kept your tone neutral, no matter how much you hated the man. Or else the beast came out. Sunny had let her live the first time she'd lost her temper. He'd promised there wouldn't be a repeat. Lexi tried not to admit that he and her mother suited each other. Both of them monsters. It would mean her mother had been right to leave her husband of twenty-three years for one of her kind. She couldn't concede that. Just like her mother couldn't acknowledge that decision had led to what had happened to Lexi. Sunny's voice cut into her thoughts before they'd gone too far down that memory lane.

"She misses you, is all. I hate to see her unhappy."

Lexi hated it too. She was her mother after all. "She's the one who gave me the ultimatum, Sunny."

There was a long pause. "Keep heading west. Toward a place called Halifax. Know it?"

It was the capital of the province she was in. Sunny hadn't bothered learning about the place to which his stepdaughter had moved? Why was she not surprised? "Yep."

"Good. I'm still trying to arrange things with the local Alpha."

***

Kerr forced back a growl. His wolf was nearly in charge, and the woman on the other end of the phone had made Lexi upset. His wolf didn't like that; didn't like when the sweet scent of Lexi was marred with distress and old pain. Her skin tasted like honey and he wanted to pull her onto his lap and nip her throat, make her forget all the bad things. Or put his head between those full thighs and use his tongue to take her to heaven. Then thrust into her lushness and take them both there. Hold her. Have her happy and content. He knew how to do that, very well. If only he could convince Lexi to play. The woman's shrewish voice filled the car. He glared at the phone again. If the woman were here, his wolf would be able to challenge her on Lexi's behalf. As it was, the urge to protect Lexi was overwhelming. Kerr fought to keep himself contained. He managed…barely.

The Alpha that had come on next wasn't as bad. He didn't make Lexi's scent turn sour with hurt. But bitter-guilt tinged it for a second. He growled at the phone but the Alpha used his Pack's power, its Argot, to murmur something to him and Kerr's wolf realized that this Alpha had lost Lexi; driven her away, somehow. How stupid. He wouldn't be as foolish. Kerr could hear his wolf's sentiments clearly: *I'm taking her as my mate, and you won't stop* me.

The sharp sting of fear, deliciously tart on prey, but vinegar and acerbic on Lexi, burned his nostrils. She was afraid of him. Both sides of him. He closed his eyes and fought the urge to shift. His wolf was displeased. But Lexi needed that restraint from him right now, more than anything else.

Wolves protected their own.

CHAPTER THREE

"And?" Lexi eyed Kerr with worry and more than a little consternation. His eyes were a reflective yellow and his tongue was lolling out as he panted in the seat beside her.

"They'll meet you at a service road. I don't think those are marked, so you'll have to keep a sharp eye. I've given them your license plate, make and model," Sunny said.

Maybe she hadn't given her stepfather enough credit. She'd bought a Canadian car once she'd crossed the border. He must have been checking up on her somehow. "How did you have all that information on hand to give them?"

A deep sigh. "You're your mother's daughter, you know that?"

"Sunny." She put all the warning into his name that she could. The deal had been no contact at all. Mum had broken that deal a hundred times since Lexi had started school, not that Lexi'd answered her calls or returned the messages. She, at least, was abiding by the rules that Mum's ultimatum had set down. Headlights flashed in her rear view, uncomfortably close. How Shifters could drive with the headlights off at night, Lexi would never understand. The car behind her flashed its lights again. She beeped to acknowledge them. A half a kilometer ahead she saw a dirt road leading off the highway, which she would have missed, had it not been for the two vehicles flanking it, hazard lights on.

"Alpha." Kerr's blissful sigh calmed Lexi. She could drop off her passenger and let the locals handle things. She didn't even need to know their identities.

"They've signaled me. I'm going to drop him off and then head home. Thanks, Sunny."

"Uh, Lexi? It won't exactly be that easy. Be submissive, don't make eye contact, and you should do OK."

Her stomach knotted. "What did you do, Sunny?"

"Nothing. Nothing, Lexi. It's just…they don't know you and now you know about them. They might feel the need to… But I doubt it. Don't do anything that challenges them. Just stay submissive."

Kerr blew out a breath. Lexi agreed. There was something that Sunny wasn't saying. He wasn't lying, because that would have made Kerr hostile, but he was not telling her something important.

"I hate you all over again, Sunny." It was impossible to lie to a Shifter. So she'd never hid her feelings from her mother's husband.

"Lexi," the reprimand in his tone was unmistakable. Kerr growled a warning.

"I'm not one of yours," she snapped and jabbed the end call button. She stopped the car just off the road. The other Shifters were nothing but silhouette faces and jeans as they shielded their sensitive eyes from the headlights. She rolled the window down on both her and Kerr's sides.

"Is the Alpha here?" She kept her eyes on the steering wheel ahead of her.

She heard the shuffling of feet, the crunch of gravel. Kerr tried to nuzzle her and she slapped him away without looking at him. She had expected him to growl at her, but he didn't.

"Babyyyy," he whined.

"Lexi," she insisted. "Where's the freaking Alpha?"

A figure came to stand at the corner of her vision, leaned on her car's roof. She avoided looking at him and any of the other men, including the two who opened her passenger side door and started wrestling Kerr out of the seat. She only knew it was two because she'd seen four hands grab the man who was determined to give her a good-bye kiss.

"I'm the Alpha." A whiskey-voiced mouth dropped into Lexi's view. "My name is—"

"No names. What I don't know about you, I can't tell. Sunny implied you were worried that I might blab. I won't. Trust me, I want as little to do with Shifters as possible."

The man bent down even farther and leaned on the open window sill. Lexi turned her head to face the gear shift. His head came close, in her personal space but not close enough to challenge her. Then he took a deep sniff. He blew out his breath softly against her neck and sniffed delicately this time.

"Disrespecting your former Alpha doesn't endear you to me."

"He's not my Alpha. He's my stepfather." Lexi chomped back on saying anything else. Counted to ten in the three languages she knew.

"You're not claimed?"

"Do I look claimed?"

"Careful." A warning, but no immediate menace. Lexi took hope she'd survive this encounter.

Lexi took a deep breath. "My mother is the Alpha's wife. Her wolf came out, they met; they got married. They mated. Some education on you guys was kinda essential if I wanted any family contact, but I only know bare bones stuff. You exist, you have mooncall, there's an Alpha who rules and you need his permission to breathe."

There was a long pause while he considered her words. "Why aren't you there?"

"I disapproved of the way my mother discarded my father." There was so much more to it than that, but for the most part, that's what Mum would tell any stranger who asked. So that was what she told him. Nothing about her moving in with her mother and stepfather. Nothing about the nightmares in the cellar or the other bumps in the night. Nothing about her father's suspicious death.

"It's the way, sometimes."

"Don't defend her to me." She couldn't stop the snap of her words at his dismissal of the most important man she'd ever known.

"This is your second warning. Officially one more than anyone else has gotten." He seemed almost amused at her cheek. She chewed her lips. This wasn't going the way she had hoped.

Lexi pinched the bridge of her nose. "Sorry, sorry. I just got one of your moon-lusty Shifters out of my car. The adrenaline's made me a little testy."

"Come up to the house."

"I want to go home."

"It wasn't an invitation."

She gripped the steering wheel hard. "Kerr got a nineteen-year-old drunk out of her head. I put her in the bathtub before he went moon wacky on me. I got him here, where he's out of harm's way. I've got to get back and make sure she's alive and well." Surely an Alpha would understand the responsibility of keeping someone safe.

He tapped the door frame for what felt like five minutes. If he wanted her to stay, she was staying and they both knew it. He finally came to a decision.

"We'll be in touch." He pushed off and strode away. She let out a breath she hadn't realized she'd been holding. Despite being worried about Tiffany, Lexi had to sit in the darkness for several long minutes after his departure. The shakes were too bad. She didn't want to be sucked in again. This life, with its constant threats and violence, not to mention the worry of discovery at every turn, was too much. She couldn't do it again. Especially if she didn't have what little protection being an Alpha's stepdaughter could afford her. Nothing she could do about it right now, though. Right now, she needed to get back to Tiffany. Focus, Lexi, focus.

When her hands were steady enough, she turned the key and headed home. The drive went without incident. That was all she could say about it. She couldn't remember much. She cleaned up after Tiffany, who'd done what Lexi had thought she'd do, thrown up while still passed out. At least the girl had been sitting upright so she didn't choke. Small mercies. Lexi debated calling an ambulance. The second round of vomiting, all while Tiffany was unconscious and unresponsive, decided her.

"She's lucky," one of the attendants told her. "If she'd been on her back or her side, we'd have lost her. Good thing you're looking out for her."

Lexi shook her head. If she'd really been looking out for her, she wouldn't have let her get involved with a much older man. "I'll follow you to the hospital."

Alcohol poisoning was much less sexy than it sounded, Lexi thought a half-dozen hours later. She'd filled out all of Tiffany's paperwork and called her parents to let her know where she was and that she was OK, relatively speaking. All the while, Lexi wondered if she was being watched by the Pack. Were the nurses wolves? The ambulance attendants? Maybe the janitor secretly ran furry in the woods behind his house at night. That was silly. It was the last weekend in September, the Harvest Moon. The Alpha would want as many as he could to run this month, rather than next month's Hunter Moon. There couldn't be any Pack members here. Could there?

Just in case, she kept her sentences short and centered on the questions asked her. No hint of Kerr's name passed her lips. The third time after she'd jerked herself awake, the nurse on duty forcibly removed her from Tiffany's room, dragged her to the hospital doors and put her in a cab, telling her to go home and sleep. There was nothing else she could do for her friend. She nodded wearily and payed the cab driver when she got home.

Three tries with her keys got her into the house. It was light outside, so she pulled the curtains as she went through the house and finally retreated to her own bathroom, stood in the shower and scrubbed her skin until it was raw. When she was reasonably sure she'd cleaned off the night's events, she toweled off. Lexi blew a raspberry at her laundry pile. Saturdays were wash days, but it would have to wait. She got her only clean nightgown, a spaghetti-strapped, flimsy number, out of the drawer and pulled it on. Finally, she flopped into her bed and was asleep before she hit the pillow.

***

Kerr stared at Forbes. The Pack had left a few hours ago, which left the Alpha and his second alone in Forbes's stone mansion, three quarters of which was underground. The only thing most humans saw was a stone farm house. A large one, but nothing like what was actually there. Enough rooms for all the Pack, and their families, along with exercises areas, libraries, common rooms, weapons rooms, and a dozen others for various purposes. This was the den, after all. A refuge for the Pack and a place they could all retreat to, if it came down to it.

"Is she all right?" he croaked out. It wasn't emotion. His voice box still hadn't fully recovered. This shift had been horrible. He'd been a wolf for over one hundred and seventy-five years and this was brand new. The residue of several years' worth of Jocky's Shifter whiskey had forced its way out of his body, a poisonous sludge excreted through his pores. Kerr's wolf had learned a new and disgusting trick. A faster way to detox. He'd showered forever. As soon as one layer was off his skin, his wolf forced out more. It was almost as exhausting as the shift itself. His Alpha regarded him coolly.

"Tiffany? She's in the hospital, recovering nicely from a shot of Jocky's whiskey. You should keep a closer eye on your glass. Her roommate got her to the hospital just in time. Our people were the ones on call, too. They knew exactly how to handle the situation. So we're safe all the way around."

Kerr cringed. Forbes's long fingers tapped a rapid tattoo on the table he'd built. It could sit a standard Pack council comfortably. And that was without any of the inserts Forbes had made. But it had been a long time since they'd needed any more chairs at this table than the original twenty-four. The Pack hadn't seen growth in a while. There hadn't been cubs underfoot for nearly fifty years. Wolves had moved out west or to the States to find work, or to keep the Covenant. There hadn't been a dominance fight in several years. Forbes was too good an Alpha, despite the fact that there hadn't been any other wolves brought into the Pack from outside the region.

"Actually, I was wondering about—"

"The Queller?"

Kerr sucked in a breath. He gave an involuntary rumble. Lexi was a Queller? Jesus. No wonder his wolf was working so hard at sobering him up. He had to be worthy of his mate. "Wha—"

"Can you explain how else you fought off a shift when it came on so quick?"

Kerr shook his head. A Queller, here, where the tides were the strongest. Someone who could push back the berserker rages of dominance fights so combatants could think straight; who could ease the rite of passage when the first shift happened in new wolves. Who could stop any witch magic from harming the Pack, or block each and every wolf from accessing their supernatural abilities to defend themselves. There'd been Quellers on both sides of the Great Noble War before the Covenant, he reminded himself. The Covenant founders had tried to eradicate the Queller bloodlines before reason had prevailed and before the humans had started burning witches and Shifters at the stake. Quellers could help you hide, even from a Hunter. And they, being neither Shifter nor witch, were nearly impossible to detect. Unless they were using their abilities. Like forcing a stupid wolf not to shift inside the car she was driving. Forbes cleared his throat, and Kerr swallowed the enormity of what his soon-to-be-mate had been fated to do for his Pack, before returning his attention to his Alpha.

"Did you forget how to listen to your wolf altogether, my friend?"

Kerr sat up ramrod straight. He hadn't listened to his wolfish instincts since 1923 and Forbes knew it. Yet Forbes didn't look angry. The bitterness of loss drifted to Kerr's nose and he realized that his Alpha and friend thought he was going to have to kill a wolf whose self-destructive behavior threatened them all. Kerr hadn't taken his responsibilities seriously for a long time, not that things had changed dramatically in the last fifty years. At least not since the twins, the youngest but not newest Pack members, had ruffled a few feathers.

He couldn't bring himself to admit to his Alpha that his wolf side had chosen to mate. He was in control. His wolf did what he said. Except on the night of the full moon. Then, and only then, could the wolf get the upper hand. And his wolf had gone and chosen a mate.

He made a fist on the table. He'd never believed in love at first sight and still didn't. You fell in love in little jolts, like with Clara Rose. He'd noticed the young waitress's beauty, of course. But love had taken months of saying shy hellos over the counter, getting to chatting after finding they'd ended up at the same church bazaars, sharing the only empty seats at the local potluck suppers and finally swaying closer and closer at the community dances. The build-up of trust between them was what he missed most. Love was complicated. Love was delicate. Love was slow to catch fire but warmed you for the rest of your life. Drops of blood welled up between his fingers.

Lust was much easier to understand. Especially for his wolf side. Wolves mated for life. Wolves kept their Packs safe. His promiscuity could have been seen as a threat to the Pack's secrecy by his wolf. That or his wolfish instincts must have decided he'd been alone long enough. Memories of Clara Rose had kept him single for this long, so his wolf had gone around them. Lexi was the opposite of Clara Rose. Clara had been boyish, waif-thin, tiny, soft-spoken and anxious to please. Lexi was louder, independent, self-sufficient. And physically very different from the women in the 1920s. Anything but boyish and with flaming hair; her temper had turned her eyes bright amber. He found his pants uncomfortably tight at the memory. Lexi would cause many a man to lose his head to desire. Throw her Queller heritage into the fray and his biological drive to mate had taken over. He released his fist slowly. Spread his fingers on the table. Took a deep breath to bring himself back under control.

It wasn't unheard of, a loveless match like this, but it was rare. Kerr had forgotten his wolfish nature. You could tell the new wolves that all you needed was the bare basics of touch, but wolves craved being part of a Pack. They were social creatures and eventually needed someone of their own kind. He'd floated around that for some time, avoided entanglements outside of the Pack and been distant to his packmates at best. He'd isolated himself. Punished himself and his inner beast. He'd deserved it, given what had happened to Clara Rose.

He and Lexi would have to reach an understanding. He wasn't going to fall in love again. At least, they would if he survived the night. He met his Alpha's stare dead on.

"It was the first time I'd met Tiffany's roommate, actually, or I would have told you, Alpha. Forgive my lapse. It won't happen again."

Kerr tried to think of all the things Tiffany had ever said about Lexi Coolen. The auburn-haired woman wasn't usually a topic of conversation. Tiffany had mentioned her in passing. Things like "my roommate made me take out the garbage" or "the cow I live with made me late for class because she refused to drive me." Things like that. Mostly what he'd heard was Lexi wasn't someone who let other people push her around.

"You're my second, Kerr. What message does it send the Pack that it happened at all? How do you explain the offspring of a rival Pack arriving unchallenged in our lands? And a Queller? How could we miss a Queller moving into our territory?"

Kerr sat back in his chair. Thought about what he could remember of his time in the car with Lexi. He was searching for her behavior, but his wolf was more than willing to remind him of how sweet her skin tasted, how warm she'd been. How good she'd smelled, how pretty her brown eyes were with their gray streaks in them before the amber had taken over. Her tank top hugged curves that begged to be explored while her PJ pants with duckies had seemed overly large. She needed feeding up, did his mate. Kerr squashed the notion. Lexi's diet was her own business. "I'm willing to bet that she doesn't know."

"The good parts or the bad parts?"

"Both." Kerr growled. Lexi had no idea what she was or how to handle it. And someone who'd managed to reach her age without finding out was…interesting, to say the least. She'd need him. Need the Pack soon enough. The need to mark her hit him. He wanted to take her back to his rooms in the den and make her his in the most primitive way. The thought nearly made him double over. He'd never felt like this, not even with his Clara Rose back in the twenties. But he'd chosen Clara, and his wolfish side had had to live with his decision. This time around, his wolf was doing the choosing.

His Alpha regarded him with that distant look again. Assessing whether he'd live or die. Kerr wasn't at peace with it. His wolf had just found Lexi. Would fight for the chance to be with her. Still, he knew his friend would make the right decision for him and for the Pack. And that was more than comforting. There was no trust like that shared between his Fundy Bay Pack members. That he wouldn't have to slay the monster in the mirror before he hurt someone was a relief. It was his greatest fear, that he wouldn't have the strength, if and when the time came. But he didn't have to worry. Forbes took care of his own.

Forbes was a good Alpha. He'd been one for over two hundred and fifty years, but there wasn't a lot of draw for wolves to come to this territory, once the province's importance in the country had waned. His Pack had shrunk. A Queller would draw wolves in droves. And not just wolves—many Shifters would love the chance for easy access to a Queller. Different groups of Shifters might want under the umbrella of her powers. Especially an unclaimed one. They'd work hard to attract her. At least the good ones would. Lexi would become a valuable draw to the territory if they could take her as one of their own.

And then there was the influence of the Fundy tides. The highest tides in the world called up the highest magics, Shifter or otherwise. It also played hell on Shifters with control issues. But if you could handle the near doubling of your power, it was an incredible rush. Most avoided the question altogether, choosing instead to honor the Covenant and remain hidden from the humans and their Hunters as much as possible.

But as long as she remained unclaimed, Lexi was a liability. Shifters of many nations would fight to the death for the right to bring her into their groups, or worse, take her back to their domains. Wars had started for far less. Forbes wouldn't allow that.

"We need to solve this. Fast."

For the first time in over seventy years, Kerr and his wolf were in complete unison.

"Yes. Yes we do, Alpha."

Chapter Four

Forbes sent Kerr off.

Kerr's first instinct was to go to the tavern. He wanted a drink pretty damn bad. The Alpha could forbid him, or worse, put a geas on him that he never drink liquor again, but that had never been Forbes's style. One wolf slacked off for a few years, another wolf picked it up until the first was back on his feet. It was the only way they made it past the death of their human loved ones. Forbes understood that. But Kerr couldn't let the Pack suffer for his shitty life any more.

"Didn't think you remembered where the den was anymore, Kerr."

Kerr looked up from his aimless walking to discover he was steps away from the male. "Graham."

The older wolf leaned against the fireplace in one of the massive living rooms of Prominitory House. He was barrel chested from age, his hair pale yellow rather than the copper of his youth. Still, his maturity was welcomed on the council, if not as one of the Warriors any more.

"Forbes going to divvy up more of your duties to the rest of us?" Graham pushed off the fireplace, his movements sharp and quick. It was the only way the old man could show his displeasure. Technically, Kerr outranked him.

"Actually, I've got an assignment from the Boss."

Graham looked him up and down. Kerr did all he could not to cross his arms in front of him in defense. Graham met his stare and held it, older eyes slowly turning shiny yellow.

"Sometimes I think Forbes is too much wolf. Our furry sides see time in a different fashion than our human sides do. Makes Forbes almost too loyal. In my day, a wolf stuck in mourning as long as you would have been dead by now."

There definitely was a challenge in the elder's tone, but Kerr grinned and spread his arms.

"Anytime you want to throw down for the position, I'm available."

The man snorted.

"Since you're back to your duties," the sarcasm in Graham's voice made Kerr wince. "I got a text from one of the witches. Their Priestess, I think, though that changes so often it's difficult to keep track."

He handed the phone to Kerr. He didn't recognize the number on the top of the screen, but the Burntcoat Coven followed the Covenant between Shifters and witches to the letter. Only high priests or priestesses were allowed to contact the wolves. So it was probably Kassia. Forbes had met her a time or two, but the Alpha had a deep-seated distrust of witches. Even more than the average wolf. So he'd given them Graham's number for contact.

What do you know about the tides in 1869?

Kerr frowned.

"Don't they keep records?"

Graham shrugged. "Perhaps they want something more detailed. Like someone who'd actually been there."

"Well, that's not me. I was only four or maybe five at the time. And not living around here. Maybe something to do with the Fundy Basin? Highest tides in the world now, but were they back then? Were you around?" he handed the phone back.

He nodded. "I was. The land hasn't changed that much. It's not just the high tides that affect us and the witches, but the fact they come in twice a day, you know."

Kerr rolled his eyes. Graham had been a school teacher once upon a time and it came out every once in a while. "Yeah, but back in 1869? Was there anything different? Anything that affected our magics? Or the witches'?"

Graham tilted his head and closed his eyes, trying to dig through his memories. Kerr remained silent. The older the wolf, the longer the memories. Kerr found that dates were less important to him than events. Sometimes fitting the two together took time.

"I'm not sure of the year, but if she's referring to the killer tides of the Hunter Moon? That was a special kind of hell. Most of it caused by a witch."

"Which one? Do you remember? What do you think they're looking for?"

There was a long pause. Graham took a step, closed the distance between them. He smoothed Kerr's hair, a gesture of affection to a younger wolf. Of comfort. He forced himself to stay still and receive the touch. He'd been with humans too long. Human males didn't touch for affection. Damn it. Time to get used to it again. Acknowledge the need for more wolf contact. Graham gave a heavy nod.

"Yes, I know the witch. With your permission, Beta, I will look into this for you."

"Don't think I can handle it, old man?" Graham's abrupt switch of attitude threw him off.

"I think you should not deal with this particular issue until you must, Beta."

"Why?" He felt like a child again. Graham had this power over most of the wolves here. Everyone except Forbes.

"Could I beg a favor, Beta?"

Kerr gave a short growl. It was tradition that if an elder begged a favor, you granted it. He didn't have to, but he'd be considered unnecessarily rude if he didn't.

"What favor?"

"Let me handle it?"

He ground his teeth. He was the Beta. High time he started acting like it, even around the elders.

"As long as I get a report at the next meeting of the Warriors."

Graham gave a short bow and left the room at a smart march. Kerr watched him go. He turned to the mantle. Something wasn't right. Something his addled brain was refusing to pick up. The mantel was lined with books of different bindings. Some hand-stitched and others machine bound. He fingered one of the older volumes, picking it up and flipping through the pages. It was about the end of the witch/Shifter wars.

The original Covenant was created in the 1630s in Europe, but the local version was signed in 1755.

Hmm. A hundred years for the fighting to stop on this side of the ocean. But the dates weren't the ones the Priestess had been asking about. He flipped farther into the book. It went into detail about the Great Noble War between the supernatural races, covered when Mud Creek was renamed Wolfville and ended with the supernatural fallout of 1835. Nothing useful. Still, Kerr's hackles were up. Witches couldn't be trusted; he held proof of their treachery in his hand.

The timing of the Priestess's text was a little too close to discovering a Queller in their midst. Had the witches discovered Lexi? Did they want her for themselves, to finally have the upper hand and control of the power in the Fundy Basin? The two groups of paranormal beings had been trying to establish dominant claims over this area for centuries. Or did the Coven want Lexi purged, so no one could have her? What was their plan?

Why would the High Priestess ask about that particular year, when the local everyday magics whirling around were so chaotic? A distraction, maybe? One that had Graham hopping. He didn't like that either. The old man was often at odds with how Forbes did things, and now he was eager to help? Too many things didn't add up. All of it seemed connected to Lexi's appearance. Just one more reason to either claim her or make her leave. The uncertainties of her status and loyalties were dangerous. He shut the book and put it on the shelf. The decades he'd spent seducing women were about to be put to good use.

***

Butterfly tongues traced the outline of her tattoo. Lexi giggled at their gentle racing round her skin. So soothing. She was limp with the simple pleasure.

"A Dragon, huh? Sexy." Lips pressed a kiss over the heart of the tail. Wait a minute, who was kissing her? She was in a sexy nightgown. *Oh God.*

The last thought yanked her from sleep. She jerked and flipped over, making sure to cover herself with her Star Wars sheets. Dear God. Kerr was seeing her Star Wars sheets. Kerr had draped himself across her bed, tanned arms folded over his T-shirt. The shirt hugged a well-muscled torso while advertising a band that had been cool in the fifties. For all she knew about Kerr, it could be an original. He might be old enough to have attended the concert with the same clothes he had on now, looking just as good in them back then. No, she would not notice his looks. Sex appeal was a trick males of his ilk used and she wasn't falling for it. She wasn't noticing how bright his blue eyes looked. Nor did she notice how his smooth, dark hair was held back off his forehead with gel. She resisted the urge to kick him in the seat of his jeans. She wasn't dressed for it. He smiled up at her, completely at home. She grimaced, and then realized she'd been doing that a lot lately.

"Kerr, get out of my room."

She pulled her pillow over her head. Kerr gave a quick tug and her sheet slipped to her waist. The pillow muffled her *eep*. Her mind threatened to freeze, but out of nowhere it also threw up a question. Could she let a man touch her after what her mother's Pack had done? Before the chill of the fall air coming in through the open window could hit her, he gallantly put his chest over her scantily clad breasts. She tested her boundaries. Was she going to panic? No, she didn't want to run to the hills screaming yet. She did firmly tug the sheet up to her neck, however.

"I can't. I have to talk to you. Get some things straight."

She flung the pillow to the foot of the bed. "Something is getting straight right now, and I want it, and you, off me. I'm not even dressed yet."

"I don't have a problem with this." Light danced in his eyes, and a slow, smoldering heat awakened, too. Charming, sexy. They were all sensual creatures, Shifters. They could draw you in. She could let him. Just let go a little and see what happened. That she was toying with the idea meant she was getting used to the thought of touching another living creature again. This was good. Could she maybe let him touch her even more?

There would be consequences. Things she couldn't see now. Kerr watched her and she found she liked it. Liked the way he gave her his whole attention. This was what must have attracted Tiffany and the other girls. Being the total focus of the man you're with. But it was the gaze of a hunter. She was the prey. Her panic started. Nope, she wasn't falling for this charming act. Not at all. He was the bad boy mothers warned their daughters about. Lexi pursed her lips. Well, not her mother. Her mother had actually wanted her to run *to* the bad boy, not away.

This was not helping. He needed to leave. She tried to bring up a bad memory from her mother's Pack—Lord knew she had enough of them—but something about the way he looked at her, the way his eyes kept watching for her slightest reaction, made her feel safe, rather than threatened. God help her. Rule one with Shifters: If you want any respect, don't let them walk all over you. Time to exercise some dominance.

"I have the problem. It's my house. My rules. I am not awake yet. Move."

There, that sounded better. Definitely in control of the situation.

Kerr lowered his head and nipped her shoulder while his hips wiggled. She gasped, which only made him move more. Suddenly the bad memories were knocking on a door she decided she'd like to keep locked. Her body froze, as did the man on top of her.

"Kerr!" She shouted. Her heart raced. He had to get off. Now.

"You're no fun." But he slid a little farther down her body. Good. She didn't feel so trapped.

She tried to take back her position of authority and growled at him. It sounded unconvincing even to her ears. His grin got even bigger. His hands slid down her sheet-covered sides and she didn't find it unpleasant. Physically. Mentally, the gerbil wheel started. What if he won't stop, what if he likes claws, what if he likes teeth, what if he starts to change, will he stop when I scream or will it turn him on more?

Stop. Nothing is happening. Shifters touched more than humans. It could mean nothing. She'd helped him keep his secrets last night. Maybe he was just thanking her, Shifter-style. "I think I'll call you *my little tiger*," he growled, and his hips started making lazy circles.

In a normal man, she'd think he had rapey thoughts on his brain. But Kerr was a wolf. They had what you could call boundary issues, especially when it came to one word: women. Possessive didn't even begin to describe how they could be.

Women were automatically considered below the men in a Pack, because they were discouraged from fighting their way up in rank. It might be that they occasionally gave birth and the menfolk were trying to protect their womenfolk. It could be that a lot of the Shifters in power were older, born in times where women were openly accepted as property, rather than people. Equal rights barely forethought. Some habits might be hard to break. Take her current sexy pain the patoot. In Kerr's mind, he was somehow entitled to his current position. The scary part was not knowing if would he wait for a woman's consent, or the orders of one of the Alpha pair like in her stepfather's Pack. She didn't know the other Alpha, but she was under the impression he hadn't thought about sex once during their conversation. So she wasn't scared, exactly. At least, she tried not to be.

This felt like it was Kerr's idea. And she knew a little about him. She'd already voiced she didn't want this; so long as she continued to say she didn't want it, Lexi was OK. And Kerr wasn't being as forceful as he could be. He was trying an almost muted form of his dominance games on her. She just had to keep saying no. Hope he wouldn't go any farther with the games. She was uncomfortable as hell, but if she let him know that, it would only get worse.

Her mother's Pack had loved making her uncomfortable. The more uncomfortable she'd been, the more fun they'd had. Her fear was that Kerr wouldn't stop pushing, wouldn't stop asking until she gave in just to get rid of him. Giving in was never a good thing. But sometimes that had been the only way to survive the night in her mother's Pack. This didn't *feel* like the same thing.

Her traitorous nipples had instantly hardened the second his chest had come down. It wasn't from the cold. The guy had a body made for sex, had used it very effectively on many women. Was trying to use it on her. She fought back another shiver as he blew lightly on her exposed shoulder and neck. She prayed none of her crazy hormones had colored her scent the wrong way.

"You will do no such thing. You're going to get up; you're going to talk to your *girlfriend*—who's in the hospital, by the way— and see if she's OK. You're going to let me get dressed and have a cup of tea before anything else happens today. Now move. Off. Off. Off." She shoved at him. He didn't budge.

"I wouldn't call Tiffany my girlfriend. She's barely my friend. I'm more interested in us. We could have some fun first. Like what we started last night."

She froze. "Fun? You call what happened last night fun?"

"Nobody died." But Kerr, recognizing his error, frowned and slid off her entirely. Not off the bed, but off her enough so she could cover up. Lexi blushed crimson when his gaze still hit her chest.

"Up here, Romeo."

His eyes met hers and the sexual heat in them was blatant. She had to cool it down or she was a goner. She snorted.

"Sure. Let's ignore the alcohol poisoning of a nineteen-year-old for a minute. Someone you call barely a friend almost drank herself to death while with you, not that it's all that important. No, forget it." Sarcasm dripped from her tone. "Instead, let's focus on me, since I'm right in front of you. I could have died, Kerr. Do you understand that? You could have killed me when your wolf took over. I know you don't give a hoot about a mere human, but you would have been in really big trouble with your Alpha—"

"I do care. About you and Tiffany. She didn't over-drink. She drank one thing she wasn't supposed to, something that poisoned her. Our people kept an eye on her. She's safe. You did good, getting her to the hospital. I was proud of you when I heard what you did for her. You're a good person. I like that about you. It'll make things so much easier. Besides, you're not really that mad, you know. You're just upset that I've seen you half-naked."

She sputtered for a full minute before she got herself under control. Taking a deep breath, she fixed him with her best glare. She was NOT half-naked, even if she did feel like it. "Do tell?"

"You'd swear if you were really mad. Or really scared. At least, that's what you did last night. I like that you do that, by the way. Swear but not swear. It was cute the way you wouldn't say real bad words."

She ground her teeth. Not for the first time she debated her decision about cursing. Kerr sat up on his knees, watching her as she struggled to stay covered and sit against the headboard. She flicked her fingers at him.

"Go see to your current girl-Friday while I get dressed."

"I already broke it off with Tiffany, Queller. You don't have to pretend, by the way."

Broke it off? A disaster she was going to have to deal with later. And what was a Queller? Some sort of insult to outsiders? "Pretend? About what? And you broke it off already? Really? You saw her in the hospital? Told her you were dumping her after a night out? How'd she take it?" Lexi'd had multiple conversations where she'd warned her younger roommate that as soon as Kerr saw someone new, he'd leave her. There was a stone in the pit of her stomach as she wondered if Kerr had done what she thought he might have done.

"Not so well."

"Imagine that. Mr. Sensitivity. What did you say to her?"

"That I was into you, and we shouldn't see each other anymore. It wasn't really a break up. More of a we-can't-have-sex-anymore talk. We weren't exclusive, you know. Besides, she lives with you. Tiffany will barely even feel it. You keep her calm, right? You don't smell like any other Pack. I want to claim you."

Lexi blinked. As dumb-men things went, this was right up at the top. She wrapped the sheet around her as she stood up. She had a suspicion Tiffany might not be as reasonable about Kerr's pronouncement. Forget about the whole I've-slept-with-a-bunch-of-people-and-I-want-you-now line.

"Not your best move, Ace."

He shrugged. "She called me a bastard. Maybe I deserved that, given what happened last night. But she and I weren't really dating, and since I've found you—"

"You gave her alcohol poisoning! Or whatever kind of poisoning. Then dumped her! I'd say you haven't even borne the brunt of what she plans. And what on Earth possessed you to bring me into it?"

"You're the reason I'm swearing off all other women. How could I not bring you into it? It's not like she wouldn't find out eventually. You're her roommate. I know you help settle her down, but she's gonna have to figure it out for herself sometime. And I wasn't totally insensitive. Hey, I gave her a ride home from the hospital."

Lexi stilled. "She's home?"

"She was. She got mad, so I think the whiskey accidentally broke whatever connection you might have had with her. She left. She might have borrowed your compu—"

Lexi tore open the door and flew down the stairs. The living room was in shambles. Her research. Books with pages torn out littered the floor. Her few memories of happy times hadn't fared much better. Pictures were smashed, shards of knickknacks were strewn around, the jacket that her father had given her, shredded. The jacket more than anything else hit her. Tiffany had known right where it was, how special it was to her and that it's loss would hurt even more than her computer and latest copy of her thesis being taken.

***

Kerr was up and chasing after Lexi as soon as he got over his surprise. He'd decided that things might be easier for her to accept if she were in love with him, even if his human half could never return the emotion. His wolf side would love her enough for both of them, and he'd see to her comforts as best he could. She'd never know the difference and he'd still be true to Clara Rose. He'd tested her a bit. She genuinely didn't know about being a Queller. Her scent was a mixture of apprehension and attraction, not a bit of deception. She was as innocent as she claimed.

He'd flirted with her, rolling his hips in a way that had most women moaning, or at the very least offering up a kiss. Not Lexi. Fear had kicked at his nose. His wolf had nipped her, playfully. She'd been the daughter of Alphas, surely she'd recognize play. Except her fear got worse. She'd been hurt. Badly. No one should be that afraid of being touched. Human or Shifter attacker? Had to be human. No Shifter he'd ever met would hurt a Queller. Maybe she'd had a run-in with a witch.

The Tiffany conversation could have gone better. But when Lexi's face had lost all its color and gone still like that, he'd felt a stone of worry drop into his belly. One rock had become a quarry when he'd seen her look at the ruins of the living room. Quellers didn't do well when they were so off-balance.

He wanted to make her feel better. A wolf would accept touch for comfort though he stopped himself from offering it that way. Lexi thought she was human. He'd seen that much upstairs. Even though he'd pushed the boundaries up in the bedroom, she'd refused. She hadn't physically pushed too hard at him, but that could have been because she knew he was stronger. His instincts told him a hurt festered in his mate. He needed to comfort her. Wanted to hold her. At least hear her substitute curse words, which he really did find adorable. He took note of the dark shade her eyes had turned and wondered if they did that every time she was sad. It was good to take care of his mate. Didn't mean he was going to fall in love again.

"Lexi?" Kerr put a hand on her bare shoulder. He couldn't help himself. She was so close, smelled so good. Citrus and lavender and a wildness that he couldn't name, all covered over in the unmistakable scent of books where she lived. Clara Rose had smelled of the flower in her name. But Clara Rose had died over eighty years ago. After she'd left him.

For the first time in a long time, the fist of pain that usually accompanied that thought didn't appear.

"This is your fault. Go get my computer! Do something useful!" Despite Lexi's best efforts, a few tears leaked out. She swiped at her face. Kerr caught her hand and held it against his chest. The tears; good God, he couldn't stand it when women cried.

"I'll buy you a new computer." She tried to tug her hand free, but he held on. "I'll buy you new books." She started walking away, hoping he'd drop his hold, but he walked with her. His wolf was practically screaming at him to do something.

"I'll fix all the pictures and we can go shopping at the cheesiest stores for the figurines, if you'll tell me what's wrong. Is it only the stuff? It doesn't feel like only the stuff. Lexi? Please smile. Tell me I'm stupid or something. Did I do something that hurt you? Lexi, can I fix it for you? Please?"

She shook her head, but the action let more tears free. Quietly, she spoke, "This is stupid." He smiled, thinking she was trying to cheer him up just a bit, but the expression fell as she burst into jarring sobs and picked up the jacket. "Just...go."

Kerr was beside himself. His wolf paced just below his skin. Their mate was deeply unhappy with him and Kerr had no insights, inspirations, or ideas how to fix it. Tiffany was OK, had been discharged from the hospital. She was mad, but she'd get over it. Kerr had "dated" a hundred young women like her before and they always calmed down after a bit. But he'd never encountered this body-shaking sobbing that Lexi was caught in right now. He was smart enough to figure out that it wasn't about the loss of her computer. Something else had been building up and this was just what had popped the cork on her emotions. That was dangerous for a Queller. They subdued others' emotions, but not if theirs were in turmoil. Or buried bone deep. He had wanted to get her to bond to him first before he tackled the Queller conversation. But if this continued there would be no choice.

He thought of Tiffany. Living with a Queller and she'd had this reaction to his announcement that they wouldn't be sleeping together again? Quellers made tempers more manageable. Even the ones who hadn't awakened to the rest of their powers often soothed those around them out of habit. A natural inclination. But Tiffany had been wholeheartedly furious with him. What would she be like without Lexi's influences?

He'd miscalculated. Badly. Tiffany was becoming a problem that the Pack might have to be made aware of, and that wouldn't be good for Tiffany. He hadn't been lying when he said he liked the girl. Tiffany was usually sweet. She'd cheered him up several times with silly little antics. But she had to have known it wasn't romantic between them. He never lied about the chance for a relationship with the women he slept with. He needed to fix this. Fast. For all their sakes.

"I will see what I can do about Tiffany."

CHAPTER FIVE

Kerr left. She held the remnants of her father's jacket close to her heart for a moment, letting the tears flow freely. Probably a by-product of her imagination, but she swore she could still smell him on the bits of collar and sleeve in her hand. She held all that was left of the man who'd raised her. *Be good to people, even when no one is watching,* he'd told her the day he'd died. *That's when it counts the most.*

She should be worried about her computer, but her logical side kicked in. She had a copy of her thesis emailed to herself. She didn't have family photos online. Didn't have any family pictures period, actually. Hannah, her best friend, was the one who'd pointed that out. Lexi didn't surf porn sites, didn't do anything but research, shop *thinkgeek.com* and check email, really. That didn't say a whole lot for her extracurricular activities, did it? She did have a Netflix subscription, but going out? It had never held any real appeal to her. She couldn't dance. And drinking anywhere but her house? Forget it. Too much could happen. Better safe than sorry with alcohol.

Besides, she'd rather stay home with a few friends than go out. Her father had been the same way. She picked the remnants of her father's jacket and tucked them away in a closet. Her mother was the one that had been adamant about Lexi going out to parties, getting dressed up, insisting she put on makeup galore. When Lexi had failed in becoming a social butterfly, her mother had moved on, to her brother. Not that her life had been so bad. Her father had always been there while she was growing up.

Now he was gone and the last thing she'd had of his was destroyed too. Because of Shifters. Everything that had gone wrong with her life could be traced back to Shifters. She wanted to scream. Thought better of it. Pulled back her hair into a ponytail, got dressed and went into the basement. Suspended from one corner of the unfinished room was a punching bag, hidden from view by stacks of trunks and boxes. She started easy, just jabs with little to no force. By the time she heard the door upstairs slam, hopefully marking Tiffany's return, Lexi was dripping sweat and relatively calm. She made her way to the kitchen, stopped and grabbed a drink of water from the pitcher in the fridge.

"I know! Gawd, you don't have to talk to me like I'm an idiot!" Tiffany was saying. Lexi froze. Someone else was here? Knots formed in her stomach. He wouldn't. She peeked around the cupboard corner into the living room to see Kerr there, arms crossed and fixing Tiffany with a fierce glare. Lexi leaned against the cabinetry for a moment. Gulped her water down. This was going to be a disaster.

"So, what's going on?" She came around the corner.

Kerr waved his arms at Lexi and Tiffany cleared her throat. Several times.

"Umm, well. Kerr here explained a few things about how you helped us both last night and I called my parents. I'm going to move out."

Lexi nodded. She'd heard that statement at least a dozen times before, whenever Lexi had become what Tiffany termed unreasonable. Usually when the rent was due or the garbage had to be taken out or the dishwasher broke. She'd met Tiffany's parents, who'd been thrilled that not only did their daughter have a roommate, but one who would be able to call them if things got a "little wild," as Tiffany's mother had put it. Given what had happened last night, it was amazing Lexi had managed to get off the phone. Which reminded her, she'd need to give the doctor on call a gift. Tiffany's mother had probably called to check on her every fifteen minutes while she was in the hospital.

"Uh-huh. Where might my computer be?"

"Um, you know that little park behind the Railtown condos, the one with the dock?"

"You threw it in the Bay of Fundy?" Lexi tried not to shriek. She'd figured that Tiffany was angry, but she never expected this. And after she'd brought her to the hospital. Not that she expected gratitude, but a time-out from a tantrum might be nice.

"No, I kinda threw it at the rocks under the dock. The tide was out. It's under about fifty feet of water now though. I watched it come in while I said some not nice things about you to anyone who would listen. Loudly. Kerr stopped the town cops from arresting me."

Lexi slapped her forehead. Covered her eyes and started to count to a hundred. Her calm from her workout was dissipating. Kerr cleared his throat.

"Oh, right. And I'm sorry for going ballistic when Kerr broke it off with me. But you didn't say you wanted him, in my defense."

Lexi uncovered one eye. "I don't want him. You shredded my father's jacket."

"Hey!" Kerr protested. Lexi ignored him.

Tiffany blanched. "Well, it was old."

"Excuse me? Right here, ladies. Part of this conversation. What about the jacket?" Kerr turned to Tiffany, who, if possible, became even paler.

"I know, Tiffany, which was the point of it. For it to be old, to remind me of things that happened when it wasn't old. When I was with my father before he died."

"I suppose it would be pointless to offer to buy you a new jacket, then, huh?" Kerr said.

"Yes," Tiffany and Lexi replied in unison.

"What about your thesis?" Tiffany picked at her cashmere sweater.

"I've got a copy of it on my cloud."

"I know a guy who might be able to fix the jacket, Lexi," Kerr tried again.

She turned to him. "That's nice. But since God couldn't find all the pieces and put it back together again, it's kinda pointless. It's gone and I will have to deal with it." Something she'd always done. Put it behind her and move on, as cleanly as possible.

"I'm moving out. You heard that part, right? Mum and Dad thought it was time for me to be on my own."

"Oh really? Where are you moving to? There aren't any apartments left now that the campus is full. Not to mention that it's the last weekend of September and the middle of the semester."

"Mummy and Daddy found me a condo in Railtown."

Of course they had. Tiffany had been after one since she'd arrived in Wolfville. They had finally given in to their daughter's unreasonable demands. That wasn't the worst part of the equation, however. Railtown was steps away from the bar where Lexi'd picked both of them up only last night. Really? Last night her world had come crashing down from normal-and-broke, to Pack-weird-and-broke. She'd awakened and there'd been a strange man who'd seen her almost naked. She took a breath. Rubbed her stomach, which gurgled and sent a spike of pain up her throat. That was becoming an issue. She'd never had stomach problems from worry before. Wasn't that what caused ulcers? Probably just indigestion in this case. She needed to pick something up at Mud Creek mini-mart for it soon.

"So if you break your lease, there is a fee you've got to pay for that. And you won't be getting your security deposit back because of the damages." She tried to sound matter-of-fact, but losing the steady income from Tiffany's rent stung. Still, she wasn't completely unprepared. The fee was something the lawyer she'd seen when she bought the house had recommended. She hadn't discouraged frosh from renting from her, but freshmen had given her wide berth. Not that she was that far off the beaten path; just that she was a stickler for quiet. College students didn't like the cramp it put in their freedom.

Tiffany nodded enthusiastically. "Yeah, they got the condo for me on Friday! And they'll pay for the fees and whatever."

Lexi took a deep breath and let it out slowly. "So when were you going to tell me?"

"Ah, today. I guess. But it all works out because Kerr can move in and I'll be closer to town and we can sorta avoid each other. I think I shouldn't see you for week at least, so stay off Harbourside Street, OK? You could probably go up to Kerr's place. But I warn you, his apartment is a mess. I could barely find the bed the first time I went there. And there's piles of old junk. Mummy and Daddy are in town now, thanks for calling them and making them worry. I was perfectly fine, now I have to go and explain why I was drinking instead of studying. But it will work out and I'll have my penalty payment here soon. They'll want a receipt and I'm meeting them for lunch, so if you could just hurry up and give it to me, I can come get my stuff tomorrow. The bed was yours anyway, so it's just my clothes and things."

Lexi was flabbergasted for about five seconds. She couldn't figure out what she wanted to say first. There were so many things wrong with this girl's life priorities. But she thought of her father's words, be kind. She'd try. She walked forward and gave the young woman a hug.

"I want you to listen to me. No money, no receipt. It's the way it works. For the record I don't want Kerr. He's a jerk for dumping you and using me as an excuse because I helped him out last night. Whatever happened between you, it's got nothing to do with me. He wanted it to be over, so it's over. You deserve much better. I hope you're happy in Railtown."

Tiffany probably wouldn't last very long there if she kept partying, but there was always hope.

"I'm sorry about your coat, Lexi. I was really angry and knew it would hurt you the most." Tiffany hugged her back with a quick squeeze. So the girl knew it would hurt Lexi. It had been a deliberate cruelty, rather than a crime of momentary fury. She'd never seen such meanness from Tiffany. It was as if the past few months of becoming first roommates and then friends had just disappeared. The girl hadn't acted like she'd been in love with Kerr. Had she just hidden it? She watched as Tiffany took off to meet with her parents.

"I'm going to just make sure she gets out OK. Be right back." Kerr bolted after Tiffany. Lexi shook her head.

***

Kerr grabbed Tiffany's arm the second she was out of Lexi's hearing and sight. "Remember the deal, Tiff."

Tiffany gave a violent shrug and pulled out of his grip. "I know. Thanks for the condo, by the way. If only all my near-death-dates were as profitable, I wouldn't need university." The pretty little blonde was looking decidedly less pretty right now.

"You shouldn't be trying to drink with the big boys, little girl," Kerr warned. His other side wanted back with Lexi and had developed a strong dislike of the female in front of him. Kerr fought back a snarl.

Tiffany's demeanor changed in a heartbeat. She ran her fingers up his side and brushed off non-existent dust from his shoulder. "You didn't think I was such a little girl last week. In fact, I was so much woman, I had you convinced that 'sugar bear' was your new name."

Kerr flushed in embarrassment and flicked her hand away. "Things changed."

Tiffany's bitch face returned. "You're gonna be sorry."

Kerr very carefully stepped on her toes to hold her in place, put his chest in her face and let a sub-audible growl fill his next words. "That a threat, little girl?"

Tiffany blanched, but didn't back down. "I'm not scared of you."

Kerr grinned and the whites of Tiffany's eyes showed through. "You should be, if you ever hurt Lexi again. Or upset her. Or inconvenience her in any way. Just stay clear of her, and me. You'll be fine that way."

Tiffany tried to stare him down, but Kerr continued to glare until she lowered her gaze in submission. He gave a sharp nod and sent Tiffany on her way, turned and ran back to Lexi. He'd have to remember to ask the staff at the hospital if they'd found an old photograph of him in Tiffany's things. It hadn't been at his apartment. Probably they had destroyed it when they searched her pockets. It was pretty standard procedure, but he'd better double check. After he settled things with Lexi.

CHAPTER SIX

Lexi probably should have put up a fight to keep Tiffany as her roommate. She was feeling just a teensy bit guilty for not doing that. To move out, on top of almost dying over the weekend, had to be overwhelming, even if Tiffany wasn't showing any indications of such. But honestly, a part of her was relieved. No more looking after someone who was supposed to be an adult but clearly wasn't one. No more late night drunk dials from Tiffany with pleas to come pick her up. No more listening to the whining about how Tiffany had to do her course work between parties. No more reminding herself that Tiffany was young and this was the time to blah-blah-blah. While having no roommate would make money extremely tight, Lexi could get another part-time job and be just as comfortable.

She heard footsteps and the door swung shut. Onto the bigger, more pressing problem. Lexi turned to face a solemn Kerr.

"So, I can pack her things up for her," Kerr said. "You have a basement in this place, I noticed. Some of the guys and I can move my video stuff down there; give me a man-cave slash office for work and gaming. We can do that tomorrow evening. I'm gonna need my equipment to work. I work from home, see—"

Kerr was rearranging her life. To suit him. Just like her mother's Pack.

"You're not moving in." Lexi crossed her arms. On this, she would remain firm. Part of her wanted to rally and scream, but the other, rational part wouldn't let her. *Was her freedom really worth the consequences to an entire race of people?*

That was *their* point of view. She wasn't a wolf; eventually, if she could convince them she was no threat to the secrecy of their race, they would be reasonable. She wouldn't betray them. She might not get along with her mother or her brother, but they were still her family. She wouldn't do anything that would endanger their lives. She just had to convince the local Pack of it.

"Yes, I am. Lexi, I claim you." He gave her a smoldering look.

This was going to be difficult if she had to spend her next few weeks with the town Lothario. Lexi put her hands on her hips. "Well, just roll me in fairy dust and call me a unicorn. What in the world makes you think you can tell me that?"

Kerr tilted his head and gave her a funny look. She knew he was partly annoyed she wasn't thrilled about his plan, but this expression held a hint of something else. Like Lexi was dodging something. She was missing part of the conversation. She needed tea, damn it. He suddenly nodded, having come to some decision.

"You know about us."

"So? I knew about Shifters before last night, too. Didn't tell anyone then, won't tell anyone now. You're not getting in here. Got any other reasons?"

"Keep your voice down," he ordered. Her stomach roiled and her left eye twitched.

OK, she could deal with this. Rationally. Calmly. She'd proven herself in the last six years. Hadn't talked to anyone about Shifters. They could check. She hadn't run into any others, either. This was the first contact she'd had. At least, that she knew of. Gritting her teeth, she walked through to the kitchen, took out some of the chopped veggies she kept in the fridge and threw them into a pot. She added some crushed tomatoes and vegetable broth. Selected some of her favorite spices. Cooking was calming. Add certain ingredients in a certain way and you usually got the same result. Following recipes helped to reset her equilibrium. Let her come up with her next argument. No one in her mother's Pack had ever helped her cook. So she was surprised when she heard the sound of chopping behind her. Kerr had taken out the chicken breasts she'd had thawing and was dicing them up.

"I'm making vegetable soup for lunch, thanks," she snapped. She'd had a plan. Her money was tight and meals were scheduled so groceries were stretched to maximize their usefulness.

"I'm adding chicken for us, you're welcome," he replied. She tried to ignore him, to formulate her arguments. But the chopping. She couldn't stand it.

"You know what I hate the most about Shifters? Especially those under the same roof with me?"

"How adorable and handy we are when it comes to household chores?" He grinned at her. Yeah, right. She'd never met a Shifter yet who knew one end of a vacuum from the other.

"How pushy, annoying, and demanding you all are. This is my house, not yours. Because I live in the same town you do, you assume that you can bully me into doing whatever you want. That you can *take* what you want. Sorry, pal. It doesn't work that way. I pay the mortgage on this house. I pay the light bill and the water and the town taxes. Don't get me started on the phone, internet and cable. I do what I want in my own house. This means, at the very least, we're having plain old vegetable soup for lunch."

Kerr's grinned widened, but he didn't stop dicing the meat.

"What?"

"You said *we're* having soup."

"So you think that's a win?"

"Yep."

He was impossible. "I hate you. You know that." She leveled a finger at him. "And that's not what I meant."

"And yet you're cooking me lunch. How sweet."

"Shut up. Get out." She pointed to her kitchen doorway.

"You know I can't do that."

"How do I know you can't do that?"

"Because you've been around Shifters before. Surely to God your father—"

"Stepfather," she corrected.

"Right, stepfather. He's an Alpha. He would have had visitors to his territory before."

Lexi shrugged. "Maybe."

Kerr gave her that look again. "Maybe?"

"What? Did I say something stupid? You going to make fun of me?"

"No, Lexi. Not stupid. Just…surprising."

"Surprising how?"

"There seem to be…let's call them…gaps, in your knowledge of Shifters."

"And these gaps let you stay in my house? You think I'm that naive?"

"No. I think your education of us had lots of interruptions."

Lexi pursed her lips, gave an enthusiastic stir to the pot and returned to glare at Kerr. "I'm not happy about this entire situation."

"I realize that."

"You can't order me around!"

"I won't. I promise."

"Liar. You've already ordered me around!"

"No, I haven't. But I do have to move in."

She could feel the panic start to rise. Honest to God, flee-for-your-life, close-up-your-throat panic. She'd run from Pack life, from being a "pet." The way her mother's Pack had treated her hadn't been fun. She didn't want a repeat, not in her own house. She was painfully aware of just how powerful the male in her kitchen was. Had seen similar males, including her own brother, rip and shred and maim. The panic in her reached a crescendo. *Breathe. Just breathe.*

"I don't want you here," she managed.

Kerr was silent for a long time. She knew he could smell her distress. "We have a submissive. She's mated though. Would you rather someone farther down the Pack hierarchy? A little Alpha, maybe?"

Lexi rocked back on her heels. Not just from the fact he was willing to negotiate with her. Or that negotiation didn't involve his fists. He was discussing members with her. Submissives. Valued members of the Pack. Everyone protected them.

But the little Alphas. Those were the Shifters who'd one day have to leave to start their own Packs or challenge the Alpha himself. Alphas were always male, she'd been told. Little Alphas were below the Alpha's Second. This meant one thing.

"If Little Alphas are below you then…you're the Pack Beta?"

He made a funny face, then nodded without making eye contact, giving her a minute to absorb that fact. She made fists so tight she could feel her own nails draw blood. She turned around and stirred their lunch. And stirred and stirred. Until her thoughts burst out of her mouth.

"But you drink and sleep around and you get into bar fights and everything!" Betas were unique, Sunny had told her. Wessel had been a pain in the ass, but a necessary one. Even she had relented and admitted that. They had the strength of an Alpha, but an intense need to follow. Not that they were cuddly. Betas were loyal to a fault, the Pack well-being the foremost concern to them, but they were vicious. Betas *always* took first shot at challengers, and they were dirty fighters. The threat of the Beta saved the Alpha lots of trouble. Saved the Alpha's energies for other matters. Like serious challenges only. A Beta had to help the Alpha maintain control of the Pack; otherwise the combination of a Shifter's animal instincts coupled with human aggression overwhelmed them. This spread through the Pack and the Pack killed lots of people. The word bloodbath had been used to describe the result to her. Bloodbaths were frowned upon because the murders brought the police and human attention down on the Pack.

Avoiding human attention was paramount. Human authorities needed to be evaded, dodged or circumvented when a human was murdered. The golden rule of Pack life was "Thou shalt not bring the cops into Pack business." That was the unforgivable sin. Shifters accepted that sometimes it was OK to kill humans. It was one of the tenets of Pack life that Lexi had trouble with, one of the reasons she'd left. Being a Beta was kind of a big deal. And Kerr was the local Beta. She shook her head. Kerr was a hedonist. He'd be the last one to help anyone control their appetites and he probably brought more attention to them than anyone she'd ever met. And loyalty? Kerr didn't seem all that loyal to her. So why was he suddenly so insistent on moving in with her? A shiver ran down her spine as a thought jumped into her head.

"Your man-bits didn't look at me and insta-mate or anything, did they?"

If the look he gave her as he walked to her stove could have been paired to one word, it would have been dumbass. Chagrined, she moved away and he selected a fry pan from the ones hanging on the wall. He deposited the chicken pieces in it and turn on the fan on the range hood.

"You're frying the chicken first?"

"It'll cook faster and I find it adds more flavor to the soup. I have cooked for the Pack before. We all take turns on mooncall nights. As to my man-bits? No, they didn't look at you and fall in love. It doesn't work that way and you know it."

No she didn't. She also didn't miss the way he'd said "fall in love" not "mate."

"It worked that way with my mother."

His hands paused, but he didn't turn her way. "Is that what she told you?"

She considered the implications of that question and her stomach gurgled painfully again.

"She lied?" It wasn't that surprising, really, given what had happened. But why? Everything else had been brutally spelled out for her. No human friends since she was twelve. Certain teachers in certain schools only. No extracurricular activities. No academic over-achievements. No talking to outsiders. Stay away from boys unless they were Pack. Human pets do the work on mooncall. Alphas were obeyed always. Betas were never to be challenged. Mates were chosen by your wolf or your Alpha. If you wanted to go on a trip, you asked the Alpha. If you wanted to save up your money for a big ticket item, you asked the Alpha. Disobey and pay with pain. Ask too many questions and you paid with pain. Cause too many problems and you paid in pain or just disappeared. Those were the basic tenets of her adolescence. Sunny and Mum had never wavered from those rules. And Shifters didn't lie. They'd never told her an outright lie; they talked around the truth, bent it six ways to Sunday, but never an outright lie.

Why let her believe the wrong thing about mating? Because it made her mother seem more like a victim than someone who'd made a choice to deliberately hurt someone she, Lexi, loved? Mum obviously loved Sunny. Why not just tell her and her brother that Mummy and Dad were getting a divorce because Mummy wasn't in love with Dad anymore? Why blame that on being a Shifter, if it wasn't true? Did her mother think that was somehow easier to swallow?

"I need to sit down." She started past him to her little table in the breakfast nook. Then whirled, spoon still clutched in her hand. She spun him around. Shook the spoon under his nose. "Unless you're lying to me. Don't lie to me!"

He made eye contact with her, held it. He nodded deliberately and slowly took the spoon out of her hand. Her rational brain made note of the fact he was moving as you would if you didn't want to spook a wild animal. That same rational part of her brain started laughing at the irony.

"I won't ever lie to you, Lexi. I won't tell you everything sometimes, but that's because I can't. Pack politics, a Warden's geas and all that. You understand about geas?"

"Yes. They're orders you have to obey without question." Sunny's favorite thing. She walked over to the table and sat down so hard it made the chair creak. Her mother had had a choice in leaving her father. Lexi had suspected it, but to hear the truth made it worse. How cruel her mother had been to her father, who'd loved Lexi and her brother more than anything. They had moved three times for Mum's job, never Dad's. He'd sometimes had to work two or three jobs just to keep up with their mother's choice of houses and neighborhoods, but he never complained. God, how could she have done that to Daddy? And to be so callous every time Lexi mentioned him? Denying Lexi the right to even talk about the man who'd raised her, trying to force Sunny on her. Oh, her poor father.

"Lexi?"

She realized Kerr had said her name a few times now. "Sorry. Just realized exactly how much of a bitch my mother really is."

"She's not all bad. She did what she could to help save you last night." Kerr put a bowl of soup in front of her. Lexi mechanically put spoon to mouth.

"You put chicken in it." She frowned at her soup. He let out a gusty sigh.

"I told you I was going to."

"But, I can't afford it," she admitted. Kerr almost brightened.

"We need protein at every meal. I can take care of that." *We* being Shifters, not we being Lexi and Kerr.

"It's a vegetable broth soup."

Kerr slurped a spoonful. Shrugged. "Tastes fine to me."

"You're not getting in here to live. None of you are." She heard the tremor in her voice, the weakness seeping in.

Kerr took out his phone. When the person on the other end picked up, he put it on speaker and set it between them.

"Alpha? This is Kerr. I'm at Lexi's place. Can you explain to her why I should move in? I think she'd appreciate the official answer."

Lexi eyed Kerr. She was pretty sure he'd just given him some kind of code but couldn't figure out what he'd warned the Alpha against.

"Lexi Coolen, you are now under the protection of the Fundy Bay Pack of the Annapolis Valley. You are not to be claimed against your will, do you understand?" The voice was a bit tinny, but Lexi could still recognize it as the one belonging to the man who'd leaned down on her car window last night.

"I don't need protection. I'm perfectly fine without—"

"You are the offspring of a rival Pack. You came to our lands without proper protocol being followed. You can see how that might be a problem, right?" The voice was smooth and deep, commanding without being harsh about it. If you could make character decisions based solely on timbre, this guy was the guy to trust. So of course Lexi was having a hard time doing that.

"Yes."

"Humans who know about us, especially in our hometown, should be monitored, don't you think? Definitely those with absolutely no ties to our Pack? No way to ensure they are loyal? That they know how to keep secrets?"

"No. I don't. I'm not going to tell anyone." He wasn't going to get her to agree to something simply because he could make it sound logical. Save that trick for someone else.

"But we don't know that. We can't know that. We didn't grow up with you, didn't see how you interacted with your other Pack. Nor do we know what made you leave. You are completely unknown to us. Do you understand why we wouldn't let you live here unsupervised, under the circumstances?"

He was being way too reasonable here. Shifters weren't reasonable. At least none of the ones she'd met.

"Because all Shifters are control freaks?"

Kerr chuckled. Bent to his soup. The man on the other end of the phone sighed. She got that reaction from Sunny a lot, too.

"Look, Lexi. You're a threat to our secrecy. Our secrecy is our security. We like being secure and safe. Don't you? We don't trust the Pack you came from. It's not personal." When he put it like that, it did make sense. Strangely, that made her feel better about all of this. She didn't want to feel better. She wanted to feel in control, not like she was being managed.

"I don't trust them either," she stated flatly. She raised her eyebrows so Kerr would get the double meaning of them.

Kerr glanced up from his soup, and his eyes darkened, but he stayed silent.

"You don't trust your own... They did that to you?" The man on the other end of the phone didn't hide his surprise.

Lexi frowned. "They did what to me? What, you think I'm special because I'm the Alpha's stepdaughter? Because the rest of the Pack sure as heck didn't think so."

"Kerr?"

"She's telling the truth."

Lexi glared at Kerr and the phone. She crossed her arms. "Of course I'm telling the truth. Hello? Lived with Shifters, know you all can smell a lie. My mother wasn't the nicest Mum after she turned, OK? How about you don't send someone to live in my house because I don't trust you?"

"How long have you been here, Lexi?" The voice was gentle, as if he'd figured out a big piece of the Lexi puzzle in one conversation. It was unsettling and she had a feeling he was going to be relentless in his own soft way. She gave a lusty sigh.

"I don't know, a little less than a year maybe." Was it her imagination, or did Kerr's spoon seem really bent all of a sudden?

"You've been in our territory for almost a year without coming forward to identify yourself?"

She had the decency to feel just a tad guilty. "Hey, it's not like you guys have a website or anything. There aren't maps issued to show where territories are. I didn't know I should have done that. Moved around a bit and never had to in other places. And anyway, shouldn't you have some sort of watch list for other Packs and their families? Wouldn't I have been on that?" Lexi eyed Kerr, who finished his soup.

"That's true. It's the Beta's responsibility." The Alpha seemed to be chastising his second in front of mere human, a woman no less. A strange woman at that. Sunny would never have behaved like this.

"Hey, Boss, she has a different last name, how was I supposed to know she was who she is?" Lexi watched as Kerr took both their bowls to the sink even though she'd barely touched her soup. He made a show of noting it and narrowed his eyes at her. He was insulted about the soup? Pfft. If he got in here, then he'd have a whole bunch of things to really be insulted about. "What?" He froze in the middle of her kitchen.

"Don't go playing all domestic god on me. I know the second I cave any little bit you'll be in here leaving dirty dishes all over the place, laundry everywhere, and your messy truck parked out in my driveway making the neighbors crazy." She pointed a finger at him on every point and he smirked.

"Tell him to stop laughing at me," she barked at the phone.

"You don't have a very high opinion of us." The voice sounded amused more than anything else.

"Shifters, men, or you two in particular?" Lexi put her elbows on the table and rested her chin in one hand. Kerr slid into the chair closest to her.

"That's partially my fault, my friend. I didn't make a good first impression." Kerr mimicked her pose, but on him it looked sexy. She was pretty sure she just looked worn out. She sat back in her chair and put her hands in her lap.

"I worked really hard to be free of my mother and stepfather and being the Pack kick-me-around back home. I don't want to let a stranger live in my house so they can put me back to being *that*."

"That's not how we run things, Lexi," said the Alpha. She had an inkling he wasn't lying. But could she trust those instincts? Experience was a much better indicator of how things would go in the future, wasn't it?

"Besides, that's not fair. I'm not a total stranger." Kerr tried to take her hand, but Lexi pulled it away from him.

"Kerr, the only things I know about you involves your sex drive, which likes the challenge of nineteen-year-olds, and the fact you drink way too much for my comfort. If I let you in here, it gives the Pack license to waltz in whenever they want, and I've worked too hard for my own space. Not to mention what it will do for my reputation in a small town. What'll Mrs. Faye think?"

"It's a university town and it's not that small. Mrs. Faye needs to get a life anyway," Kerr growled.

"She has a point, old friend." The voice from the phone seemed highly entertained. Apparently seeing his Beta in a snit made his day. He sounded relaxed. Definitely not worried about making her feel comfortable in her own house. But not a dictator. At least not one like Sunny.

Kerr frowned at both of them, but Lexi stuck her chin out, determined.

"I'm not letting her live here, unprotected," Kerr pouted. He was digging in his heels. "Wait, unprotected? What do I need protecting from?" She fixed Kerr with a fierce look that usually quelled rowdy students, but had no effect on a Shifter. She knew it wouldn't, but she gained nothing if she didn't at least try.

"That's one of the things we won't be talking about, right off the bat. You need to trust me first." Kerr leaned forward, his face kissable close. The scent of him hit her, making things tighten that had no business tightening for a Shifter. Still, she was tempted. Sorely tempted, just to see the look on his face, but she shouldn't. Kerr's nostrils flared. Her moment of crazy passed and humiliation surfaced. He must know. She should lean back, but that would be the same as turning her head, which was a sign of submission. A sign she couldn't give. A low rumble of a challenge vibrated the table between them. But Lexi wouldn't turn away.

"Not answering questions...great way to inspire trust. And you're going to force me to trust you how, exactly?"

"Here's my pronouncement. Ready?" The Alpha's voice interrupted before Kerr could make a retort. "Kerr moves in for two months. He pays exactly half of the bills, does at least half of the chores, and he sleeps in a separate room. If, by the end of that time, he feels that you are not a threat to our Pack, we can negotiate another arrangement where you get checked on regularly with no one from the Pack living with you. You are entitled to call on Pack for aid at any time, for any reason, while you are here. Sound fair, given the circumstances? 'Cause the only other way to do this, is to move you in here with me and the other full-time wolves—"

Never again.

"Three caveats." Lexi thought quickly about what she could ask for.

"I'm listening." The Alpha waited patiently. No wonder he could handle a drunk for a Beta. He was managing her from a distance and she didn't even know his name, hadn't seen his face. And she was *listening* to him. Falling back into old patterns. Wait. Was she? Maybe it was just the most logical thing to do in this situation. She wasn't being a push over and wasn't keeping silent. Even she had to admit she probably wouldn't win this fight. They were already in her home. They knew who she was now. And a Pack's safety overrode her comfort. She could see that. Couldn't admit it out loud, but she could see it.

That scared her. How she could accept a Pack back into her life? After all she had been through? But it was only for two months. She could do this. A person had to be careful of how hard they pushed a Shifter. Lexi swallowed and watched Kerr closely for his reactions. The wording had to be just right.

"He cannot consume or bring alcohol onto the premises, nor can he be drunk here. He stays sober for the entire two months." Lexi doubted he be able to make it two weeks. It might give her some brownie points if they saw she was doing OK for those two weeks. If that condition fazed either male, they gave no indication.

"And the second?" Kerr asked.

"He cannot, under any circumstances, continue any activity if I tell him to stop." Lexi's mouth was dry by the end of that sentence, but she got it out. There were all manner of things that Shifters liked to do. Shred furniture with their claws, push you out of the way so hard you hit your head, snap razor-sharp fangs millimeters away from your throat and dry hump you if they had a good day. That last one was Wessel's personal favorite. She instinctively knew that as a Shifter, Kerr would be sneaky about everything in this house. That he'd try to find some reason for the Pack to have permanent control over her. The Pack would try to get to her finances; her few friends; her freedoms. Anything to make sure she was controllable.

As confirmation of her suspicions, Kerr gave her a slow, devious grin. She felt herself pale. But she had no recourse. She knew if she fought them too hard, they'd just get rid of her. If she rolled over for them, they'd take over. Experience had taught her that the hard way. She had to do this just right so she could live as Shifter-free as she could. Two months of possibly out-of-line behavior she could stop with a word was infinitely preferable to the rest of her life spent in the Alpha's house.

"Kerr?" The voice waited for confirmation.

"Agreed. What's the third, Professor?"

She grimaced at the nickname, but didn't correct him. "You can't ever enter my bedroom or bathroom without express permission."

Kerr held up his index finger. "That one might be difficult, Professor. I'll need to search them regularly. And what if there's an emergency? You pass out or are hurt?"

"If I pass out, leave me. Call 911 or someone from the Pack to help. You are not to be alone with me in those two rooms, ever. As for searching, that's fine. Just not while I'm in them. OK, drunkard?"

She thought the insult might make him a little angry, might make them slip up. But no. The grin was back, with interest. She shook her head, tried to review what she'd said to see where she had messed up, but wasn't quick enough.

"I'm fine with it, if you are, Boss."

"Done. We'll help you move the bulk of your stuff in while she's at her classes on Monday."

Kerr ended the phone conversation. Her head throbbed with the threat of a massive headache and her shoulders were tight. The next two months were going to be interesting.

CHAPTER SEVEN

Kerr danced into his apartment. He was allowed in her space. His next job was to convince her he could touch her, and then he'd seduce her, stealing her heart as he pleasured her body. He couldn't wait. Not that it was going to be easy. She'd accepted him in her home. That was a huge first step. But not the biggest. He knew that. Logically, he knew that, but his wolf was sure that getting in the door was going to be the hardest part in getting her to accept him into her life.

She was attracted to his scent, his wolf side pointed out. Kerr nodded as he grabbed a duffle bag and tossed in clothes. The room he was going to stay in wasn't Tiffany's old one, but a guest room that wasn't even on the same floor as Lexi's bedroom. That was a problem. Distance was unacceptable to the wolf and less than ideal for the man. He paused, considering. Her old Pack didn't sound like they'd treated her well. Mistreated her, in fact. He shook his head, searching for his favorite T-shirt. It wasn't in the drawers, nor did he discover it hanging in the closet. He got on his knees to look under the bed. Nope, not there.

Mistreating a treasure like a Queller was simply not in his or any other wolf's nature. The shirt in question appeared beneath a pile of manuals he moved. He pictured Lexi wearing it and nothing else and had to take several deep breaths until his very male response was back under control. The very thought of Lexi made him stir. And she was so skittish. He wanted to chase and tease and coax her into loving. Lexi's sexual appeal had never been an issue with this mating. He was sure he could perform admirably, satisfying them both. His initial impression was she was less than thrilled about that idea. He'd met women like that before, ones who said they didn't like sex when really, it was that they hadn't met a decent partner, one who'd given a damn about their needs. He definitely cared. He was proud of his skills. If and when Lexi gave him a shot at showing her, he'd wow her with them.

He hefted his overflowing duffle out to the truck. Had to make it look heavy so he'd appear human. He took the stairs back to his floor three at a time to compensate. He was in her house. He could charm his way into her bed in two months. The longest it had ever taken with his university bunnies had been three weeks, and that one had been much pricklier than his Lexi. He frowned and dropped his keys. Bending over to pick them up, he wondered if she'd be angry at any mention of other women he'd been with before her. All that was over now. He let himself into his apartment again. She'd had to have been around enough of their kind to know that, right? Slamming the door behind him, he jangled the keys in his hands. He had a lot of questions. Why didn't Lexi know the basics about mating? Or how to move from territory to territory? Didn't she know how to find the Alpha of an unfamiliar territory? Why were there so many gaps in her knowledge? He picked up one of the empty boxes he'd collected from Promontory House and started filling it with his books.

The car ride to the Moon Gathering had cemented him to her. He was hers and she was his and that was that. He grabbed another box and started to fill it with books. He hadn't lied to her exactly. His "man-bits" as she'd called them, weren't mated to her. His wolf was. She'd gotten so upset about it that he'd backed off the word mated altogether. He stacked the book boxes by the door and attacked his desk, throwing things in haphazardly.

In any case, she hadn't been around wolves in a while. Let her re-acclimate to the touching, the care-taking wolves often gave to those humans who'd been taken into the Pack for whatever reason. Treat her as human for now. Carefully, he balanced the boxes with one hand and locked his door. The stairs were empty this time of day, so he ran down with the boxes, put them in the truck and ran back upstairs.

He'd save the higher-status Queller stuff for later. This was the last cardboard box he had. Moving out to his living room/dining area/kitchenette in his little apartment he'd used to separate himself from the other wolves, he picked up an older photo in a frame. Humans, mated to the Pack, all smiling and laughing at the camera at a Pack picnic. He tossed it into the box. That might calm his Lexi.

His Lexi. The thought should have made him run for the hills; instead it put a stupid grin on his face. He put the box on the floor and deposited his game system, carefully wrapped in blanket on top of the low pile inside. The controllers slid down the sides nicely and there was plenty of room left. He'd had nearly a century of being by himself—as much as he could be alone in Pack like his. His wolf brought the picture of Lexi leaning close, staring at his lips and her nose flaring, her own arousal beginning to emerge. Excitement bubbled up in him. He rubbed his hands together. But it was just a physical reaction, he reminded his other half. One that had brought Lexi instant embarrassment. He hoped it was the reaction to his wolf, not Kerr that bothered her. But if he needed to adjust her to being with him first, not his wolf, so be it. To be mated was permanent. It was more than sex. More than a partner. And in this particular case, it was out of both his and Lexi's control. There was no choice. He lifted his arms above his head and stretched until he felt his backbone pop.

A wished-for mating was different. A desired mating was a pairing of the souls. To be truly mated, you were bound together, spirit to spirit. A thing of true beauty. Mating was a step beyond marriage. Clara Rose and he had been well on their way to this bond before her disappearance. But mating was something that Lexi didn't seem to know much about. It sounded as if she'd only seen the worst his kind had to offer. She needed to know it wasn't all bad. To know that Kerr wouldn't hurt her, wouldn't abuse her. That in his Pack, she would be cherished and respected, the way she should have been in her own. Sweeping the pile of games into the remaining space, he folded the lid over on the box. He peeked out into the hallway. Still no sign of anyone. Cocking his head, he confirmed that the building was empty. Using the box to brace the door open, he lifted his leather lazy recliner easily and rushed down to his truck, darting back up before anyone was the wiser. The bed was easier to dismantle and carry. He lashed both down to the bed of his truck and sprinted for his game console and flat screen. Those he put into the cab, not the back.

Even if there might not be love of the human-to-human variety, their connection would still be intense, once fully formed. If he could get past the barriers she'd set up around herself for protection. The fierce stab of anger that anyone had treated so precious a resource as a Queller, let alone Lexi, poorly, made his gut burn. He dropped down and started a few push-ups to burn off his mood.

He'd have to explain that to her as well. The extremes of his nature were pushed even further here. The tides from the Bay of Fundy were the highest in the world, something about this area that was special. Unique. Just like the Pack that lived here, they were affected by the moon's gravity. The push-ups weren't cutting it. He moved to the bar he had installed in his bathroom doorway and began pull ups.

The results of the tides were more…dramatic here, however. Stronger, more dominant wolves who needed to control their already tempestuous natures protected their more submissive members with a passion that could be frightening. Abilities, some supernatural in nature, that elsewhere would have developed over the course of a person's life, came crashing down with the strength of a tsunami overnight without warning. He locked his feet on the bar and tried curl ups. Some talents would have remained undiscovered altogether, if not for living here on the Fundy Basin. And there was always the danger of going too far. He let himself drop off the bar and fished a protein snack out of the box on his shelf. The fridge was always empty here. Plates were paper, forks were plastic, nothing permanent. What was the point? Having company over meant heading to the bedroom as quickly as possible. It wasn't important enough to make a home here.

Oh, your average wolf could overextend himself, drain the human half of his soul's energy so low that there was no controlling the beast until the human could regroup. It could take days, maybe even a week to recover while the beast rode the body's battery into the ground. Snagging his tools, he disassembled the workout bar, putting it into one of the clear plastic bags he had for garbage. Bedsheets, two pillows and a handwoven rug from his mother followed. But here, the Fundy had a way of feeding directly into your beast's soul, like some sort of cosmic battery you were plugged into. Kerr had heard of wolves being trapped on four legs for indefinite periods of time. You ran the risk of forgetting your upright self altogether. Never a good thing. Forbes was rumored to be the only wolf in living memory that had been on four legs for an entire human lifetime and returned. He was Alpha for many reasons. Pine scent burned Kerr's nose as he attacked the floor with a mop and the cleaning fluid.

The trick to survival here came in teaching the younger wolves how to feed their upright half from their four-legged half when need arose. Training began years before their first wild turn. How to deal with the influx of energy that the natural world created was difficult enough, but here it was magnified a hundredfold. He could only imagine what a Queller would be feeling. Especially an untrained one. The bathroom just got sprayed. No scrubbing would help those tiles.

Unexplained insomnia that ended as abruptly as it began, mood swings for no reason, clawing hunger in your belly that nothing could satisfy, and the feeling of being so buzzed, having so much energy and nowhere to put it were only a few symptoms she might be experiencing.

Hefting the last of his things, Kerr locked up. There was no question that Lexi hadn't had any training in her old Pack. Getting her to open up about any symptoms might be problematic. Teaching her to deal with the symptoms without a full explanation even more so, but those had been Forbes's orders. At least until they knew Lexi better.

He'd have to play the Queller stuff quietly. If it hadn't surfaced yet, and she'd been here for a year, she must be suppressing it. He didn't want her hurt, so he and Forbes would have to bring out her abilities slowly, hoping the dam that Lexi had built herself would hold long enough for her to survive the cataclysm that her awakening abilities could cause if they crashed through. It could devastate all involved.

He looked down at the keys to his imposed den of isolation. First, the claiming of his mate. Then they'd figure out why the Queller in her had been drawn to this area. Forbes was very interested in her sudden appearance, how she'd hidden from him and what that portended for the Pack. Also, why a woman with her smarts had chosen a small university like Acadia to do her master's degrees. She could have gone to Yale, Harvard or Princeton. Canadian universities were relatively cheaper, but Forbes couldn't accept that as the sole reason for her appearance. Acadia was predominantly an undergrad university, something the Pack took advantage of frequently.

A little voice in his head warned Kerr that Lexi might not be so easily seduced as his last girlfriends. Kerr was choosing to ignore that assessment. He would be in the house, a tacit claiming as far as other Shifters were concerned. He'd have a year to prove his claim after any declaration at the Moon Gathering. And he wouldn't declare anything until Lexi was fully involved with him. It would be easier if she were on board by the end of their two months of relative peace and quiet. It would be way more fun if it were sooner.

He needed a few things from his office at Promontory House. He kept what he called a go bag for when he had to travel out of the territory on business. The rolling case wasn't so heavy to him, but Lexi might have trouble moving it. He could set his work area up so everything he'd need would be in one spot and would take up even less of her house's space. He'd have to use that somehow. His strength was dangerous at times, but she was as weak as a human right now; he could impress her with it and the fact he wasn't taking up as much space as he'd originally said he would. That would earn him points. He headed up to the house.

He wondered if the Pack she'd come from had used their strength to intimidate her. Shook his head at their folly. Their loss, his gain.

***

Lexi couldn't remember the last time she'd lived with a man. Not that she had tons of dating experience or man experience or even making friends experience, but right about now any experience would have come in handy. She'd been out of her mother's house for twelve years. She was a Master's of Psychology student. She'd survived a wolf Pack. Surely to God she could figure out how to deal with a guy in her house, make him want to leave. Except she wasn't having any luck. Tampons and Midol in every bathroom didn't faze him. Picking up his cell phone and scrolling through his calls didn't seem to bother him at all. He kept the toilet seat down, there was no dirty underwear anywhere she could see, and when he put away groceries they were neither chucked into the pantry helter-skelter nor obsessively neat. He rolled the toothpaste tube down from the bottom but didn't care when she squeezed from the middle. He never left dishes lying around. Never turned the TV up so loud she couldn't hear herself think. He had even done the dusting. He'd dusted. What the holy hullabaloo was she supposed to do with that? She was running out of ideas.

"Those Cheerios are getting mighty soggy."

Lexi blinked and looked at her bowl. She couldn't eat the mess, not that she'd been enthusiastic for breakfast in the first place. He made her breakfast. Every. Day. What the heck? Nobody had made her breakfast since her babysitter and she hadn't had one of those since she was nine. She picked up her spoon and moved the sludge around. "Right. Thanks."

"You stare off into space a lot. You OK with all this?" Kerr put his own bowl down across from her. He'd been here a week and had asked this question in various forms at least a dozen times a day. He inquired about how she'd slept, if her stomach was upset, if she'd had a headache last night, did she have a good day at work, had she broken a nail or stubbed her toe. It was starting to get annoying. No, scratch that, it was already phenomenally annoying.

"If you'd been really concerned about my opinion, you wouldn't have moved in in the first place, Kerr." She pointed her dripping spoon at him but couldn't maintain the eye contact for too long. "You should put on a shirt." She sounded sullen, even to her own ears.

"Wolves run hot, in case no one ever told you that. Don't you like the view?" He leaned back so she could get a better look. She sighed dramatically, hoping to sound uninterested, but she was human. The man had abs like stairs, a dusting of hair that arrowed from his navel to disappear down his jeans. She tried not to drool into her goop. Maybe it was time for a dose of the truth.

"You're sexy as hell and you know it. That's the problem, Kerr. You think of women like amusement park rides. You spend money on some, but the vast majority of us don't thrill you after the first ride."

"Some won't let me on at all." He let the heat reach his eyes, but she didn't take it seriously. The man had women calling him all hours of the night. She hadn't gotten a single full-night's sleep since he'd moved in. At first she'd figured it was a way for him to show off. *See me, Lexi? How wanted I am? You should be thankful I'm here.* Except he never once tried to rub it in her face. He would just pick up the phone as soon as he could reach it and close the door or leave the room and go somewhere she couldn't hear the conversation. If she was in bed, she watched the handset go from green ring-light to orange in-use-light and then dark in under two minutes. Every time. And he stayed in the house. Every time. She couldn't figure him out.

Wolves needed sex and petting and she was providing none, so where and when was he getting it? Who was he getting it from? Why hadn't he tried anything on her other than joking and innuendos at the breakfast table? A week of waiting was making her cranky and jittery.

The train of her thoughts hit her and she felt like smacking her own forehead. She was thinking about him. Maybe that was his plan all along. Well, she wouldn't play. She picked up her bowl and dumped the contents into the compost bin under the sink.

"Want my advice?" she asked him.

"All help is appreciated." He gave her that winning grin. She shook her head.

"Get in line for different ride." She put her dish in the dishwasher and went up to her room to get ready for the day. A few minutes later, she heard the ancient dishwasher start up. Lucky she'd already had her shower. She sighed. He was as good as his word, doing more than half of the chores, inside and out. Her lawn had never looked better. He'd even dug up the gardens in back and the front. There were empty bags from bulbs in the garage, waiting for collection day. The back looked ready for winter. She hoped he wasn't here that long, though she might ask for his help when it came time to plant in the spring. She wondered if he was old enough to remember when the area around Wolfville had been nothing but farms. How old was he, in the first place? Dang it, she was doing it again! *Stop it, Lexi. No thinking about Kerr.*

She gathered her books, notes and the papers she'd graded for Professor Engles, her boss. The man was the very definition of curmudgeonly and she absolutely loved him. He taught all his own classes and graded the freshmen papers himself, though he gave her the occasional class to cover when he wasn't feeling well. When Lexi came through the living room, Kerr was sprawled out on the couch, still shirtless.

"What do you do all day?" It slipped out before she could stop herself.

He looked up, remote aimed at the TV. "I go online to look at porn," he deadpanned.

She rolled her eyes. "And after those five minutes are up? Or am I being too generous?"

He chuckled. "You haven't been with the right men at all, Professor."

"Jack hole." She'd noticed her swearing had picked up the minute he moved in. Needed to make a conscious effort to curb it. She rearranged her bags on her shoulders, getting comfortable for her walk. She didn't look in his direction, did not care what he was doing right this second.

"I check the stocks, do some of the cleaning. We need more groceries today, so I'll do that. Anything special you want?"

She tilted her head. She could be princess-y and continue her campaign of attempt-to-annoy but she hated grocery shopping. "Pineapple, please. Maybe you could pick up some strawberries too? I've been craving fruit. Fruit salad. Fresh. How old are you? Wait a minute, stocks. Did you say stocks, as in Wall Street?" She put her bags and papers down to pull on her walking boots.

His jaw dropped and he stared for a full minute as she hopped from one foot to the other pulling on her footwear. His eyes better not be dipping below her collar; she could feel the girls jiggling. She knew they belonged on a woman with better curves than hers, but she couldn't help what God gave her. At least not on her income. Then he threw back his head and laughed.

"Fruit salad. Got it. Yes, stocks and investments. I actually run the Pack's finances. It's how I make my money, too. How old do you think I am?" He watched her pick up her things. She put some of the papers into a plain tote bag on her left side and a few in a similar bag on her right.

She pursed her lips. "Were you around here for the Acadian expulsion? That was 1755, I think."

"Not born yet."

"What about when Acadia University was founded? Eighteen…"

"1838. I wasn't in the womb yet, but my brother was here."

She brightened. "You have a brother?"

"Had."

"Oh. Sorry."

He waved a hand. "It was a long time ago."

People said that all the time, but it struck her that for him it might not be hyperbole. He was staring at the television, avoiding her gaze.

"Literally?"

He didn't respond. She swallowed and thought of her own brother before all the trouble had started. After the babysitter left, she'd been the one responsible to see he ate breakfast, got dressed, and made it to school.

"A hundred years or five, losing your brother hurts."

His gaze cut to her. "I thought yours was still alive."

She grimaced. Was there nothing they hadn't checked out about her? "Figures you'd know that. But he turned five years ago."

"You stopped speaking to him?"

She shook her head. "Other way around. He turned, was angry at me for not supporting Mum. Not trying the turn myself."

"Trying the turn? They tried to force you to turn?"

"Yeah, so? It worked on Rafe."

"I'm sure it did. But you never tried to blo—"

"I'm human. I've always been human, will stay human just like my father, whether my mother likes it or not." She didn't need to hear how he would have turned someone.

"I see."

She doubted it. "You're as bad as they were. They were so furious when I failed." The memory her mother's rage, cursing her for being so weak-blooded and human burned across her vision before she blinked it back.

He turned back to the TV, carefully avoiding eye contact. Flicked the channel. "I'm going to be honest. I am a little disappointed they didn't manage to trigger your gifts back then, but I'm not angry at you. It would have made things easier. You are not an unaware." His eyes flickered from blue to yellow for a moment. Yellow eyes in a human face meant angry. So who was he mad at if not her? She took her keys and left the house, making sure to slam the door, before he saw the prick of tears his words had caused.

"Unaware? Unaware of what? The dangers in changing? In becoming a monster like my mother?" No, he'd said he was disappointed in her. That hurt. Like Kerr would know anything about her relationship with her brother, anyway. She'd been close to Rafe. Why was what Kerr said bothering her so much? To heck with him. She really didn't understand men at all.

***

Kerr shook his head after the door slammed. Lexi was pissed, that was for sure. He wasn't really clear about why. He'd give her time to cool off and try to talk again. At least the discussion had been enlightening. One, her Pack had tried to scare her Queller abilities out of her. That never worked out well. Two, Lexi had no idea that she was born even more different than her brother. Three, she didn't realize that humans who had no idea about the supernatural world were called unawares. That last one he thought was pretty standard, but could have been different in Lexi's Pack. He'd call Forbes, let him know what he'd found. Maybe he knew of some regional differences. He had a call in to a few more sources to check out Lexi's history, anyway. Time for him to get to work, too.

CHAPTER EIGHT

She'd fallen in love with her little two story house the second she'd wandered down Eden Row and seen the for sale sign. It was old for the area, at least a century. She'd been scared she'd have to clear all her renovations with the town council, which would have been a nightmare of begging Mrs. Faye to wander around her home so she could fix the roof. Thankfully, she was just outside of town, able to avoid Wolfville council altogether, while still being only a quick walk to work. The BAC, the Beveridge Arts Center, where she taught and attended classes and where the majority of the English and some of the Psychology professors had their offices, was an uninspired, red brick building. Of much more interest to her were the three farm markets she had to pass on the way.

The bounty of fresh fruits and vegetables offered by the markets paled in comparison to the Victorian houses that had been turned into bed and breakfasts just inside the town limits, however. She often fought the urge to turn down the B&B driveways and take a quick tour. But she didn't have the extra cash to spend at the markets or the B&Bs and she'd just be wasting their time. There was the Acadia Athletic center to the left, another boring brick and steel construction save for the large river stones that surrounded the outside of the pool. Mrs. Faye's pride and joy, the Atlantic Festival Theater, huddled in a corner just before you crossed over at the old cemetery to the BAC. Not a bad walk to work every day.

Today's trip took twenty-five minutes, fully loaded down with papers and books. She could feel the sweat steam off her. Disappointed in her. Kerr thought her brother was right to feel that way about her. Or that he was entitled to an opinion about it? Why? Why did it matter so much that she be one of them? Out of some sort of Shifter sense of loyalty? Sure, she could see how a human might think that, a little bit. Everybody on the same team, all having the same problems. She couldn't help being different. And she couldn't change the way they had treated her. She'd left her brother with Mum and Sunny after…everything that had gone down after the divorce.

Goodness, she missed her brother. She'd been in that town for six years after high school graduation. Trying to make it work after her father's…accident. Rafe couldn't fault her for not trying to keep the family together. She'd tried her hardest to keep them all together, and still stay sane. What he hated, and Mum too, was her need for independence. So she could never be part of the Pack by becoming a wolf. She could have contributed in other ways. She'd gotten a crappy job working the night shift at a gas station to pay the bills, not taking anything from the Pack, and saved as much as she could. She hadn't been a drain on the Pack resources. She'd had her own place, well, as best she could with the Pack coming and going as they pleased. Her brother had always been welcome.

There had to be a line somewhere. She'd refused to become what her mother had. Refused. Rafe had always respected her choices before the turn. Talked to her, calmed her down sometimes and tried to explain their mother's side of things whenever she'd get bullied by the Pack. He gave Lexi some perspective. She might not have agreed with him, but he'd always listened to her, saw her point of view. He'd been on her side in her efforts to fit in as much as a misfit could. When he'd told her that Sunny and the others were going to change him, make him like them, she couldn't believe it. How could he, after what they'd done to Dad? After what Mum had done, how could Rafe even trust her? She'd thought he was more like her, less like Mum.

The betrayal had cut deep. She'd only stayed those last two years for her brother. The only true family she'd had left was him. Her mother had stopped being her mother the moment Lexi had found out about her father's death. Lexi had gone, taking her half of their father's inheritance with her. The handful of times she'd tried to talk to her brother since then, he'd been angry, aggressive, and as bad as the rest of the Pack. Because he'd been so disappointed in her.

She wasn't disappointed in him, though. Hurt, yes. Betrayed and never going to trust him again. But she did understand. Keeping his head in the sand was one way to deal with the fact that their mother had been responsible for their father's accident. If her dad had been accepted by the Pack as her biological father, he would have been protected. He'd never have been walking alone at night. He'd have been safe. But their mother had withdrawn her protection and their father had been run over. Yet Rafe kept insisting that the only monster in the family was Lexi.

The more Lexi thought about it, the more she realized that was what her brother had always done. Rafe had always been closer to Mum than she had. He couldn't leave her. But Lexi could. Had no problem going, once she'd made sure her brother survived the transition.

Disappointed in her? What really burned was the fact that deep down, she knew Kerr was right. Rafe did blame her for not being able to forgive Mum. But she just couldn't. Dad had always been her best friend. The one she could talk to without worrying if she was going to hurt his feelings or him being so mad at her that he wouldn't speak to her for days. He was always there. Always. Until one day he wasn't. Rafe was angry with her for not shifting, for being less than what their mother wanted, for leaving when he couldn't. Lexi could never forgive her mother and Rafe could never forgive Lexi. Because in Rafe's eyes, Mum was always right, even when she couldn't be more wrong.

"Oh, excuse me!"

Lexi had bumped into a blonde ponytail; she'd been so intent on her internal rampage, she hadn't been paying attention to where she was going. Or who might be going in the same direction. Her tote bags exploded onto the cement.

"Hi, Lexi! How's life with Kerr?" Bright, bubbly, smiling at her like nothing was amiss, Tiffany helped Lexi pick up her bags.

"Err, they're OK, I guess." Lexi tried not to make eye contact.

"Un-huh. You were muttering to yourself and slammed into me. You're red in the face and puffing. I'm guessing he's driving you crazy."

"Um, a little," she admitted.

"Is he walking around the house naked yet?"

Lexi blinked. Tiffany burst out laughing. "Wait for it, it's coming." Both women stood up.

"I've got to be going."

"Let me help you carry these up to the department. I've got a few minutes before class."

The elevator seemed to take forever to get to the fourth floor. Lexi had no idea what to say to the young woman now. Certainly not what had been on her mind.

Lindsay, the department secretary, seemed to be waiting for them. She pounced at them as soon as the doors were open. Well, pounced on her. Tiffany, she regarded curiously.

"Dr. Engles left a message. Could you cover his classes? He's had me take detailed notes on what he expects covered. I told him to email all this to you, but he's so old fashioned, don't you think? Anyway, I took down the old man's wishes for the classes this morning. Basically he wants you to go over the papers you graded this weekend. You're all red-faced. What's wrong?"

Tiffany spoke up. "She's got a new roommate. Kerr MacDonald. I moved out once I dumped him. Got a condo in Railtown."

Lindsay did a double take of Lexi. Lexi bit back sarcastic comment. Lindsay would ensure that tasty little tidbit about her new roommate made the rounds of the faculty before noon. Oh goody.

"Thanks, Tiffany."

"Just trying to help. Anyway, I've got to get to class. Later!" With a cheery wave, Tiffany was off, conveniently handing Lexi's papers off to a more than willing Lindsay, who accompanied her to Engles's office. Lexi had a key to this door as well as to the elevator.

For the first time since she'd moved in town, Lexi wondered if Lindsay might belong to the local Pack. Lindsay was from here. She was an intelligent woman and could have picked up on a lot of things. Or she could have been recruited by the Alpha. Lindsay would have been perfectly placed to move certain students in or out of the department, and no one would know the difference.

Lexi shook her head. She was being paranoid. She'd been free for the year she'd been in Wolfville. Hadn't had to answer to anyone but herself, or so she thought. Hadn't actually considered the possibility that she might have moved into another Pack's domain. She'd just put her head down, studied and worked her butt off. She'd already gotten a Master's of English before coming here. She'd thought her Master's of Psychology would be the same. Wolfville was totally different than the city she'd grown up in. People smiled here. They said hello to strangers. The town held festivals that everyone attended, not just big shots and hoity-toity types. It had felt safe. Historic and peaceful.

But now that illusion was shattered. Being around a Pack again wasn't going to be blissful, and peace might be a fairy tale at this point in her life.

"Kerr MacDonald, huh? Nice catch. Wouldn't mind a red face at work if he was the one who gave it to me." Lindsay fanned herself.

Oh my God. "No. That's not…he insulted…he didn't give me this, I just walked too quickly to work. That's all, Lindsay."

Lindsay's eyes grew round. Then she giggled as she left Engles's office. "Right. Mum's the word! I won't tell a soul. You go, girl." She gave Lexi a quick tap on the shoulder and marched down to her office.

"He's just a roommate!" she yelled after Lindsay.

"Of course he is!" Lindsay hollered over her shoulder. Lexi groaned and banged her head against the wall. She could almost hear the phone being dialed as Lindsay's office door closed tight. *So the end of my reputation begins.* At least it was Lindsay. She wouldn't spread it outside of the faculty and lord knew everyone in faculty kept the dirty laundry in house, so to speak, lest someone fling a nasty rumor back. Mutually assured destruction and all that. She made her way down to her office, a room with several cubbies that the grad students all had access to. She dropped off her research books and went to the professor's class.

Who among the class were students and who were actually wolves? Before today, when she'd looked at the names she hadn't wondered if any howled at the full moon, or got furry and curled up on their dorm beds. For the last week, she'd had to stop herself from asking if Lucas wanted a milk bone or did Julie need a chew-toy when she checked them off. It was the first week of October, nearly three weeks until the next full moon. Would she be able to tell just by looking? Would there be other clues? Why hadn't she paid more attention back in the city?

Because, she answered herself, she'd been too busy keeping her head down and her eyes away from anything that resembled challenging authority— the one exception being her mother's orders. She hadn't wanted to learn so much about Pack physiology. She handed out papers in the class. Grinned at those who'd gotten a lower grade and put up some suggestions on the board.

But she must have noticed *something* useful. Compare what she knew back then to what she saw now. How pervasive was the Pack in a small town with a constantly changing population? She hit the remote and showed six slides from Dr. Engles's previous presentation, pointing out key words again. More students took notes this time.

The university must have been a Godsend here. Fresh supply of fresh faces, fresh workforce, ever-changing businesses, young people who were constantly coming and going. The Pack could have been hiding in plain sight for years, if they shared their wealth and bought some of the local land with plenty of forests.

She put up one of the papers from a previous year and went over that student's mistakes. More pens flew across pages and fingers tapped keyboards loudly. A few students took pictures from their phones. Some of the students she'd seen around had been very attractive. Not that attractiveness had anything to do with being a wolf, but most were not barking up the ugly tree. But she'd run into the students at the gym and thought their appearance was genetics, working out and good eating. There were at least three health food stores she could name in town. She picked up the text book and showed the students how to pick out the important details that Dr. Engles would undoubtedly use on quizzes. There was a mad scrambling for highlighters.

Nothing spoke to the extra that being a Shifter gave you. Her brother had gone from being 298 pounds to a slim, muscled 195 in less than a month when he'd first turned. And he'd increased his bad eating habits, if anything. She shook her head. So much for feeling peaceful.

The first class went relatively smoothly, but as soon as the second group drifted in, the digital projector in the classroom went wonky. A call to tech was useless and she refused to just send the students the notes in an email, so she had to go old school and write on the whiteboard. The groaning from the classroom echoed and she stifled a smile. The notes were still up for the third class, which gave her more time to lecture. Except they weren't paying attention to her voice. They mostly just took pictures with their phones. The more serious students typed while she gave a bit of a historical background for the case studies they were going to discuss in the next week. She spotted one student's head lolling as he snored loudly. Annoyed, she slammed a book on the table. Everyone jumped. She reminded them they'd be responsible for the information whether or not she finished her lecture. She erased all the notes and asked students to come up to the board individually, to come up with examples in their lives or modern culture of the topic they were studying in the texts. She held them overtime to make sure everyone had a chance and they knew how to apply some of the information they should have shown in their reports. They all bolted from the room when she said she was ending.

Sighing, she gathered up her books and the papers of students who had missed class this morning and headed upstairs to her office. If a Shifter made it past the death of everyone they'd been born with, they were generally well adjusted. So she'd been told. It was one of the reasons they'd been pressuring her to turn, especially her stepfather. She was perfectly happy living her very boring, relatively short life without being part of the Pack politics, and to heck with her mother having to deal with the pain of her death. Mum had chosen her path, let her live with it. Even as she thought it, Lexi knew she was kidding herself. If there was one thing she and Shifters shared, it was a phobia about losing control of one's own life. If Sunny could control his mate's happiness, he would. If her brother could get her back home, he would. And her mother wasn't out of the game yet. Not with Lexi being in someone else's territory. But would these wolves play her Mum's game? Was the game here the same?

She sat at her desk, pulled out one of the books for her thesis and tried to focus. After about five minutes of staring at the same paragraph, she let her head hit the desk. Her biggest mistakes in her mother's Pack had been when she'd threatened the order by disobeying so many of her mother's decrees. Humans were subordinate to submissive wolves. Submissive wolves were subordinate to dominant wolves, who were subordinate to Betas who were subordinate to the Alpha pair. Lexi had fought too hard not to be submissive to her mother to let that get very far. Mum had always been somewhat demanding, stubbornly convinced she knew the correct course for her daughter's life, no matter what Lexi had wanted. Lexi had wanted to be a writer. Mum had said she couldn't make a living that way. So Lexi had decided to become a counselor. Reluctantly, she put her book away and headed downstairs again.

The fourth class of the day was a test. She passed out the papers and reminded everyone to keep their eyes on their own work or she'd give a zero. No talking or leaving for the bathroom until you were finished and had handed in the paper. Nothing for her to do but watch that no one was cheating. After the fiasco with the phones from last class, she had everyone put their cell phones at the front with their names written on the board above it. No computers, no iPods, nothing except a pen and their test papers. Many students tried to say she was infringing on their freedoms. Well, they were free to walk out the door and complain to the Head of the Department and she told them so. No one did. Satisfied, she crossed her arms and watched the whiners closely.

When Mum had told her she couldn't go to university because they didn't have the money, Lexi hadn't given up. She'd gotten loans, taken what she'd managed to save during summer jobs during high school, and worked hard for scholarships.After graduating with both her Bachelor of Psychology and English degrees in a record three years, Mum had *decided* Lexi would pay off her loans by substituting and living at home. Lexi had gotten a job in Dubai for a year instead. Then northern Canada for a year while she took online courses for her Master's in English. Every cent went toward her bills. She'd vowed the money her father had left her would only go on the place she wanted to call home.

She'd paid off her loans herself and held on to her father's inheritance, built up a nest egg before coming to Wolfville, only to start up the whole process again with loans and working while studying for her second master's.

It had been hard to escape. She hadn't told her mother her plans. Hadn't had any friends in the Pack, that was for darn sure. They'd kept her isolated and terrified whenever they'd met. All she'd done was work, study and sleep.

Kind of like now, she mused. She took the papers from the classes back up to Dr. Engles's office. Mondays were the busiest for both she and Dr. Engles. And it wasn't over. She still had her own research to do. She went to the library and got a few more books for her thesis, wrote a few pages, but nothing serious. She graded a few papers but her brain gave out after her fourth C-. She sighed, got up and gathered her things, locked the office and headed over to the arena on the way home. The whole day felt like a wet sock in her boot: icky and miserable. A workout would clear her head.

At least, that had been the plan. The lower level of the BAC held a gallery open to the public and sure enough, Mrs. Faye had decided to partake of the arts today. She flagged Lexi down on her way out the door.

"Ms. Coolen! Ms. Coolen, a word."

The woman always wore large hats. Today's ensemble had one of the broad-rimmed head gear in burgundy, with long, black feathers. It topped off a brown wool coat, which must have been sweltering in the early October heat, over a muted flora skirt, finished off with sensible, black, flat walking shoes. The woman dressed like she was in an episode of some British period television drama. She had apparently appointed herself the Dowager Duchess of the town's propriety.

She was also one of the largest "anonymous" donors that Acadia had. Faculty were instructed to "humor" her whenever she arrived. To Lexi's knowledge, the woman wasn't even alumni.

"Ms. Coolen, what's this I hear? You've taken up with that scoundrel, Kerr MacDonald?"

Lexi ground her teeth. "My roommate, Tiffany, left abruptly. I took the only available renter applicant I had." It was none of her business who lived with Lexi. Though why Lexi felt the need to defend Kerr to Mrs. Faye escaped her at the moment.

Mrs. Faye's nose rose to the sky, as did the insufferable woman's voice. "You should have consulted me. I could have found you a much more suitable housemate. I trust that the relationship is purely professional?"

Lexi took a deep breath. "What it is, Mrs. Faye, is none of your business."

She marched away as Mrs. Faye sputtered and hissed something unintelligible after her. The farther away she got, the more she regretted her hasty words. Mrs. Faye could make things uncomfortable for her. Since Lexi had been in town, Mrs. Faye had, allegedly, smeared the local Victorian expert's reputation so much, she'd had to move to another university. Lexi had just painted a big target on her own back. And Lexi wouldn't have been in the woman's cross hairs at all if it hadn't been for Kerr. Her stomach did a roll followed by a loud gurgle and she fished in her bag for a peppermint. A workout. That would help. A true and proper workout. It had to, didn't it?

The fitness center was state of the art, but the change rooms were in an older part of the building, so they weren't very close. Lexi rented a locker there. It housed a fresh set of workout clothing just for days like this. She changed quickly, pulling on runners, and stretched. The changing room was connected to the pool, the smell of chlorine was strong and her locker and the one next to it were rusted on the bottom. She heard a bunch of girls giggling at the lockers behind hers and figured there must be a meet for the local swim team, the Wolfville Tritons. How many of those kids were gonna grow up to become Shifters, if their parents had anything to say about it?

An apple hit her lightly between her shoulders and the giggling increased as her patience plummeted. She frowned and picked up the offending fruit.

"Professor!"

Kerr. In the women's locker room? No. He wasn't allowed to come in the bathroom when she was...well, technically she wasn't in her bathroom, so she had no right to expect privacy here. It was the last straw. She peered around the lockers and saw him, his hand over his eyes, peeking through his fingers with a bag dangling from his elbow and another apple in his hand. He looked cute, she had to admit, but an image of her mother barging into the bathroom as she showered flashed through her mind. There was never any privacy with Shifters around. Shifters were to blame for it all. And here was the very latest insult and injury acting like he gave a damn about her modesty, ready to make more demands on her.

The giggling ensured this would get back to Mrs. Faye's ears. She wondered if the Pack saw the old woman as a threat yet. Her head pounded and she saw red. If she wasn't careful, she was going to do something that would upset her deal with the Shifter-locals.

A tiny voice said that Kerr wasn't really to blame for everything that had gone wrong in her life, but he made a damned easy target right now. Something was building under her skin, something that had no claws but would cut whoever or whatever she directed it at nonetheless. It frightened her. She had to control this sudden explosion of rage bubbling in her brain. She was a good person, but she'd never been this angry before. Violence. She wanted it. She slapped her thighs until they stung without release. She clenched her jaw, wondering where she'd put this energy.

Exhaustion might work. The energy that was surging to her limbs might make it take a long time, but she could try. Kerr, Mrs. Faye, her rude students, none of it mattered more than breaking this wave of rage.

"I'm going for a run around the rink. There's a track especially for it, playboy. Go away. I'll see you at home."

Kerr looked at her like she had three heads. "Can you come out, please? I've got something important I want to talk to you about."

Lexi slammed her locker closed, spun the lock and stormed past him, out the door and stomped up the cement steps. She didn't stop when he called her all the way down the hall. She plugged into her cheap MP3 player, drowning the outside world. She wasn't fit for company right now. The kicker was, she knew it. She knew she was being unreasonable, but couldn't seem to stop herself from being offensive and rude.

She just needed some peace. A little space and she could shove this ragewave back down. Stop the spikes of violence from erupting from her skin. She was starting stretches against the arena seats when her earplugs were yanked out of her ears.

"What the hell did I do?" Kerr shouted. His voice echoed in the nearly empty rink.

"Moved in," she shouted back. Dang. She hated giving in. Losing control. She grimaced. She could hurt him. She didn't want to hurt people. Not like this, not in public and not because she was losing control, but there, under the surface, the rage swelled. *Deep breath, Lexi.* Get back under control. She made fists. Her skin burned, tight and hot. In a minute, she worried others might see steam rising from her.

He put his hands on his hips, bags flaring to the sides deliberately making himself look ridiculous. "Sorry, princess. You're stuck with me." He smiled, trying to be charming. She shook her head. He needed to understand how out of control this was for her.

"I need space. Leave me alone. We can talk when I get back home."

Kerr cocked his head at her, took a deep breath. Then another. A very Shifter movement. Her mother had done that, right before she'd blasted Lexi with a verbal tirade or a couple of blows. Since Kerr was male, she was betting the blows were coming. She tensed, ready to drop into fetal position.

"If you're going to hit me, knock me out. And expect charges when and if I wake up."

He rolled back on his heels, eyes wide. It took him a minute to come up with something to say while she glared. "Don't you have a high regard for me? Or is it men in general?"

"Today, it's your entire race." She could taste the bitter venom she spat at him with that sentence long after she put the headphones back in and started running. And she hated that. Hated losing her temper and lashing out, the way her mother had.

She wanted to punish herself, so she pushed, running at her top speed. Not for a burst or a measured interval either, but running for as long as she could. Five laps turned to ten, turned to twenty. Forty. Fifty. Her muscles ached, but she wouldn't stop. She couldn't talk to a therapist about her situation. Couldn't write it out in a journal for fear of the journal being discovered. *Stop thinking, Lexi. Run. Just run until there's nothing left.*

When she thought she was going to drop, she let herself find a slower rhythm, so long as she was still running. She wasn't easy on herself. This was going to hurt tomorrow, which suited her mood fine. It wasn't a perfect world. Maybe she could run until it was a better one.

CHAPTER NINE

Kerr paced the living room. He'd been so surprised by Lexi's agitated state he'd completely forgotten the inane reason he'd drummed up to go see her. She'd been close to exploding. The waves of emotion coming off her smelled burned, angry. And the closer he'd been, the higher the emotion had gotten. So he'd backed off, but called in a favor and had one of the other wolves' human mates go for a run around the track.

She didn't know how to tell a Shifter from a human yet; he was pretty sure his surveillance had gone unnoticed. She'd said as much when she admitted to traveling around the world. He'd checked and no one had registered that she'd been in their territory at all. Granted, according to his information, she hadn't left the international school she'd been teaching at in Dubai much. She'd stayed close to her apartment or sighting-seeing with other staff members only. The extremely cold and long winters in northern Canada had kept her indoors much of the time. She must have gone stir crazy up there. All the while suppressing her Queller abilities.

He checked the clock. Three hours. She'd been running too long. He ran his hand through his hair. He was absolutely certain that she had been supressing, rather than them being latent. Latent implied biological or developmental difficulties, while this stoppered-up, ability-stifling fear he sensed in Lexi was definitely psychological. Because just like his wolf was harder to control at high tide, Lexi's temper had been flaring when the waters were at their peak this afternoon. The

Queller rose to the surface like the wolf did, but Lexi hadn't done any of the things a Queller could do to alleviate the pressure. Here she was, exploring all sorts of psychological healing methodology and not applying any to what had happened to her.

He was just as certain about the type of abuse she'd received from her former Pack. Little things tipped him off. The fact she slept with the bed arranged so she could see under the doorway in case of a potential attacker. How she kept the window curtains closed but the outside lights on whenever she was home so there was no chance of someone not casting a shadow if they approached her house. An early warning system. She always locked the door behind her in the day, even though she couldn't live in a safer neighborhood. No one could stand behind her without Lexi moving so she didn't have an unknown at her back. She'd fidget unless she could see and face the doorway when she was seated, like she'd been caged with no escape. She hadn't been safe in her own home and had had to be vigilant against attack. She'd been terrorized.

His wolf was nearly out of his skin with worry, but that was the last thing Lexi needed to see right now. He went to the door and peered through the curtains, a useless gesture because he would have heard something before he'd seen it. If she did suspect his wolf had mated to her, she might bolt and that was not an option he was willing to consider. He'd either drag her back to where her abilities might explode out of her control or he'd be her supernatural stalker for the rest of their lives. Because Quellers lived as long as the Shifters they were claimed by. And Lexi was unequivocally his.

The Pack healer was currently away on a conference in Chicago, otherwise he'd have asked her to meet with Lexi. Kerr had done everything he could think of to make Lexi feel safe around him. He'd left his favorite soap in every room with a sink so she could get used to his scent. Padded around making lots of noise as he walked so she wouldn't feel like prey around him. He'd even let her have total control of the TV remote even though he hated HGTV. He DVRed his stuff anyway.

He did his own laundry, but only because he'd have to go into Lexi's room to grab hers and he didn't want to do that yet. He didn't want to break her caveats. His wolf was going crazy over her too-thin frame so he'd taken over the cooking duties, slowly discovering her favorites. He vacuumed the upstairs hallway carpet every day, just so he could wake her up every morning and be the first to see her. Maybe he could wear shirts more often, but his wolf was insistent that he display himself for his mate. He wanted to hold her and tell her she was safe with him, but he couldn't. She flinched at even the most casual, accidental contact.

And the Queller inside of her was rising. He would swear she threw off heat in her sleep; she woke soaked in sweat every morning. Today the air around her had shimmered. She could hurt not only him but his Pack if she kept going unchecked, not to mention fry her own mind to hell in the process.

And any witch in the vicinity would be alerted to her presence immediately. That would be bad for all concerned. But could telling her what she was be enough to trigger an even bigger episode? With all that wild power inside of her and Lexi unable to point it in a safe direction, she might as well be a loaded gun. The Alpha and his mate might be able to help her direct it until she got her abilities under control. His wolf's connection to her might be enough if he had help. This meant that she needed to get to know Forbes, way ahead of Kerr's schedule.

He snatched his cell phone from the charger and punched up Forbes's number.

**

Lexi found Kerr sitting on the couch when she got home, waiting for her. Before he could open his mouth, she held up her hand. She dropped her bags by the door. Stripped off her boots. She shuffled over to the chair facing the couch and him and fell into it. The salt from her sweat stung her eyes. She let it drip.

"OK." She braced for the blasting she deserved.

Kerr took a deep breath again. Stood up. Sniffed in her direction like a dog. A dead giveaway of what he was. But there was no one else here. She would have mechanically smiled at the action if she didn't feel a blip away from malfunctioning. He didn't try to disguise what he was doing. Which she appreciated, just then. She'd seen the same behavior in the men of her mother's Pack, right before they'd try to knock some sense into her. On her mother's orders.

"Body shots only, please. Bruises are easier to hide."

He froze. Something flitted through his eyes. She thought it might be outrage, but it was too much to hope for. "Your mother's Pack beat you."

She nodded. "I wouldn't toe the company line."

He sat down and made fists on his knees. He kept his head down. Lexi frowned. This was either going to hurt really badly or something else was going on. She tried to muster the will to care either way and found herself unable. She was too damned exhausted. After several minutes, he got up and went into the kitchen.

"I made supper." His voice sounded odd.

A tendril of fear skittered up her spine. He wasn't acting like the other Shifters she'd pushed. She'd assumed the only thing that had kept her from being dragged out of the arena was the chance of making a scene. She heard drawers open and slam shut. Dishes clattered. Cupboards rattled from being banged closed. Lexi never moved. Kerr reappeared around the corner with two plates. Steak, fried potatoes, asparagus and corn salad sat artistically arranged. He set his on the coffee table in front of what she now thought of as his place on the couch and held hers out until she rose to take it from him. The second her hand met the plate, he refused to relinquish it until she met his gaze.

"We need to clear up a few things. Sit next to me."

"I'd rather stay out of swinging range if you're going to start off yelling. In case things escalate."

Kerr growled, his eyes glowed amber briefly before becoming blue again. He faced her. "Listen, because you obviously aren't picking up on the signals I've been trying to send. I'm *never* going to hit you. Not in panic, or in anger. Not because I'm bored or because you annoyed me or hurt my feelings. Never because

I disagree with the choices you make for your life. You don't have to fear violence from me, Lexi."

"You're angry," she pointed out. He gave a forceful shake of his head.

"Not at you. At the people who turned a strong, smart, passionate woman into someone who expects to be beaten because she has feelings. Please sit by me. Please?"

She blew a raspberry. It was the only thing she could think to do in the moment. No one had ever said that to her. He saw her as strong? Her mother's Pack had emphasized how weak she was to them. Smart, she understood. Most people made the mistake of assuming a couple of degrees meant you were at a certain higher intelligence level. Passionate? He saw passion in her? Where and when did he see that? Could she trust it, the way he saw her? Or his word, about not hitting her, even though he was a Shifter?

He'd kept his word so far. He hadn't entered her room while she'd been in there. Hadn't "accidentally" walked in on her in the shower. The worst he'd done was vacuum too damned early, waking her up out of the nightmares she'd been having, but that was a blessing in disguise. The Alpha had kept his word so far too. Was she actually going to take a chance and put her faith in him not to hurt her? It was worth a shot. Besides, given her terrible behavior, she owed him at least the benefit of the doubt.

She sat down on the couch facing him, her back against the arm and her leg curled under her plate. He handed her a knife, fork, and paper towel. He seemed embarrassed at the paper toweling. "You didn't have napkins."

Her jaw flapped open. "You're here in my house to make sure I don't talk. Trust me, I've been well trained. I know the consequences. And you're worried about the napkins?"

"Why did your mother reveal herself to you, do you think?"

The question took her off guard. Reveal herself? That was an odd way to put it. Mum had told Lexi she was a Shifter because she had to, she supposed. It was the only way to explain to twelve-year-old Lexi why things would be different and why Mum was leaving Dad for another man. Well, not the only way, but the only explanation that her younger self would have remotely accepted.

Or was it? To tell the truth, Lexi had asked herself the same thing several times and could never seem to come up with an acceptable answer. On charitable days, she thought maybe it might be to warn her about what was out there. Others it was that she wanted to keep her under her thumb. Lexi shrugged.

"I was her pet," she said. The title had burned. Sometimes an endearment, other times a curse, Lexi had never been sure which meaning was intended on any given day. She thought her mother might have flipped a coin in order to decide.

"You should have been given a much higher title than that."

She frowned. "Because I was the Alpha's mate's human daughter? My brother didn't get special treatment, even after he was turned."

He nodded, as if she'd confirmed something. "She didn't tell you."

"Tell me what?"

He pointed to her meal. "Eat up. I want you to meet the Alpha tonight."

She drew in a sharp breath, her spine like a fence post. "And if I don't want to meet him face to face?"

He took a bite, buying himself some time to consider his answer. "We could watch a movie?"

Watch a movie? Really? He suggests that the Alpha wants to meet her, which can only mean she would be getting disciplined in some painful way, and when she balks, he says they could turn on the tube? This was shaky ground. Anger, she understood. How sad was it that kindness was unfamiliar. The ragewave she'd managed to send back out to sea threatened to return again. She felt her mouth move without her brain.

"Wouldn't that interfere with your social calendar? They've been calling all weekend." She turned her head and looked at him sideways.

He didn't grin at her attempt to wound him, but he didn't look offended either. "What do you want to do?"

"What if I wanted to go to bed?" she shot back.

This time he did grin. "Any time, Professor."

Darn it, she'd walked right into that one. "By myself, Fluffy."

He nodded, all signs of teasing gone. "Just be aware that I'm going to ask every day until you're ready."

She took in a breath, appalled. "To sleep with me?"

He chuckled. "To meet my friend. You need to meet the Alpha, face to face. Then the whole Pack. The sooner, the better."

"So I should just give in now while I still have my sanity?" She snapped. The ragewave was closer. She took a couple of deep breaths and it seemed to recede again. This was…unacceptable. That wasn't a strong enough word to describe what was going on in her brain, but she couldn't think of anything else just yet.

"That might be easier on both of us," he joked. He put a hand on her knee. Slowly, and with plenty of time for her to pull away. She fought the urge to jerk away, and was rewarded with a sigh.

"Seriously, though. You don't have to be afraid here, Lexi. It's your home. I'm not here to make you leave. The Pack might not trust you, but I'm not…we're not about to let anyone hurt you, either." He lifted his hand and returned to his meal. He had such dainty manners for a big guy. He cut the steak with quick, efficient movements. Then he leaned the knife against the plate, held his back straight as he raised his fork to his mouth and took the bite. This quiet ritual was repeated until his meal was finished. It was as if he sat in some blue-blood dining room and not at her coffee table. She closed her eyes. Ignored him, as a test at first, but he didn't make any more sounds after he'd finished his meal. Just waited. She let the quiet of the house seep into her mood and it stilled some. Her anger turned to weariness.

"I don't want to go tonight," she said, too afraid of his reaction to open her eyes.

"OK. We'll see tomorrow."

There was some shuffling, her untouched food taken out of her hands. When she opened her eyes again, she was alone in the darkened living room.

**

Kerr watched her for a few minutes. Lexi's body was still much too thin and she really needed to eat some of the food he'd made her but he wouldn't push. Not tonight. Something had set her off today. Something had brought all this close to the surface. He needed to get more information. He needed to see to the Alpha and bring him up to speed with what was going on; how hazardous Lexi was to herself and to others. He needed his Alpha's help to come up with a plan. Because as it stood now, Lexi was dangerous. If her abilities exploded without any direction or purpose as they burst out of her for the first time, she could kill herself, or someone else. Maybe the Alpha would decide she was too dangerous to live.

Kerr's wolf couldn't live with that decision. And Kerr was afraid he might not be able to either.

Chapter Ten

Lexi went up to bed after rising the last cup in the sink. Kerr had assured her he'd do the dishes before heading out for a few hours, but he'd already done dishes for the day. It was her turn. She'd do them by hand. She felt a little guilty and lazy anyway, since she was used to doing everything. She'd taken quiet pleasure in washing up, and it gave her an excuse to ignore his presence in the room with her.

He stayed close for the half an hour she puttered around the kitchen. She'd sneaked glances at him every once in a while. His eyes were still tight around the edges, but he didn't display any other signs that he was upset. She'd made a cup of tea for herself after he refused one, watered her herbs on the window sill, and swept the floor before attending to the food. She'd wrapped it all up, put it in the fridge, in what had become a companionable silence. After the dishes, she'd left Kerr just sitting there and walked up her stairs to her bedroom. She was almost calm again. A nice feeling after the day she'd had.

When she flicked on the light, a parcel sat on her bed. Double dog poop, what had her mother sent her now, trying to tempt her to come back? The ragewave made spots dance before her eyes and she doubled over, trying to push it back. But she had to do it silently, lest Kerr come charging up the stairs, trying to help her. She'd feel like even more of a numbskull if he saw her with one of her headaches; a sure sign to Sunny that she'd been too weak to attempt the turn to Shifter.

Breathe, breathe, she coached herself. In through the nose, out through the mouth. Focus on the breath, on her feet planted firmly on the floor, on the rage and fear draining away.

***

Kerr slipped out quietly, locked up, got in his truck and headed for Promontory House. It wasn't a very original name, given over two hundred and fifty years ago, but it had stuck. He loved that you could see the giant farmhouse only as you made the final turn down the long driveway. It was old, by human standards. It had been lined on the outside with river stones, rounded and multi-hued grays, browns and blacks. He always thought of it like an iceberg—what you could see represented only a small portion of the den. And it overlooked the lowlands around the river. Wolfville was in a valley after all. Promontory House gave the wolves a sense of security in times of trouble, was far enough away from any other houses that strange, inhuman sounds wouldn't carry even on the clearest night, and the lands were lushly wooded. It had a number of service roads that the local game hunters were unofficially permitted to use so long as they didn't abuse the privilege or the wildlife that regularly stalked Forbes's land. There were a few other dens hidden around the valley, all connected to this main one, but this was where the wolves gathered every moon. To hunt, to laugh, to connect with one another and the Alpha. This was where Kerr often found himself whenever he was troubled.

Truth be told, it had seen better days. Not that the grounds weren't immaculate. The gardens, both floral and vegetable, would have been the envy of the local gardeners, had they been permitted to see them. But the stones seemed extra shabby tonight, the wood a little too weather-worn. There was no welcoming light in the windows, giving the appearance of the gaping maw of a skull: inhuman and inhospitable. No humans, other than mates, had crossed the threshold for as long as Kerr had known Forbes. Humans were the unknown, were not to be trusted, and were just shy of being the enemy of the Pack. They were the reason Kerr had to be careful around Lexi, why he had to keep so many secrets from her. Right now he wanted nothing to do with them. He hated the unawares.

Lexi didn't count as human, on so many levels, yet until she'd earned the trust of the Alpha and the Pack, she wasn't permitted to know about this place. This safe place, where no one would hurt her, where she'd find a place to belong. One of his greatest treasures and he couldn't give it to her, show it to her, tell her about it when she obviously needed it the most. He parked his truck and stomped into the house. So many things about this whole mess could be cleared up with just a simple conversation, one he was aching to have and had been forbidden. Forbes hadn't even answered his phone call, just sent a one-word text. *Later.*

"Forbes!" The darkness echoed his voice, made it seem harsher.

"He's gone. The Warden summoned him this morning." Taskill Starrett rubbed his copper head and yawned as he rounded the corner. He was barefoot and wearing a pair of plaid pajama bottoms. His tan from his time in California with another Pack was visible when he flipped on the kitchen light.

"Jesus, man, when did you get back?" Kerr thumped his packmate's back in a hearty embrace. It was good to see him. Pack practice was to send problematic or too-visible members to another friendly territory for twenty or thirty years, long enough for human memory or photographic evidence to fade or be explained away by relatives coming to visit. Task and his twin brother Dax had been gone for twenty-five. Task grimaced.

"Dax and I were the ones who delivered the summons this morning. The 13th Warden is fading. Things are getting a little unstable in some of the other territories. People vying for the guy's job before he's even gone. It's disgusting, man."

"Sounds like a change of Alpha in any Pack, son. You've just been spoiled, having Forbes for so long. So what's *our* Warden want with Forbes? And why didn't he tell me? I'm the Beta after all. You shouldn't have been up here alone." Kerr was annoyed beyond all reason at the surfer-boy in front of him. Something he couldn't really express with Forbes right now.

Rather than be offended, Task barked out a laugh. "Dude, last time I saw you, it was all about chasing the skirts and Jocky's moonshine. You weren't exactly up for Beta duties."

It was Kerr's turn to grimace. Up until a few nights ago, he would have had to agree with the younger wolf. "Didn't you get sent away after that grand affair with the Paquet twins?"

Task gave a sheepish grin. "Well, one good twinset deserves another."

"They're *witches*!"

Task laughed again. "Worth every bit of trouble we got into. Haven't seen them around, have you? Dax and I might want to re-connect."

Kerr swallowed. "Forbes didn't get a chance to tell you? Never told you while you were away?"

Task's bright face fell slowly as he put the pieces together. "They're sway-locked?"

Kerr nodded. "Not that the Coven shares much with us, but it happened two or three moons ago. They were in the hospital in Halifax for a bit, before the Priestess moved them to Seawind House. Sorry."

Task's face squinted and scrunched as he made his peace with losing two of his oldest friends to what amounted to a magic coma from working the Fundy tides. "Damn. Isn't that permanent?"

Kerr nodded.

"Son of a bitch."

"There's a lot of that feeling going around." Kerr sighed. He didn't love being around witches, but neither did he wish them any harm.

"Only two ways I know of to blow off steam. A rut or a run. You up for either?" Task danced from foot to foot.

Kerr eyed the young Shifter. Most of the Pack was bisexual when necessary, as wolves generally preferred their own kind to human mates. Kerr had never been bothered by human women and he preferred females. As did Task. Not that that was what the boy had been asking. The "boy" had been born in the late 1940s; his human family hadn't died yet. His body looked twenty-five to Kerr's thirtyish appearance. Task had been his wingman on more than one trip to Jocky's bar. Kerr didn't like to admit he might not be as young as he used to be. Not like he couldn't take Task if it came to it though, and it might be a good idea for both of them to spar afterward. But maybe he should stop acting like a friend and move into the big brother role he should have been fostering with the young man. He nodded before he pulled his shirt over his head. "Run. Definitely a run."

***

The two of them stood naked in the back yard. The stone fencing was high, just in case prying eyes were around, so they shifted in safety. Kerr waited for the younger male to finish first, before he began his transformation. It was more than common courtesy. He was older, was the protector. A Shifter was never more vulnerable than when he was changing from one form to the other. The process was beyond painful and took on average ten minutes. Forbes could push his to a fast five and Kerr had once managed eight, but it was excruciating. So one wolf always stood guard while the rest shifted. After a few moments of recovery, Task would watch over Kerr in his current form. Never shift alone if you can help it. It was Pack rule number one. Pounded into the young ones' heads early on.

A gray and reddish wolf with ghostly yellow eyes came around the corner of the Juniper bushes that Task had disappeared behind. The young wolf wasn't comfortable being vulnerable with another male around. Kerr gave him a sharp nod.

"Nicely done. My turn."

He didn't bother moving. Shame of being naked around another living being had long ago disappeared. And he had learned how to defend himself, mid-shift. He didn't begrudge that part of Task's personality however. The man was young and brought up in a very traditional household.

Kerr's spine rolled and elongated inside his skin. His fingers popped themselves out of joint and his knees started to slip around so they bent the opposite way. He could no longer stand upright so he fell forward. His palms became pads; his bones liquid and on fire at the same time until he had paws. Elsewhere on his journey through agony, his skin stretched, his shoulders rose, then snapped and reformed. His neck pushed out through the skin that had become like rubber and his jaw cracked and reformed. His ears slid up and grew bigger. Then the itching started as dark brown fur erupted all over his body. The last, most painful part was the tail. There was no human equivalent, so flesh finally crawled up the naked bones protruding from his spinal column. It took a while for everything to settle and then he was up, sniffing the air.

People said canines couldn't see colors. Kerr had always wondered if it was the result of domestication or if regular wolves were also bereft of the rainbows. He saw colors just fine as a wolf. It might be one of the benefits that wolves got when they entered a man. He knew he loved being able to see scents when in wolf form.

Enough. My turn, Kerr's wolf side seemed to say. The wolf wanted free rein tonight. Kerr decided to let him.

He took off at a run, not waiting to see if Task was ready. The youngling would keep up with him or not. The fresh earth under his paws felt good. A misty yellow cloud led into a low clump of weeds and Kerr slowed enough to determine that a hare had bounded away from them as soon as the two men had come out of the back of the house. Scents didn't lie. He kept going. Wasn't interested in hunting just now. Now was the time for running.

He pushed. Faster through the birch stands, over the pile of pine trees that had been cut down for winter wood, through the clearing where the Pack usually gathered, into the deep woods themselves. Moss-covered boulders left over from the last ice age occasionally appeared, not as barriers but fun obstacles to leap and hide behind while the youngling caught up to him. Occasionally he'd jump out and force Task to the ground in a round of play. The two of them got along. Task had been away from the territory so long and needed to run the trails again. Kerr needed to retrain the adolescent, so he led them through tracks that had been cut since Task had been away. Showed the youngling where older paths had been stopped due to the housing development that had sprung up in the past ten years. They ran up the mountainside until, panting, Task whined for a break. It was a little cold this autumn night, so Kerr curled up beside the cub, making sure he was warm enough. When Task fell into a fitful doze, Kerr stood guard. He waited until Task was ready to head back to Promontory House before he took off to check on his mate.

***

Lexi lifted the brown box, trying to guess what had come in the mail, but it was from a local store, one she passed every day on Main Street. No postage, so it must have been hand-delivered. She often wished she could splurge enough for one or two of the upscale items within the shop, but she couldn't afford it. Driftwood Treasures wouldn't have anything in her price range even on sale days. It was only through window shopping that she recognized the label.

Curiosity was like a tick under her skin; she had to get it out. So she opened the parcel, against her rules for dealing with anything from her mother. A leather satchel brief case, complete with extendable handle and wheels, sat there with an envelope on top. Very posh, very sophisticated, very professional. She knew she'd have a hard time sending this one back to the store if her mother had sent it. The bribes hadn't shown up for a while though. It could be from someone else, couldn't it? She was in love already. She stroked the rich chocolate sides and played with the handles before she sighed and resigned herself to opening the letter so she could form a decent refusal and return. The poor shop keeper. He was going to be as disappointed as she was; this had to be one of their more costly items. Still, Lexi didn't want to fuss.

Every Professor should have a decent briefcase – K

A plethora of emotions skittered across her mind. Anger that he'd crossed the boundary of her bedroom door, even if he did have permission when she wasn't around. Excitement that he'd thought of her; she felt her cheeks heat. A flutter of butterflies in her stomach she couldn't quite explain. But most of all, guilt. Her heart was in her throat. She'd treated him horribly. While she'd been juggling her boots this morning she'd thought he was ogling her boobs, and instead he'd been noticing her tote bags. OK, maybe he was ogling her boobs *and* noticing her tote bags. He was a guy, after all. And he'd decided that she needed something more practical and pretty. This had been sitting up here the whole time she'd been acting like a…her mind rejected half a dozen names, some too harsh, and others she probably deserved, but didn't want to claim.

She lifted the case out of the box. It was big enough for all her things, for the knickknacks and papers and space for a laptop she usually dragged back and forth every day. He'd bought her something she'd use daily and think of him. Clever. But it was so pretty. And useful. She loved gifts that managed to combine the two. This was the perfect just-because gift. Her face burned, her jaw tightened and shame welled up in her gut. She felt like a heel. She had to make things right.

She went down the stairs two at a time, clutching her new bag to her chest, ready to thank Kerr. Except he'd left already. He must have heard her coming. Left before he'd had to deal with her changeable moods. Not that she blamed him, given her behavior. She wanted to do something to make up for it. She looked at her tote bags by the door and the case in her hands. She didn't know him half as well as he knew her. But that could change. A few days of paying attention to him, discovering what he liked instead of trying to get rid of him would help. It would take a long time…but not if she snooped through his stuff. The sly thought made her grin. There was nothing in her caveats against that. Then she'd give him a gift too, one that set the scales right.

She happily spent the next hour transferring everything from the two totes to her spiffy new case. Then she put it by the door, so Kerr would notice when he came back. She'd thank him in the morning.

She went up the stairs much more cheerful than when she'd come down them. She glanced out the window to see a pair of yellow eyes glowing up at her. She let out a startled gasp and the creature came more fully into the light. Chocolate fur, the same rich brown as her bag, covered the large wolf sitting in her backyard. She blinked. He was beautiful. It had been a long time since she'd seen a wolf of any kind; she should be afraid, given her history. She wasn't. The creature before her exhibited no malice. He was simply watching her. Like he was making the rounds and he'd stopped to acknowledge her. Kerr? Before she could so much as mouth his name, he was gone. The floodlights stayed on long enough to illuminate the swaying branches, and then night cloaked the yard. The strange appearance should have made sleep impossible, but she barely managed to change and slip between the covers before she nodded off. She'd snoop tomorrow, once she worked up a little more courage.

When she woke, she wandered, fuzzy-slippered and fluffy-bathrobed, to his room and knocked, shy about seeing him in his bedroom. Did he sleep naked? She was half-hoping, half-terrified he did. She needn't have worried. He wasn't there.

"Oh," she said aloud. Guess he'd been out all night. With one of his girlfriends. That wolf in the back might just have been a dog. A very large dog. That made sense. He was probably sick of her. It was a bitter pill to swallow.

Lexi wandered back to her own space in the house and got ready for work. She went to the office, had a relatively easy day, stopped by the gym on the way back again, and was home by four o'clock. To an empty house. Again.

Why was she so disappointed? Because he'd bought her a gift? Because she hadn't seen him yet today? When did he become so necessary to her life? Short answer, he wasn't. Long answer, he could become important, if she let herself feel. And she wanted to explore those feelings now, except he wasn't around. Frustration left a bad taste in her mouth. Lexi tried to shake off her mood, but it was difficult. She'd been an awful roommate and didn't like it. Maybe she could start to fix things by doing her share of the chores while he was away.

She made hamburger soup, a big pot in case Kerr came home hungry from wherever he'd gone. She watched a DVR'd episode of TV, vacuumed the living room, read a chapter of one of her Nalini Singh books and went up to her office to work a little.

This got her to roughly six thirty. It was a miracle when her cell rang. She checked the display. Hannah. She accepted.

"I've got two words for you, Professor. Pumpkin people."

"What?" Lexi laughed. Since "discovering" her in one of the coffee shops, Hannah had made it her mission to show Lexi the wonders of the Annapolis Valley. She never ceased to amaze.

"Every October the next town over picks a theme and the whole of Kentville businesses and homes set up displays of pumpkin-headed scarecrow thingies for tourists. I didn't know you last year around this time, so I missed showing you this charming spectacle of the valley. There's also the gourd races this weekend. We should go around the pumpkin people and then catch the races."

Lexi tried to picture what Hannah was talking about and came up blank. It was a common occurrence. "How, exactly, do you race a gourd?" She had a vision of a spaghetti squash herd being rolled down some hill.

"You grow super big squash, pumpkins and other assorted gourds, hollow them out and put them in the river, get in one and see who can paddle it to the finish without sinking." Hannah always sounded so matter-of-fact when explaining the ridiculous.

"Of course, how silly of me not to know that. Sure, sounds like fun."

There was a long pause and Lexi wondered if her friend had forgotten what she was going to say. It had happened a few times.

"Stop playing around, smart ass," Hannah said finally, chomped on something and chewed loudly. "I'm waiting, you know."

"Waiting for what?"

"Fine, we'll do this the hard way. So, what are you doing, Professor?" The bubbly voice made Lexi smile.

"Nothing, Vet. How about you?"

"I've heard a rumor. One that could not possibly be true."

Lexi cringed. "What rumor would that be, Vet?"

"Well, Professor, I'll give you a hint. I ran into Mrs. Faye in the grocery store."

Lexi's head hit the wall; she had a funny feeling she knew where this was going. "Uh-huh."

"She had lots to say." Hannah hummed, delighted.

"Yeah, I'll bet."

"How can you have a new roommate?" Hannah finally exploded. "Forget about that, how could you not have told me the second it happened? Never once offering to give a girl a bit of the gossip so I can be first rather than Mrs. Patricia Faye. Kerr MacDonald! Are you crazy?"

"Don't you have to neuter or spay some poor animal?" Lexi grimaced. The cafe she'd been sitting at had been full when Hannah had sat down at her table without an invitation over a year ago. The two of them had started chatting and despite Hannah's words, she was anything but a gossip. She hadn't pried into why Lexi had chosen to move to Canada, hadn't thought she was weird because she didn't talk about her home. Hannah had talked her ear off and told her all about Wolfville and some of the surrounding areas, her job, and her obsession with romance novels. Lexi had been more than willing to listen. Hannah had made her feel at home immediately. It didn't hurt that Lexi had some of the same favorite books. The two of them had struck up an easy friendship. One that didn't tax either woman's sometimes-unpredictable schedule.

"Nope. I have a wonderful, free evening. And no idea what to do with it. Want to meet up at Rosie's for some nachos and a pint? My treat."

Lexi found that she did. She agreed to meet in an hour, changed into something that could pass for eveningwear, put on a bit of makeup and walked to the restaurant. It was only a block or so from her work building. Hannah had already grabbed them a table in the back and started on a plate of nachos. Lexi grinned at her friend.

"Skipped lunch again?"

"We had an emergency. Guy backed up and ran over the tail of his neighbor's cat this morning. Been with the poor thing all day. The cat, not the guy. Neighbor's away. He works at the tire plant. Twelve-hour shifts and he was late. At least this guy will be able to pay."

Hannah motioned for the waitress to come over and take Lexi's order. She got a Raven Ale and an order of crisp wings to go with Hannah's nachos. The two chit-chatted for a half an hour and another beer.

"OK. What's wrong?" Hannah asked, rubbing her belly after demolishing the platter. Lexi shook her head.

"What do you mean?"

"Don't play with me. Something's up. Besides having a hot guy in your space."

"Hannah!"

"Oh shut it. He gets the girls for a reason. He's sexy as hell, well versed in the ways of seduction, and from all reports, fantastic in bed. Normally this would be enough to get you all bothered and frozen, but this isn't the case. Something else is wrong. So give it up."

Lexi toyed with a half-eaten wing on her plate, debating. She couldn't tell Hannah the whole truth, after all. If there was anyone she was sure wasn't a Shifter, it was Hannah. The vibrant woman attracted too much attention by simply breathing. No way would any Alpha worth his salt allow that.

"Been a little weird lately. Out of sorts. You know?"

Hannah shook her head. "Explain." She snagged the wing from Lexi and took the rest on the plate too.

"Well, my temper's been out of sorts."

"How so?" Hannah paused, wing dripping above the barbeque sauce.

"Just…I don't know. It's been getting worse. And my fuse is shorter. I get this feeling in my stomach. Burns, actually. It rumbles and tumbles and normally I feel sick, but lately it's been churning and I get this…kinda…ragewave."

"Hormones?" Hannah tilted her head and pursed her lips. "Nah. Don't even dignify that with an answer. Before or after tall, dark and handsome moved in?"

"Before, but it's been getting worse the past week. I nearly took the poor guy's head off for coming into the women's locker room to ask me something."

Hannah's eyes grew round. "He came in after you? Were you naked?"

Lexi sighed. "No. I wasn't naked. It hasn't got anything to do with him. At least I don't think it does." She pulled at her lip.

"When's the last time you had sex?" An elderly couple enjoying their meal nearby gasped and glared at Hannah. Hannah dipped her wings, unperturbed.

"I thought you were taking this seriously?" Lexi hissed.

"Sex is serious for you. You're not like me, you don't do casual sex. You're more like a camel when it comes to doing the deed. You can go for years between drinks. Or maybe camels can only go for a year. Now that I think about it, that might be impossible, but they can go for a really long time without something the rest of us find necessary in greater frequency. Grr. Let me try again. So how long between the last time you had sex and this guy moving into your space? And when are you going to take a drink of that man?"

"Do you think that could be it? Not something else?"

"It's the only two things that correspond to when this started. You have a long dry spell and then a Greek god moves in, it's bound to make any symptoms you were having before much worse, very fast."

"Not anxiety or an ulcer or any of the logical things I was going for. It's gotta be about a man, huh? You don't think I should go see a doctor?"

"I am a doctor."

"You're a vet!"

"Vets go through just as much education as people doctors, and it's harder to get into vet school. Don't you watch Sherlock?"

"What?"

"Never mind. Anyway, that's what I think. And I'm your friend. You should have some fun and see if that cures what ails ya."

"Right. I should book an appointment for the clinic. Gotcha."

Hannah sighed dramatically and Lexi laughed. "Look, vet, I have another question for you."

"I'm all ears." Hannah sipped her beer.

"I was really terrible to him. And he gave me a really nice gift. A leather briefcase on wheels. What can I do to make it up to him?"

Hannah waggled her eyebrows and Lexi tossed her serviette at her.

"I'm serious."

"I'm just saying, the boys like it when you play with them."

The plates jumped as Lexi's head hit the table with a loud thud.

"OK, OK, OK. What does he like?" Hannah took another sip of her ale.

"Nineteen-year-olds?"

"Now who needs to get serious?"

Lexi shrugged. "That's just it. I don't know that much about him."

Hannah's smile was full of mischief. "Well, then that, my friend, is what you need to fix."

***

Lexi had showered, changed into a nightgown that looked like an old boyfriend's shirt but wasn't and straightened up the kitchen, then the living room. After an hour or so, she admitted she was stalling. Time to implement Hannah's plan. She tiptoed to Kerr's room. Opened the door and took a deep breath.

This went against everything she was trying to establish with him. Crossing the threshold would mean she'd made a move she couldn't take back. Not that he wouldn't know she'd been in there. They knew. Wolves always knew if you'd been snooping in their stuff. That didn't worry her so much. What worried her was there was the chance she'd get caught in the act. She could make up any number of reasons she'd had to go into his room. None of them sprang to mind at the moment, but she was sure she could come up with something. Getting caught would make it so much worse. She hesitated in the doorway. Was her shame worth the price of admission? If that's all it was, shame at how she'd treated Kerr, then she could skip this exercise, apologize and do better in the future.

No, she admitted to herself. This wasn't about her. She was genuinely curious about the gorgeous guy living in her home. And she was using her bad behavior as an excuse to snoop. She took note of where everything was, memorizing the layout. Stalling, again, she realized.

"Come on, get on with it," she told herself.

The room was rather large. It had originally been designed as a dining room, but since she didn't know that many people and couldn't really cook well enough to feed a dinner party, she'd turned it into a guest space. He'd brought his own furniture, or bought new. The bed was king-size, and made up, brown and burgundy colors with a fluffy duvet she couldn't help but touch. Velvety and luxurious. The pillows were huge too, and she lasted exactly three seconds before she crawled into the middle of the bed and put her head down on one. Hmmm, a little soft. But comfy. This didn't really tell her much about his likes. She glanced around. He'd turned an old sideboard into a desk, taking out the drawers and hanging them on the wall to use as shelves and filling them with books and other things to surround his monitor. Clever. He'd cut the drawer slots to make room for a re-upholstered dining room chair. So, new bed, new pillows, new sheets, repurposed desk. He was handy and practical. Not much help. The shelves might hold more clues.

No pictures, but she didn't expect there to be. The digital age had hit the wolves hard, with cameras being everywhere. Smaller towns like this one that couldn't afford the new CCTVs and security measures must be tough to find. Hmm. An old pocket watch, what she thought might be a musket ball, and a geode were on the other shelves. No help there. She touched the computer keyboard and was in luck. It was on, just not unlocked. She sat down and blew out a raspberry. The screensaver came up and she watched as pictures of paintings rolled forward. She recognized one. A black horse running toward a train. She pulled her phone out of her shirt pocket and did a bit of digging online. It was called *Horse and Train* by Alex Colville, a local artist. She tried to think why the images floating on his screen were so familiar and snapped her fingers when she got it.

When she'd bought the house, the great-grandchild of the original owner had insisted that Lexi was now responsible for clearing out the whack of everything left. She'd had a massive garage sale, but there was still a huge amount of things that she'd had to put away in the basement. Among them, she remembered seeing this image on a print, as well as a few others in a trunk filled with tons of prints. She went downstairs to see if there was anything else in the boxes she might find. A coin set, with the same artist's name, was wedged at the very bottom of the trunk. She pulled it up and found the print too. She smiled. She'd put the print in a frame and present both to Kerr. Pleased with her discovery and decision, she raced upstairs, the threat of being caught was still fresh in her mind. She ducked into her bathroom, a room of refuge.

She found a bar of Kerr's soap on her sink. The bathroom opened out to the hallway. She had to use a robe to walk between it and her room. So he might have occasion to use *her* lavatory and he probably didn't want to smell like a girl. She could see that. She had given him permission to enter if she wasn't in the room, after all. She picked up the bar and brought it to her nose. Hmm. A bit of patchouli, a dash of sandalwood, some subtle hints of amber musk. It smelled so good. She took a deeper sniff. The scents were exquisite. The soap was hand-made, which was not unusual for wolves. Commercially made soap often contained harsh odors and additives that made their noses curl. The Denver Pack had even had their own soap maker.

Lexi wasn't sure if soap could smell expensive, but she thought this stuff did. How much must the man pay for a pound of the stuff? Twenty, thirty dollars? More? It was almost too faint for a human to notice, except Sunny had tried to teach her about scent during a more stepfatherly moment. One more deep lungful and she'd go back to her room. Go to sleep. She wondered what it would smell like when Kerr was in the shower. How it would smell when freshly applied to his skin, worked into lather over his abs and look as it traveled lower while he rinsed…

Whoa. The mental imagery was making her temperature rise. She squeaked and put the soap firmly back. Maybe Hannah was right, at least as far her being in a dry spell. She forced herself to march off to her bedroom, slide under her covers and turn off the lights. She closed her eyes. She could not believe she'd been thinking about Kerr naked. That was not good, off limits, a no-brainer.

She remembered him on the couch before she'd left for work. She'd wanted to reach out and touch the sparse curls on his chest. Feel the heat of his skin.

"Darn it!" She turned over, trying to think of pink rabbits or purple butterflies or grading papers or anything other than Kerr MacDonald naked. Her nightshirt felt tight. She took it off. Lay there in the dark for a full minute looking in the direction of the ceiling. The buzzing at the base of her spine was a dead giveaway. She was never going to sleep all hot and bothered over Kerr. What could it hurt? It wasn't like he was here. She'd never tell him. What the hell?

She ran light fingers over her collarbone, making lazy circles where the swell of her breasts started. She took one finger into her mouth, ran a wet line down her throat, between the valley of her flesh, over her stomach. She ran her hands over her breasts, imagining they were Kerr's strong fingers caressing her nipples. They contracted painfully at her touch and she gasped. Imagined Kerr's smile when he got that reaction out of her. In her mind's eye, she saw him take the hard peak of one into his mouth and she rolled that nipple the way she'd want him to roll it with his tongue. The other hand traveled south, parted her flesh and started stroking. She imagined it was Kerr's hand instead. His finger that found the right spot inside her, touching that one spot until it had her breath quicken. His tongue on the nub outside and his rumble of approval as she started panting in time to his efforts.

That's it, Professor. You like that, don't you? She imagined the sound of his voice and hummed.

Want more, baby? Want me to make it better?

"Yes," she answered imaginary Kerr.

Say please.

"Please, please, please," she begged. The image of his grin sent her over and she turned her head to cry out into her pillow, in case he was back in the house. Dear Lord, the orgasm went on and she shuddered, riding the waves until she could do more than lay there and gasp, spent. It took her a few minutes for her legs to firm up enough to walk to the bathroom again. She cleaned herself up as quickly as possible and snuggled back down into her bed.

Sleep came fast.

Chapter Eleven

"Lexi. Lexi, wake up." Rough hands shook her awake. Snapped on her light. Lexi clawed at the hands, flipped over in a hurry, pulled away from whoever was in her room.

"Shh, it's OK. It's Kerr. Lexi. I need you to put on some clothes and come with me. Now." Kerr sat on the edge of her bed, a pair of jeans and a shirt in one hand, his other on her blanketed legs. He was patting her through her covers absently. He looked around the room and she had a wild thought he might see her gifts before they were ready until she realized she'd tucked them under her bed.

Lexi rubbed at her eyes. "I thought you weren't going to push me to meet your Alpha."

"I'm not. This is something else. Please?" No jokes. Not a smirk in sight. Nothing but deadly seriousness in his gaze.

Lexi blinked. Had he just said please?

"Umm."

"I need your help, Lexi. Please?"

That did it. She couldn't very well say no now, could she? Not without seeming like an even bigger jack hole than she'd been earlier today.

"Where are we going?" She flipped back the blankets and held out her hands for the clothes. His eyes wandered down her frame and she felt her cheeks flush. "My eyes are up here, Kerr."

"There's a lot of you I've never seen down there, though."

She frowned. "Was that a comment about my weight?"

"No." His voice was thick, husky and he hadn't hesitated in the slightest. He gave his head a sharp shake. "Right," he said aloud. But he didn't hand her the clothes. He stared at her body and his eyes took on a yellow hue.

"Kerr?" She crossed her arms over her breasts and pulled her knees up. A frisson of something crawled up her spine. Not entirely unpleasant. Kerr's breathing increased, as if he was fighting for control. That was never good. On instinct, she leaned forward and stroked his arm lightly.

"Kerr. I need Kerr, not the wolf."

Kerr caught her fingers and brought them to his mouth. Nibbled at the tips, his eyes never leaving her face. "You've got me." He glanced down at her hand in his and she wondered if he realized at the same time she did that she had touched him, not the other way around. "I'm going to protect you, Lexi. Remember that."

A cold storm erupted in her stomach. She took the clothes from him and Kerr finally clued in that he was making her nervous. He got up and walked to the door, gave her his back so she could pull on the jeans and shirt. Thank God, her tank had a built-in bra.

"So..." her voice trailed off. Kerr turned around and nodded. He took her hand and hurried them down the stairs. Handed her boots to her and jingled his keys while she tugged them on. She brushed her fingers through her hair. "Do I have time for a brush?"

He pulled her close and plunked a kiss on her lips. "You look great," he said absently.

Lexi blinked three times. What just happened? Before she could process, he took her hand and tugged her outside, locked the house quickly and handed her a helmet. She eyed the bike. Hadn't he had a truck in her driveway, earlier? When did this show up? He got on and started it, looking at her expectantly.

"I borrowed it from a friend, Professor. Don't worry. Shifters are excellent riders." He patted the seat behind him, impatient but taking the time to try to calm her down.

"Yeah, I'm not worried about you and your driving. Kerr, I know I owe you, but this might be pushing it."

"One of the group is in trouble. I think you can help. Please?" he held out his hand, palm up. She raised her chin. He meant Pack. That was where the kiss came from. Shifters were more touchy-feely when they were worried and Kerr was obviously worried. She slipped her hand into his and he put it on his shoulder so she could balance as she straddled the seat behind him. Then he wrapped her arm around his waist. Thank God, it was cold out. The instant her hand slipped over his abs, her nipples got rock hard. Kerr reached back and found her other hand, put it over his heart.

"Hang on tight. I'm gonna go faster than you might like, your first time with me."

He's talking about the bike, she reminded herself. But she was glad she followed his advice. Her head whipped back when he took off and she flushed at the little squeak that escaped her before she snuggled against his shoulders. *Purely for safety's sake*, she tried to reassure herself. OK, so the guy was built like a god and smelled like heaven. He used it. It was a set of tools he used to get what he wanted. He went from woman to woman and she had to live with him for another six and a half weeks. She'd have to deal with him after that too.

They hit the highway quick and traveled toward Halifax again, but rather than head straight to the city, they pulled off at an exit marked Falmouth. She didn't think much of the town, if it could be called that. The beam from the bike's headlight was the only illumination that Lexi saw for miles. Then again, it might just be her perception. All too soon, he pulled into a driveway that had several cars in it already. Lexi couldn't see any neighbors around. It made her nervous and she sat too long on the bike, even after Kerr had shut it off.

"Lexi, I'm not going to let anything happen to you. Trust me." He kissed her palm and put her hand over his heart again. She took a deep breath. She'd dealt with Shifters before and Kerr was the Pack's second. She was the daughter of an Alpha's mate. She could handle this. Centering herself, she got off the bike and waited for Kerr. He slipped her helmet off and ran his fingers through her hair. He was touching her too much. But it didn't mean to him what it meant to her. Shifters weren't human. He must be really anxious. She smiled weakly at him and he winked at her. He twined his fingers in hers and led the way.

They didn't knock, but several men and women came forward when she entered behind Kerr. He made sure she was behind him. "This is Lexi. She's here to help Elyse."

That's when Lexi heard it. They were growling and howling, but the sound was muffled. Pack magic could do that sometimes; reduce the noise inside a single structure. She'd seen Sunny do it once. She'd been able to see the fight through the window, but hadn't heard the two wolves outside at all.

There were voices around her, but Lexi kept her eyes downcast. She waited until someone entered her field of vision to challenge her right to be here; until then, she relied on Kerr to deal with any attacks. To her surprise, a pink manicured hand reached into her space, touched her shoulder, and withdrew. Kerr pulled her into the next room behind him, and another hand, this one with grease encrusted in the nailbeds, repeated the action. Blood red nails, cut short, followed. A man's hand with a silver Celtic wedding band stroked her elbow as she passed. There must have been twenty hands that touched her as Kerr helped her stumble along. None of them threatened in any way. It was almost as if they were asking for her help too. Everyone was so anxious.

She was completely confused. Every time she'd been around her mother's Pack and their gatherings, they'd snarled and snatched at her hair, scratched her with hands half changed or snapped at her heels. They'd hurled insults at her, made fun of her for being human. If they had seen her in public, they'd "accidentally" bump into her, knock over her cart at the grocery store or make a scene somehow.

But not these wolves. There was no hostility here. There was worry. And lots of it. They stopped at a door from which the loudest sounds emanated.

"Lexi. Elyse is down here. She's chained, but it's for her own safety. And yours."

Lexi swallowed. The name set a spark of recognition sputtering in her brain, but it went out before she could remember. "What do you think I can do?"

"Do you remember what you did for me in the car?" Kerr held her face between his palms. Lexi shrugged.

"I talked to you. Tried to keep you calm enough to get to the Alpha. Is your Alpha coming?"

Kerr shook his head. "He's out of town right now. He'd never have left if he knew that Elyse was going to shift. It's her first, but something's gone wrong. Can you please try to help me get her calmed down? Like you did for me?"

She swallowed. A wolf caught between human and not human—for the first time. There must be so much pain. And fear. The poor girl must be so scared. Wait, how could she be having her first shift if the Alpha wasn't here to make her?

"Who turned her if the Alpha isn't here?"

"Lexi, I don't know what you know about us, but Elyse is something called a dormant. A generational dormant. That means she doesn't have any family to help with this part, which we call the turn."

An animal's howl of pain that ended on a woman's scream echoed up to them. Lexi shivered.

"What can I do?" Her voice sounded reedy and desperate. She squeezed Kerr's hand as hard as she could and he let her. Put his forehead against hers.

"Just what you did for me in your car, Lexi. Do you remember? Was there anything going through your head?"

"I had to get you to your Alpha."

"Good. Anything else?" He was being patient with her, which she appreciated, but the young woman's screams weren't helping her calm. She tried to think. She was not going to call her mother for help in this. What had she been thinking?

Driving. Calm. She remembered him licking the inside of her elbow and a warm fuzzy feeling came back.

"Don't think about that. Whatever that was," a new voice said from behind her. Kerr growled a little, but she turned to see a swimmer's frame on a blond man with warm brown eyes. The man smiled and tilted his head to the side, exposing his throat. Kerr stilled instantly. The man spoke.

"I'm Task. I've met someone like you before. He said he tried to control his scent when he had to make people calm. Try that, see if it helps."

"Someone like me?"

Kerr pulled her back against him. His voice commanding and all business. "Focus, Lexi."

OK, a mystery for another time. She tucked it away for later. Thought of what she must smell like. The ride over her had been wild. She'd smell like the fall leaves. The cool temperature. And Kerr.

Kerr put his hand on her hip as he whispered in her ear. "Good. Concentrate on that. It will help. You have no idea how much that will help her. Keep that in your mind for as long as you can, OK?"

"I'll try."

CHAPTER TWELVE

Kerr gave one sharp nod then took her hand in his and led the way down the staircase behind the door. They went into a basement and the sounds coming from the she-wolf were deafening. If not for Pack magic, there would have been police, fire trucks, and ambulances crawling all over this place.

Lexi covered one ear with her hand and, since Kerr wasn't letting go of her other, buried the exposed ear in her shoulder, just so she could make it down the stairs. The lights glowed brightly down here, so the cement, steel and cage in the center of the room were clearly visible. At least that was the quick impression she got just before whatever was behind the bars lunged at her. She peeked over Kerr's shoulder, her nose brushing his shirt, which smelled like *her* laundry soap. For some reason that little detail helped her get it together. Kerr smelled like her a bit. She took a deep breath and walked out around so whoever was in the cage could get a good look at her. And she could look at them. She thought of the autumn night, cool winds and Kerr's scent again.

What she saw was a young woman, probably in her twenties. At least she looked like that now. Shifters often looked much younger than they were. This girl was muscular, strong. If this was her first shift, any natural healing ability she'd gotten wouldn't have taken hold yet. Neither would her muscles have developed as a wolf's would. Clearly she worked out. Young for a Shifter's first time. Most didn't turn until they had reached their forties and sometimes fifties. Unless you were like her brother and asked to be turned early. So this woman had changed before she was supposed to. At least that was what Lexi had always understood. Maybe it was different for other Packs? Maybe they didn't have generational dormants or whatever in her mother's. She waited for Kerr to introduce her, but she didn't look away from the girl in the cage.

"What do you feel?" Kerr crouched down before the cage and tried to get Elyse to look at him, but she wouldn't take her eyes off of Lexi. Lexi took a deep breath. So the injured wolf was staring. That was OK. She'd been stared at by hungry wolves before. And there were the bars between them. They'd held so far. Lexi was encouraged. Kerr looked at her expectantly over his shoulder.

"What, do you mean me?" Lexi asked.

Kerr nodded and turned back to Elyse. He'd slipped between them, so Lexi guessed he was going to keep his promise that she wasn't going to be hurt. Some of the others were drifting down from above, but Kerr made a slashing motion with his hand and only two came down.

"I'm a little scared," she admitted. Kerr shook his head.

"From Elyse. What do you feel from her?"

"I don't feel anything from her." Lexi frowned. "I'm not telepathic or anything. Are there telepaths in your world?" She felt foolish for having to ask, but she wasn't quite sure.

"No. Not like the movies." He reached behind him, asking for her hand without words. She stepped up and put her hands on his shoulders instead. Kerr seemed to relax a fraction. Leaned back and pressed against her legs a bit. He motioned for Lexi to do something, but she wasn't sure what. What had she done with Kerr in the car? Just talked to him, really. With a shock, she realized she'd met the young woman before. At Dr. Engles's home when she'd dropped off some work. She had a connection, albeit a small one. This might actually work. So she tried.

"Elyse, my name is Lexi. We met at your father's house. Do you remember?" Was her father a wolf? No, Kerr had said she was a generational dormant. No one else in her family had been a wolf. No sign the girl heard her. She tried again.

"I'm here with Kerr. He's your Alpha's Second. Do you remember?"

Elyse snarled low in response. She paced the cage, her eyes never leaving Lexi. Kerr vibrated against her but remained silent. She squeezed his shoulders.

"OK. Let's start from scratch. My name is Lexi. I'm not here to hurt you. I doubt I could. I'm human. My mother is one of you but she's kind of a bitch. No offense, but you know how mothers can be. Mummy dearest. One second the PTA woman of the year, then Bitchzilla on steroids the next. But she taught me some things about wolves. Maybe I can help you, if you let me. Kerr seems to think I can. Will you let me try?"

Elyse squatted down. Watched Lexi's every move. But at least she'd stopped the howling and growling. Kerr patted her hand on his shoulder and Lexi took it for encouragement. *Think calm thoughts*, she told herself. Calm thoughts. Autumn winds, fallen leaves and Kerr. Elyse stuck her nose out, searching.

"So, you've just started your shift. Which, above everything else, would probably really hurt. But you're not a wolf right now so I'm guessing you just changed back to full human. But is it Elyse I'm talking to or your wolf? See, with my brother I can just tell which one is looking out at me. His eyes change color as soon as the wolf is anywhere near to taking over. But your eyes are brown. A really nice brown, by the way. I bet you get lots of compliments on them. Sometimes Kerr's wolf comes out, but it's more difficult to tell. Sometimes his eyes don't change color. It's the way he looks at you that changes. A sort of feral glint, I guess. Except when it comes to sex. Anything to do with sexy stuff that gets him the least bit excited and out come the yellow eyes."

Several chuckles came from various shapes around the room. Kerr grumbled. She stepped out from around him and toward the steel a bit. She stopped short of touching the bars at Kerr's warning growl and sat down cross legged on the floor. Might as well be comfortable with things. *I am calm*, she thought. *I am safe, this is OK.* She let her breathing slow before she continued. "I can't see the glint in your eyes. So I'm going to guess that maybe it's Elyse, the human, I'm talking to and not Elyse's wolf. The wolves I've met can be really scary, mean and angry most of the time. Even the ones I was related to. I couldn't imagine having one in my head. Or my body. You're very brave to be able to stand that."

She paused to see if her words were having any effect. Her own heart rate had slowed considerably. Elyse turned her head slowly to the side, like a child too tired to hold it upright. She unclenched her hands and leaned backward, as if she was going to lean on the wall behind her. Lexi took it as a good sign, until Elyse leaped forward before anyone could react and grabbed Lexi's ankle. She gave a good yank and half of Lexi's leg was in the cell with her. Kerr was at the door with keys, two others moving as well. One behind her ready to pull Lexi back and the other behind Kerr, ready to aid him in stopping Elyse from whatever she was about to do to Lexi. Lexi focused on her breathing. Slow and steady. Calm thoughts. Fall leaves and cool winds. Slow and steady. Kerr was here. He'd protect her. He promised. Elyse pulled again.

"Ouch!" Lexi bellowed, Elyse moaned and everyone halted. They all looked to her for instruction. But Lexi was clueless. What was supposed to happen now? It felt like her leg was in a bear trap.

"Elyse, please let my leg go." But Elyse whined again, lifted Lexi's jeans up and put her cheek against Lexi's skin.

"What's she doing?" Lexi asked.

"Getting comfort or getting ready to feed." The keys dangled from Kerr's hand. He looked afraid to move. Elyse gave another yank and Lexi yelped.

"Elyse!" Kerr barked. The command in his tone was unmistakable. The new wolf looked up at him.

"Let Lexi go." Kerr enunciated every word.

Elyse growled and started to lift Lexi's leg at an angle that the human body did not bend. Lexi couldn't stop the yip of pain escaping her lips. "Elyse, you're hurting me. Do you want to hurt me? Wolf or not?"

"No."

The rough gravel in the woman's voice made Lexi's throat hurt in sympathy. She motioned for Elyse to put her leg down and she did. She started to pull it back and Elyse's hand darted forward, the hand on her ankle firm as stone. Lexi gave a weak smile to the woman. She wanted to be close. Lexi could do closer. As long as the others were there.

"I'm not going anywhere, Elyse. I'm going to come into the cell with you, if it's all right with Kerr. Would you like that?"

Elyse looked up at Kerr, eager and hopeful. Kerr glared at Lexi, she could practically see the dark thoughts he threw her way. He fought with the decision for a few heartbeats. Finally, he motioned with his hand and Elyse scooted back. He entered first and motioned for Lexi to come in slowly, sit on the floor behind him. She did. Elyse waited patiently.

"Sit here." Kerr's voice roughened and Lexi watched him tap the concrete. Too much force and he'd set Elyse off again. Too little and Elyse might not be as careful with Lexi as they needed her to be. Lexi was impressed with the amount of control he demonstrated around his Pack. Now, if only he'd do that with what was in his pants she wouldn't be so worried about having him as a roommate.

Over the next two hours, Kerr and Lexi coaxed Elyse to come over and put her head in Lexi's lap, then onto the bed, and finally to close her eyes to get some sleep. By the time Kerr took her hand and led her up the stairs again, Lexi's own eyes were drooping. She dreaded getting up in a few hours to go to class, but she hadn't missed a day in all the time she'd been here. She climbed onto the back of Kerr's bike without a word, barely managed to hold onto him on the ride home. She didn't even remember climbing the stairs to her bedroom, but she did come awake long enough to kiss Kerr's cheek as he pulled the cover up under her chin. He kissed her lips again. She sighed.

"I didn't mean to start anything like that."

He grinned. "Then why did you kiss me?" he said as he tucked a piece of her dark hair behind her ear.

"It was a thank-you."

"In Professor language?"

She blew him a raspberry and he snorted. She felt the bed dip as he rose.

"You did good, Professor," Kerr whispered by her doorway.

The light went out in her room and she closed her eyes.

CHAPTER THIRTEEN

Once Kerr had gotten Lexi to bed, he left Findlay outside her house to keep an eye on things while he was gone. Then he'd headed up to Promontory House. There was to be a quick meeting of the Warriors, the highest ranking wolves in Forbes's Pack, in the dining hall. Everyone agreed that this was another indication that *something* was happening, but no one knew what, yet. They all agreed to check out their sources and return. No one made a comment that Kerr was leading the meeting. He saw the majority to their cars. One or two had stayed behind to welcome him back to his duties. The others and their families cleared out quickly, but the kitchen still seemed full. As he expected, several of the dominants had gathered. Taskill and Dax were there, Graham, Aidan, Wallace and Ellar too.

This many dominants in Forbes's kitchen without Forbes was usually a bad idea. Tempers flared, testosterone flowed and bloodshed was usually followed by bruises and beers for those who stayed behind. Kerr grimaced. It shouldn't have been like that. Whether the Alpha was here or not, business should have gone on as usual. God, he'd been lax. He paused in the shadows of the kitchen archway to gage what he was up against.

"I think we should—" the older Graham was saying, his peer Aidan already nodding his head in agreement.

"Why don't we wait until Kerr comes back? See what he thinks." Task interrupted his father. He was the only one who'd get away with it.

"Ha! The guy's probably in the Queller's panties by now. Or a bottle of Jocky's junk." Dax was less a fan of his than Taskill, it seemed. He shrugged. The younger twin often took a contrary position to his brother. Fraternal twins, Dax was quick to point out.

"Dax!" Graham's voice cut across any reply the others could make. "If you've got the fangs to insult the Beta, challenge him and take his place. Otherwise, keep your opinions to yourself. The man found the Pack a Queller. If he does nothing else for our packmates, he's earned our gratitude for life." Graham might be a stickler for traditions and a bit prickly around him, but he apparently respected Forbes's choice for a Beta until Kerr gave him a real reason not to. Kerr wandered out from the shadows.

"Anytime, you want a go at me, Dax, let me know." He grinned at the pup.

"Drunk bastard." Dax muttered, but didn't make any other move to challenge him, so Kerr turned to Ellar.

"How's Elyse?"

Everyone in the room sobered. Elyse's Shifter gene had been discovered through blood tests three weeks ago. The Fundy tides had brought on her turn, without aid of an Alpha and in the middle of a great number of Pack members. Those two things should have prevented a generational dormant from breaking through. Unless that dormant was an Alpha, but Elyse wasn't. She wasn't anywhere near to being a dominant.

"Sis is calm, thanks to the Queller." Ellar took off his bandana and wrapped the red cloth around his grease-covered hand. Ellar was also a generational dormant. He hadn't been found before his decision to leave the valley after high school and explore the country on his bike. When he returned five months ago, everyone had gotten a surprise when he turned for the first time. Elyse had found him mid-change and called their father, who'd been aware of the family history. So the Pack had gotten a new member five moons ago, if he decided he wanted to stay. Kerr didn't think Ellar would go anywhere before his sister's situation was settled. He'd been fiercely protective of his sister before the turn. Afterward, the urge had been even stronger, though he'd been checking the edges of their territory on the night Elyse had changed. "Tell her I owe her one."

"Yeah, about that. Why do *you* have unlimited access to the Queller when the rest of us——" A snarl interrupted Wallace.

Ellar growled again, the challenge clear. Ellar and Wallace were heading to blows soon. There'd be a fight to see which one was higher up the food chain. Right now, they were on equal footing and it was chafing both men raw and raging. Wallace didn't have a sister to talk to or a lover to take the edge off. He could have used a few meetings with Lexi. So long as Wallace understood he couldn't charm Lexi. She was Kerr's.

"Here's the truth, boys. She's not exactly ours. Yet." Here was where things got tricky.

There was a pause as all the assembled men absorbed that. Then everyone burst out talking at once and it took a minute for Kerr to calm them enough for individuals to be heard.

"How long has she been in the territory?" Aidan sliced an apple with a knife and ate it off the blade. He refused to meet anyone's eye just then, but there were waves of confidence rolling off him.

"A little better than a year." Suddenly Kerr was immensely grateful he'd been the only one to move his things into Lexi's house when Lexi had been gone. His wolf saw these men as a potential threat to claiming Lexi. Aidan was very much like Lexi: studious, calm demeanor, but a poor teacher.

"A year? You've known about her for a year?" Dax cried.

"No. We just found out a few weeks ago. The last moon."

"She was the one who brought you back to the Pack," Graham surmised. He'd taken on a calculating look as well. Kerr was going to have to watch the two older wolves.

"My father's TA?" Ellar exclaimed. He had everyone's attention now.

"*You've* known about the Queller for a year?" Dax's voice was much more subdued. He'd only just gotten back into the territory and didn't know Ellar yet.

"I've known Lexi since he hired her, end of last year. Met her over the phone before I knew her in person. She's nice. We geeked out about Shakespeare once. Dad bought me tickets and I invited her when I was in Stratford, Ontario for the festival; she came up and we hung out. Never got the sense she was a Queller. Could she have been the one to activate the gene to turn me?"

"No. Quellers don't do that. They bleed away a wolf's surfacing, make it easier. They don't make things burst," Graham said. Next to Forbes, Graham would know.

Kerr started coffee brewing. He had to do something with his hands or risk throttling Ellar, who'd been near his mate for a weekend. "You didn't feel any calmer around her? Better control after being in her presence?"

Ellar shrugged. "Elyse and I only met her a few times at the house. Maybe half a dozen for me after the play and dinner, up in Ontario. She seemed normal. Especially when I saw her here. She dropped off my father's papers and then left. Quiet. Not much to the conversation if it didn't concern Shakespeare." He cocked his head, searching through the exchanges. "Now that you mention it, those were the few times my father and I seemed to get along tolerably."

Kerr's lips twitched at Ellar's choice of words. Shakespeare and motorcycles, that was Ellar. Right down to the long dark hair and leathers. Yet he had the mannerisms of a poet. Except around his father, where the foul-mouthed, disrespectful biker came out.

"Hmm," was all Kerr said.

"What are you thinking, Beta?" Graham's voice was soft. He took the coffee Kerr poured for him without looking at it, but his head was tilted down in a non-threatening posture. The earlier exchange kept playing in Kerr's head. He'd need to talk to the man again, in private.

"The tides are what I'm thinking." Kerr grabbed more mugs off the hooks on Forbes's walls and began pouring for the rest of the group. Caring for the other members of the Pack was a dominant's responsibility, but it was also a privilege, and something that Kerr had denied himself for long enough.

Graham blew on his coffee to cool it, waiting. The others in the room followed his lead, and all eyes focused on their Beta.

"The witches who went into sway-lock, it happened in the last few moons." He took a sip of his coffee and considered his words. No one hurried him. They waited for him to hunt out an explanation. "Elyse's turn happening without an Alpha. My difficulty controlling the shift while with a human after nearly two centuries of practice. The Queller suddenly appearing on our radar after being here for a year… It all speaks to something else. Something *other*. Like the Fundy magics are working their way up to something big."

"Like what?" Taskill's voice was soft.

"I don't know. Nothing's ever happened like this while I've lived here. Findlay might have heard stories on the Reserve when he went to visit his grandfather. I'll get him to ask if he doesn't know of anything off-hand. The witches' High Priestess might have an idea, but the only one on any kind of speaking terms with Kassia is Forbes." He raised an eyebrow at Graham, but the old man held his tongue. They definitely needed to talk later.

"What if the witches are behind it?" Wallace asked.

Kerr nodded. "Another possibility. There is reason for concern, but it doesn't feel like things are ramping up fast. Witches would need to strike first and strike hard. This is different. Things are…accumulating. Gathering. We have enough wiggle room for Forbes to bring us back more information."

"So…the gist of your wisdom is we wait for Forbes to get back from the meeting with the Warden. Maybe he'll already have the answers." Dax nodded. "Brilliant."

Taskill gave his brother a sharp jab to the shoulder and their father sent another menacing stare at his youngest son.

"My answer is for the rest of us to get off our asses and do some sniffing around. See if there are any other occurrences, anything to add to the pattern. Magics that might not have worked out, Shifters acting strange, natural phenomenon amping up or down or simply appearing out of place, ghosts making house calls. Whatever. Look for *anything* out of the ordinary. We need to bring more meat to the Alpha's table, wolves, so he has enough to ensure the Pack's survival." It was one of Forbes's favorite sayings.

"And you? What do you intend to do while we're scouting all this stuff out?" Dax asked.

"Who, me? I'm gonna claim me a Queller mate, boy. I'll have my hands full, trust me. Now snap to. Everyone else, good hunting."

***

Lexi woke up the next morning, the sun streaming in her window and the dulcet hum of a lawn mower just outside. She sniffed the aromas sliding in through her curtains. Fall, unmistakably here and in full swing. Sunshine warmed the comforter on her shoulders. Someone was up early if they were up with the sun. She took a sip from the cool water waiting on her bedside table and snuggled back down under her covers.

Wait a minute. Her bedroom window faced west. So it wasn't the early morning sun streaming in. The lawn mower cut out. She rubbed her eyes and grabbed the clock next to her bed.

"Good evening," Kerr said as he bounded in, shirtless, sweat-soaked and his shoes leaving moist grass clippings behind him.

"I missed my job! How could you? I helped you last night!" Lexi was sure her neighbors could hear her bellow several streets away but she still couldn't control herself. This was unbelievable, and she'd actually begun to think that Kerr's Pack might be different. Things might not be so bad as they had been in her mother's cluster of mongrels, but obviously, the care only went so deep. She flipped back the blankets and was about to leap out of bed when she realized she didn't have a stitch of clothing on. She yipped and dove back under the covers.

"Wh-wha—you ass!" she managed, flustered beyond comprehension. Kerr was grinning from ear to ear as he toed off his sneakers and plunked on the foot of her bed, crossed his legs and waited for her to stop sputtering.

"You about done, Professor?"

She crossed her arms over her chest and glared.

"I'll take that as a yes." He laughed at her, leaned forward quicker than she could blink and laid a kiss directly on her lips before retreating to the end of the bed.

"That was for Wednesday night. You probably saved Elyse's life, if not her mind. The entire Pack thanks you. Elyse is very much loved."

"Great, how does that save me from being fired?" She frowned, alarmed at how pleased his gratitude made her. She pulled up her knees. He leaned up on his and pushed down the barrier she'd put up between them. Then he sat on her legs so she couldn't do it again. Try as she might, she couldn't move him off her. Truth be told, the scent of him was kind of appealing. Sweat, grass clippings and something that was just him. Not to mention she hadn't had a man in her room for far too long. *Stop*, she thought to herself. *This is so not the guy to break your celibacy streak with and you know it.* Still, she couldn't stop the butterflies that danced in her belly because he was here.

"I like you. You're definitely unpredictable."

Her eyebrows shot up. "Then you're gonna love me when I miss my mortgage payment from being unemployed and get us both thrown out on the streets."

"You will never need to worry about being on the streets again, Lexi. Not as long as you're with us. We take care of our own." He leaned forward and snagged her hands, "And don't worry about Dr. Engles. I called him yesterday and let him know you wouldn't be coming for the rest of the week. You were ahead of where you needed to be, thesis wise, and I think the old guy was actually looking forward to doing some of his own grading."

She took a shaky breath. "He just bought that? I'm sick for three days?"

Kerr shrugged. "It doesn't hurt that Elyse is his daughter."

She disengaged one of her hands and smacked her forehead dramatically. "Why did you let me sleep so long? You've totally ruined my rhythm for bed now, you know. Not that you care."

He grinned at her and she felt an answering smile stretch her lips. He was still touching her, holding her hand, his finger making lazy circles on her wrist and it was giving her the shivers. She didn't want it to stop. In fact, she wanted him to lean over and give her a real kiss. Her heart was beating so loudly, he probably heard it. She felt like flying.

Wait. Dr. Engles had a daughter that was a wolf. He was one of their people. She blew out a long breath.

"How long have you guys been aware that I was here? That I was who I was? And you've been watching me?" She had been so stupid. Her boss was in on the whole damn thing. She'd overloaded on courses during the year, worked eighteen hour days over two summers and even with the online courses during her time in Dubai, she'd just barely completed the requirements, but had it mattered? Had she even *earned* her master's? Or did the Pack ensure she got it to keep her happy and in the town?

Kerr ran his thumb over the knuckles of the hand he refused to let go, then lifted it to his mouth. The second he started to gently nibble on her skin, her stomach tensed along with things much lower. She tightened her grip on the sheet around her.

What was worse was Kerr knew exactly what he was doing to her. Curse her own body for tipping him off to her arousal. He smiled against her skin, his eyes darkened with sensual promise. Even that turned her on and there was no hiding it. The jerk.

"I asked you a question." She wanted it to come out angry, not breathy. But it was getting difficult to remember exactly why she was angry with him.

"You asked me several." He ran his lower lip over the back of her hand, back and forth.

"Pick one and speak, doggy." She tried being deliberately insulting so he'd back off and she could think straight, but Kerr's grin widened and he shimmied closer on her legs. Hell's bells, why didn't she push him away? He was invading her space, he was a player, and he was a wolf, for goodness sake. All valid reasons to make him leave her alone and she couldn't even get a word out.

Her heart had kicked up a notch and she could feel her skin warming. He leaned closer in, and she could feel his arousal against her thigh. She wanted to rub against him, mark him like he'd mark her. It took every ounce of self-control to keep still. Dear God, where was her brain?

"Eep."

"You're cute when you panic, Professor. Anyone ever tell you that?"

She managed to swallow against a dry mouth. She couldn't speak so she gave a sharp shake of her head. He put a hand on either side of her shoulders, his knees now holding his weight on either side of her legs and got close enough to kiss. Her breath stuttered. *Kiss me, please*, then realized what she'd just told herself. *No, don't kiss me.* He licked his lower lip and she watched it slowly slide across his mouth and heard a breathy *oh* escape her. She was losing this battle. Space, she needed space. She wiggled as far back as the headboard would allow.

"Well, I let you sleep in late because the other night would have been exhausting for you. I want you rested and full of energy." He let one hand trail down her shoulder and the heat of it felt so good she curled her head toward it before she could stop herself. *Pull it together, Lexi.*

"How very kind. What do I need the energy for, exactly?"

"Tsk, tsk, Professor. It isn't nice to tease. I was just going to express my thanks."

His fingers moved over the swell of one breast on the outside and she couldn't suppress the shiver. Her brain, trying to help her out, produced one fact to latch onto.

"What do you mean, you called him yesterday?"

"What?" The hand on the outside of the sheet froze.

"You said you called Dr. Engles yesterday. I'm assuming it wasn't at the ungodly hour we got home. That means it was during the day. A day I have no memory of at all. So how long have I been out, exactly?"

Kerr's fingers curled. "Um, you've slept a full day."

"Oh my God."

"Lexi, calm down. It's OK. I fixed everything until you woke up. Remember?"

"What was wrong with me?" She pushed at him, but he didn't budge. Got closer, in fact. Leaned into her, but stopped short of taking her into his arms. She had to look up to meet his gaze.

"Nothing's wrong with you. The same thing that affected Elyse affected you too while you were in the room with her. That's all. You're safe." He stroked her cheek again.

She pleaded for space with her eyes, but he was either not inclined to give it or was deeply ignoring it. She caught his hand, brought it down to her hip.

"The Pack magics are affecting me somehow?"

"Sort of." Kerr cupped her face. She wanted to put her forehead against his, but wasn't brave enough for it.

"Sort of? Explain sort of?" Terror crept through her veins at the thought that things were changing in her. This Pack had a use for her. They had been respectful, even grateful. They had protected her. Kerr had protected her. She was beginning to rely on him. Usually that's when the floor boards got pulled out from under her.

"Ready to meet the Alpha, then?"

She hiccupped.

"Lexi. You're safe."

Her mind refused to consider Pack magic playing with her so she focused on another of her questions. "So how long have you guys actually known I was here? Did Professor Engles let you know?"

"Engles isn't a Shifter. Until you brought me to the last full moon ceremony is how long. That's when we found out you were here. You were who you were. Are. That you're a…rival Pack's daughter. We haven't been watching you, Lexi. I swear."

She narrowed her eyes at him. What had he meant to say? His charming grin tried to distract her from the fact that she knew he'd slipped up. She needed to distract herself from how much she wanted him to get under the covers with her.

Before she could answer, he dipped down and kissed her lips. She tried to stay stiff, tried to remember all the reasons she should hate the man in front of her, but his lips were soft. He ran his tongue along the seam of her mouth and nipped gently until she opened for him. He stroked inside, sweetly at first, then with more need. She slipped her arms around his head, threading her fingers through his hair and tilted her mouth to give him better access. He took full advantage. Just when she thought he was going to push the blankets down and settle against her bare skin, he pulled away. It took effort, if his growl was any indication. She gave a cry of protest, gulping air that burned her lungs. She wanted heat. Wanted him.

He was breathless above her and his eyes had nearly gone black, the pupils were so wide. But a thin ring of blue remained. It wasn't his wolf that had kissed the wind out of her just now. This was Kerr. The fact the man had seduced the hell out of her was wildly more thrilling to her senses and she let the sheet slide a bit. The curve of her breasts were exposed, a silent invitation. Kerr's eyes hadn't missed it. He closed them and shivered. When he spoke, his voice was thick.

"I can't, Lexi. Not yet. You don't trust me. God, I want you so much right now. But with what your mother's Pack did to you, it wouldn't be fair. Wouldn't be enough for me."

She leaned up, ran her hand through his hair and kissed his neck. "I want you, Kerr."

He groaned. "I need more than you wanting me, Lexi. I'm in this for the long haul. I want you to be, too. Get dressed, Professor. We need to talk. Downstairs." He leaped off the bed and nearly bolted from the room, leaving Lexi confused and very, very turned on.

CHAPTER FOURTEEN

Kerr's abrupt departure confused her, since he'd seemed as affected by their encounter as she felt. Lexi turned the faucet to Arctic and loaded soap on the loofah. Should it matter? She started scrubbing her face until the skin stung. The fact she was annoyed as hell that he'd pulled away meant that it troubled her. It was a complication and it shouldn't be. What the hell was her problem? She couldn't get involved with a wolf. Could she?

Even if she was going to, it shouldn't be this wolf. He was a player. Dated nineteen-year-olds. Was totally hot. Oh God, could she just control her raging hormones for a second so she could think? It wasn't like he was going to take her to mate. Was he? No, he had said it wasn't anything like that and it wasn't like any of the matings she'd witnessed back in Denver…why was she even thinking about the *word* mate? That was crazy. But wouldn't her mother love it.

Long haul. He'd said long haul. As in long term. She was barely halfway through the first month with him. Was two months long term to a wolf like Kerr? Was he thinking beyond their two months?

Crap. She dressed in sharp, crisply ironed black slacks and a flowered peasant blouse. The outfit looked professional on her and gave her a sense of grounding. Maybe whatever had knocked her out for a day was still affecting her. Maybe this was still Pack magic. Maybe it was the ragewave. The stillness in her blood told her she'd be lying to herself if she believed that to be the truth. This was plain, old fashioned lust. She wanted Kerr MacDonald in her bed. That much she was willing to admit.

The phone rang, making her jump. She checked caller ID. Figures her mother would call at this precise moment. She debated for a second about whether or not to answer, but her guilt won out. The woman had helped her when she needed it this full moon past and she was her mother, after all. She picked up on the fifth ring.

"Hi, Mum."

There was a pause in which Lexi could hear her mother drawing breath, like a storm gathering. "You little witch." A lightning strike to the libido. Her mother wanted a fight. Great.

Lexi plunked down on the bed again. "And to what do I owe the pleasure of that particular insult?"

"You need to come home. Now." There was the unmistakable command in that sentence. From someone used to instantaneous obedience. There was also a tiny thread of fear. Lexi had never heard fear from a wolf before, especially directed at her. How interesting.

"Umm, no. Because I am home. I live here, Mum. So I am home."

It was as if she hadn't spoken. "I'm sending your brother to come get you. He's on the way. Be at the airport to pick him up."

"No." She hung up, worry spreading ice through her entire body. Trouble was coming, fast. She put the phone back in its cradle and bolted for the stairs. Whatever else was going on, she had to warn Kerr that her brother was coming. And beg him not to kill Rafe for entering another's territory without permission.

Kerr was sitting calmly at the dining table, a steaming cup of tea at one seat and a beer in front of him. The beer was the only acknowledgment that the episode in her bedroom had happened. True to his word, he hadn't touched a drink in this house since he'd moved in. That he'd grabbed one now said he wasn't as invulnerable as wolves had always seemed to her. A little flutter of feminine satisfaction stirred before she squashed it. Serious matters needed immediate attention.

He took one look at her face and his soothing demeanor faded. "What?"

"My mother is sending my brother here to come get me." She wrapped her arms around herself, ashamed that she was shivering. But she couldn't help it. She couldn't go back. Not ever. Not to that. Not now.

He stood up and opened his arms, though you could tell from the look on his face it was a struggle not to close the gap and make her accept his comfort. She wanted to, oh, how she wanted to believe that he could hold her and things wouldn't seem as bad. He wasn't growling at her or raging that there was another Shifter invading from a hostile Pack. He wasn't blaming her. He wasn't anything like her mother's world. He was good and kind and he was worried about her and how she felt. Something broke inside her, a wall that had been there for so long she couldn't remember if it had been built brick by brick or slammed down fully realized. But it crumbled inside of her now. She pushed the heel of her hand into her heart and fought back tears. Because she was absolutely terrified her mother would find a way to take her away from someone who was rapidly becoming the most important person in her life. Fear froze her to the spot.

This left a rather awkward scene occurring in her kitchen. Her terror wouldn't let her go to him and his pride dictated that she make the first move. Kerr recovered first and dropped his arms. He appeared to remember they hadn't negotiated any change in his right to touch her. But he never broke eye contact with her. His next words seemed dredged up with great effort, but he said them. "Do you want to go?"

"Where?" That drop of his hands almost had her rushing to him. Until the fear clawed up and wrapped itself around her throat and she fought to breathe for a second.

"With your brother. Do you want to leave this territory?"

Leave the territory? She finally owned a house. Had a few friends. Was possibly falling in love with the worst candidate in the world for her. No, of course she didn't want to leave with her brother. But she couldn't find the courage to say that. Not yet. Not all of it. *Get mad, Lexi. Shake yourself out of this and get mad.*

"Excuse me? I have a life here, you know. I've got students. If I've still got a job, that is. I haven't been on the winery tour yet. Or up to the Lookoff. I hear you can see the entire valley from there. And there's Canadian Thanksgiving next week. I love that I can celebrate it twice. I don't want to miss it. Hannah's supposed to take me to see the pumpkin people and the gourd races, and Halloween's coming. I already have my costume for Hannah's party." She was rambling and she knew it. Damn it.

He gave her a Cheshire grin. "For the record, that's a no. Right?"

She sighed and put her hands on her hips. Took another deep, shaky breath. "No, I do not want to go anywhere with my brother. Please?"

He pulled his cell phone from his pocket and speed dialed someone who picked up on the first ring. "Airport. Lexi's brother, a wolf from the Denver Pack, is flying in for an unwelcome visit."

Lexi pulled at her lip. It had been a few years since she'd seen him. He was her brother and she missed him. Not all of her memories were bad. She held up a finger and Kerr turned. He intuitively seemed to know what she was going to say, however.

"Bring him to Lexi's house. We'll put him up for the night and put him back on the first plane out of the city in the morning. So long as he doesn't cause any trouble, he's not to be harmed, OK?" He ended the call, but gave a little bow when he spoke to Lexi. "That is, of course, if it's all right with you, Professor."

Lexi bit back a smile, choosing instead to roll her eyes to hide the relief. She was really starting to like his nickname for her. A huge weight lifted off her shoulders. Kerr understood her emotions were split between the love of family and self-preservation. "I'll get the blankets and a pillow for him. He can take the couch."

"Wait a minute. There's no rush. I have an idea."

Lexi stared hard at the man who had insinuated himself into her life in so short a period. She realized she could barely remember not seeing him every day. Was even more surprised to find she wanted to see him daily.

"And what would that be?"

He was lightning quick and pulled her hand toward him, catching her as she tripped on the carpet. "Let's go dancing. We've got a few hours before your brother shows up, no reason we can't enjoy them."

She gave a nervous little giggle. "Dancing? Hello, have we met? My name is Lexi, I'm the Professor. Professors don't do a whole lot of dancing."

Kerr pulled her body up against his and held their arms aloft like some Ballroom dancer. "I can partner anyone, Professor. And it'll be good for you to get out of your routine, get your mind off your troubles. Relax and have some fun with me, Lexi. At the very least let this old wolf try and teach you a new trick." He twirled them around the room. She threw back her head and laughed.

"I'm not sure you're up for the challenge I'd present, wolf."

He dipped her. "How can you be so sure?"

"How about a move from this millennium?"

He spun her and proceeded to do a few moves directly from Dirty Dancing. Again, she laughed. She was a bit embarrassed about the bedroom. Maybe she'd misread the situation entirely. She wasn't exactly an expert in that area. And he was certainly not aroused right now.

"So is that a yes?" He pulled her close and sashayed them around the room again.

"Isn't it a bit early?"

"We'll eat, and then we'll go dancing. If you are willing, Professor." Kerr gave her a puppy pout.

"Sure. Why not?"

True to his word, they had a decent meal at Paddy's Pub. It was still nice for the second week of October and she'd brought a shawl Hannah had made her, so they chose a spot on the patio out back. Her shawl was a great multicolored thing with fringe made from chunky yarn. She loved it. Rather than poke fun at her for it, Kerr smiled and fingered the wool, running his hand over her arm where it rested on the table.

"Soft," was all he said.

She nodded. Pulled it tighter around her. "A gift from my friend."

***

Kerr bit back the stab of jealousy that someone else might elicit such a warm smile from his Lexi. His Lexi? Holy crap, was he in trouble. He liked it when they fought. He liked it when they rode the bike. He loved it when she touched him. He ached to be the one she trusted enough to let him comfort her. He found he couldn't stop himself from touching her. Found any excuse he could, like a soft shawl that showed her wild, colorful side. Or dancing in the kitchen when she wouldn't come into his arms moments earlier. He knew how hard it was to choose the Pack over her brother. And a strange Pack at that. But she knew the consequences of a rival crossing their borders without proper tithe and permissions. Perhaps the concern had been over her family and she smiled out of happiness that he'd spared the pup a great deal. Or that she could see her brother again after such a long absence. But his wolf wouldn't let him lie to himself.

No. She likes me.

Like. Not love. Lord help him, it was eating his heart out of his chest to feel the truth of those words. To know it was the man who was falling under Lexi's spell, not the wolf. He wanted her. And he wanted her to want him back. So he fed her up, as much as she'd let him order. She even relented to 'trying' some of his dishes. He had the exquisite pleasure of feeding her from his fork. It made the wolf in him rumble in satisfaction to take care of his mate. To watch her mouth curl up on the corner when she found something she truly enjoyed eating. Or when her left eye squinted just a bit at something she found too sour.

She was not a fan of chocolate, he discovered. But of fruit. Apples in particular.

"Is that why you came to Acadia? The apples here?"

She nodded. "Partially. It really is a great opportunity to work with some of these professors. But I met an older woman when I worked in Dubai. She was from here. The way she spoke about the valley and the Apple Blossom Festival, I wanted to come and see. And once I got here, I just kinda…fell in love with the place. It felt, I know this sounds cheesy, but it felt—"

"Right," he finished for her. And nodded in agreement. "I felt something similar when I got here, way back when. Although it had lots to do with the people I was with at the time too."

"Your brother?"

"And my wife," he agreed.

"Your wife?"

He shrugged. "She left me for my brother. They moved down to New England."

They were both silent for a while and he wondered if she would let it lie. He almost grinned when, as she casually toyed with her left-over dessert, not making eye contact, she managed to ask him the question he could see vibrating through her smaller frame. She was just a tiny bit jealous and he was a tiny bit thrilled with it.

"Did you go after her?"

"I did."

"And you fought your brother for her?"

"I did."

She looked up at him then, met his gaze. He'd tell her anything she wanted to know, as long as there was no geas against it. Hell, maybe even if there was. He wasn't sure he was strong enough to tell her anything that Forbes had specifically forbidden him to, but he'd try. For her, he'd try. He gathered breath to tell her of the awful night in question, when he'd lost his brother and any chance of his loving wife returning with him. But she put her hand on his arm and squeezed gently, then ran her fingers over his forearm before taking his hand and holding it.

"I'm sorry. It sucks when the people who are supposed to love you the best are the ones who are the worst to you."

His heart was hers. If he'd had any doubts up until then, those words, her simple acceptance and understanding of what had shattered him and made him vow against caring for anyone deeply ever again, had him. She got it. She knew.

He'd been staring at her, into those amber eyes, for a long time. So long in fact, that he hadn't realized that anyone was standing beside their table, waiting.

"Um, check please."

"That's great, Kerr, but I don't actually work here. Or did you forget when you brought me for a romantic dinner for two? It was only a couple of weeks ago."

Lexi looked up at the young blonde woman with the blades in her voice. "Hi, Tiffany."

"Lexi." The coed's voice couldn't be colder. Lexi pulled her shawl closer around her and shook her head. Tiffany was right. She couldn't fall for the man's tricks, at least out in public. But she hadn't the sense that this was some ploy. He certainly hadn't told anyone else about his family. Had he? No, he couldn't risk it. What if one of the young women he dated decided to go looking for him and found his wife had died decades ago? Or even a century? Better to tell them nothing at all. It must have been so lonely.

"So, I guess I should tell you, I have an STI, Kerr. You should go and get yourself tested. You too, Lexi, if you've been sleeping together." Tiffany announced loudly. People from other tables glanced over. Lexi actually chuckled.

"Should have gone with the pregnancy scare, Tiffany. That one I might have believed." Lexi's answer was too quick for Tiffany. More onlookers turned to watch, but Tiffany was their focus, not Kerr and Lexi.

"Think I'm lying?" Tiffany was stalling. Lexi let her stew, mostly because she couldn't tell everyone how Kerr couldn't catch diseases because his metabolism was too quick. His body broke itself down and rebuilt itself at least once a month. A human disease? Didn't stand a chance. Since she couldn't say it, she let the certainty bleed through her relaxed body language.

Tiffany wasn't giving up without a fight. "What if I got it from him? You ever think of that?"

Lexi shrugged. "Well, the clinic is a block away. Let's go get tested right now. When it comes up negative, and you've only been broken up, what a week or two now? We'll know what you've been up to. And I guess you can't play the pregnancy card now. It would have shown up in your tests already."

The couple across the way snickered and Tiffany glared daggers. But there was nothing she could do. She'd been publicly caught in a lie. Someone Kerr had trusted enough, even casually, to sleep with had tried to stab him in the back. Lexi stood, pulled Kerr up with her.

"Why don't we go in and pay, then we can continue on with our night, Kerr. Have a good one, Tiffany. Good-bye."

Tiffany's jaw dropped a fraction. This was Lexi's time with Kerr, after all. Tiffany had given him up without a fight. She was trying to wound him now, for spite. Kerr didn't deserve that. No one did. Lexi was learning so much about the man behind the wolf tonight. It sounded like he'd been deeply damaged by family too. They had a common wound, they just dealt with it in different ways. He seemed so much more human now, so much safer and intriguing all at the same time.

The Wolf's Den wasn't what she'd had in mind when Kerr had suggested dancing. But the dark atmosphere combined with oldies rock blaring from the speakers was somehow just right. True to his word, Kerr was a perfect partner. Spinning her effortlessly, jiving with her and keeping her on the beat as best he could, she found herself laughing and enjoying the music. He pulled her close during one of the slower songs.

"Careful, Professor." He pitched his voice lower so she could hear it. "A guy might get the impression you like him."

She pulled far enough back so she could look up into his face, so he could see she meant what she was about to say. "I do. I care about you, Kerr. Please don't... don't do anything to spoil that."

They stopped swaying to the music. He put his forehead against hers. "Never, Professor. I'll never do anything of ill intent against you. I give you my vow. I am never going to hurt you, Lexi."

She couldn't breathe. His promise was a warm weight she wrapped around her. Because she believed him. Felt it in her very cells.

"Now who's teasing," she managed, and leaned forward for a quick kiss that sizzled between them. She'd been trying to lighten the moment, but Kerr groaned.

"Don't, Alexandra. You have no idea how much control it takes not to whisk you home to have my wicked way with you."

She licked her lips, surprised at how brazen she felt just then. How powerful. How utterly feminine. "So why don't you?"

He growled. "Be good, Professor."

She wrapped her arms around him and brushed her chest against his, the friction making her nipples harden instantly. "I don't want to be good. Take me home, Kerr." She brushed her lips over his, the slightest touch. "I promise I'll be good at home."

"I've only got so much control, Lexi. Please."

He shook his head, but she could feel his erection straining against his jeans. So she leaned in.

"I want you, Kerr." She bit his earlobe lightly and he snarled, yanked her off the dance floor, and they practically ran the length of Main Street back to her home.

Once in the door, Kerr was in front of her in a flash, slipped one of his arms around her waist and lifted her off her feet to bring her lips in reach. He slid his other hand behind and tilted her head just right. She didn't have time to fight him, even if she'd wanted to. He leaned in and gave her the sweetest, softest kiss. She wanted more. She wanted to tell him the things she was feeling, how much it meant to her that he understood. That he was on her side. That he was here. The words wouldn't come. This was fine because her mouth was busy, anyway.

Her hands griped his shoulders, pulled him toward her again. This, he'd understand, wouldn't he? The kiss heated swiftly, Kerr catching onto her mood, and he was thorough. When he plunked her down again, he didn't let go of her waist. She didn't really want him to release her, but then again, she didn't want to be interrupted later.

"Let me go set up the couch for my brother."

Kerr refused to let her go.

"We can be nice. Give him the spare room, since we'll be in yours…" he let the sinful promise into his voice as his fingers trailed over her face and neck to linger on her collarbone. Exactly the way she'd fantasized him doing. It did exactly what she fantasized it would.

"You. Um. What?"

His masculine pride and possessiveness sent her head spinning, especially when his kisses trailed down her neck and settled on her collarbone where he'd been playing seconds before. This was even better than the fantasy.

His breath was hot and she shivered, his voice vibrating all the way down her spine. "Let's go back to your room, Professor. I've got a lesson for you."

There had been something she was going to say, but his lips were on hers again, his hands on her bare skin and she couldn't think. She gave up trying and slipped her hand under his shirt, up his chest, his fevered skin driving her mad. His stomach was strong and when her palm grazed his nipples, the intensity of his kiss changed. A low growl came from his throat and he picked her up without breaking contact, wrapping her legs around his waist and walking them over to the couch. She heard a tearing sound. That was important and she should probably figure out what that sound was, except her mind forgot about it when he covered her bared upper body with his own. She sighed into his mouth and he laughed.

"You feel so good," she whispered.

He smiled again, kissing down her throat, past her collarbone to circle her right breast, spiraling closer and closer to her nipple while he teased the other with nimble fingers. She arched when his mouth closed over his target and his tongue ran over the pebbled nub. Something jangled and she blinked. What was that sound? Kerr redoubled his efforts at distraction and slipped his thumbs into the waistband of her slacks. The zipper had magically come down already. He tugged the garments past her hips and the jangling came again. It took Lexi's brain a minute to realize it was her phone.

"Phone," she gasped, and tried to push him away. But he kissed down her stomach, inching lower with a wicked gleam in his eye.

"They can leave a message." He kissed lower and lower. He was so close, if he'd just move a little farther.

"Jackpot," she panted as he found just the right spot and stroked once, twice with his tongue and then she was exploding out of her skin, stars dancing across her eyelids. When she could think again, she felt a gentle tap against her cheek.

"Hey, Professor. Open those hazel eyes up for me. I want you to know who's giving you bliss."

She cupped his cheek. "How could I not know, Kerr?"

Kerr held himself above her on the couch and gazed at her as if she was the most amazing thing he'd ever seen. She didn't want to consider the flip-flop her heart was doing, lest her fear she was falling in love spoil the moment. She managed a lazy smile in return.

"I'm that good, huh?"

"What, you doubt your own skills?" she teased.

"Never in a million years, sweetheart. My turn."

He was slow and gentle as he sheathed himself in her, but bigger than anything she'd ever had before and she was glad he'd let her go first. He paused, letting her adjust to his size, kissing her the whole time. She wrapped her arms around his neck and held him as he groaned.

"You're so good, baby. So right. So mine." He nipped her chin, her ear lobe and bit her shoulder gently as he finally pushed himself to the hilt. She groaned then, and he chuckled. "Ready?"

"Mmmhmm."

***

Later, after several missed phone calls and ecstatic turns for both of them, he finally collapsed on top of her as they tried to catch their breath. It didn't stop him from exploring her skin with feather kisses.

"You're mine, Lexi. All mine. I'm not ever gonna let you go." He kissed her shoulder, her throat, everywhere he could reach without moving off her. Repeating the same words over and over. His, she was his. Instead of feeling scared that he'd try to control her, she felt loved. Safe. Happy. Had it really been so long since she'd let herself feel this happy? The phone wouldn't stop ringing, though neither of them could move just yet.

"Whoever it is, I'm gonna kill 'em," he growled. A laugh bubbled out of Lexi's throat.

"You're on top, you have to get up to get it."

He shook his head against her shoulder. "Nope. They will forever live in bewilderment, wondering what happened to you."

She chuckled again and pulled his arms around her. She kissed his mouth and he hummed in approval. The phone stopped as it went to voice mail. Seconds later, it began again. She ran her hand down his hair as he snarled at the offender.

"You're interfering with my cuddling, buddy," he told the phone. He faced her again and pouted. "We haven't even gotten to the bedroom."

"Maybe we should sleep on the couch and let my brother have the bedroom. I don't know if can walk that far, anyway." She laughed as he rolled off to fetch the offending device. He was standing naked, dead center of the doorway when the door exploded inward and her brother stood framed by the street lamp outside.

CHAPTER FIFTEEN

"You Queller slut!" Rafe shouted. The first time she'd seen him in a little over six years and that was the first thing he said to her. Not to mention he'd just destroyed her front door. What would the neighbors think? And she was naked. Her clothes were ripped. Too many conflicting emotions and thoughts crowded her brain in too short a time.

Kerr didn't even bother growling a challenge, simply launched himself at her brother, claws and fangs instantly extended. In full view of the neighbors, again. Lexi didn't even have time to yelp, but snatched the afghan from the back of the couch, wrapped it around herself and started screaming at the two men to stop.

"It's all right, Lexi, we've got 'em," a slightly familiar voice said. One of the men from Elyse's house was in the doorway; the kind, blond one who'd said he'd met someone like her before. She forgot his name, if he'd given it. As he reassured her, two of his fellows grabbed the combatants and parted them. There were strangers in her house. Pack strangers. They had been watching her. They'd been watching them. She swallowed. They'd heard. They'd heard all that had just gone on inside her house. She felt so violated.

Wait a minute. Then how had Rafe gotten past them? Unless they'd been chasing Rafe, not waiting for Kerr. That was it. They must have lost Rafe at the airport, somehow, and been forced to follow him. She needed to let go of the paranoia. It wasn't necessary in Kerr's Pack. He didn't want to keep her as a pet, like her mother. She was safe with him.

Kerr was first to regain some of his composure, shifting back to normal. She darted to his side, watching as the minor cuts and bruises he'd received healed before her eyes. His eyes were bright and out of focus, as if he didn't see her, and he was snarling softly. The instant her hand touched his bare chest, he stopped dead in his tracks, looked down at her and sighed. The fight went out of him like blowing out match. He pulled at the afghan, tugging it above her shoulders. She raised an eyebrow at him.

"You're mine. You said." He ran a strand of her hair through his fingers and played with it.

"Technically, you said and I didn't argue with you."

"Why not?"

She shrugged, in the mood to tease him and torment her brother while making sure Kerr knew he had a place with her. "More interesting things to do with my mouth at that moment." *See what I have now?* Her gaze said, as she met her sibling's eyes.

Kerr exhaled again and hugged her close. She wrapped him up in the blanket too. She was human enough to want to cover his nakedness, but he didn't seem to mind at all. They turned as her brother was dragged farther into the house and the men who'd broken up the fight attempted to close the door. Or find what was left of it.

"The latch is busted," one of them said.

"Are you nuts, Dax? The *door* is busted. We've only got the top half."

"Shut up, Wallace. Go get some lumber so we can fix this up."

"Not with a strange wolf in the house. Taskill can go."

"Looks like you owe me a new door, little brother. Fork over some cash for the nice men." She held out her palm.

Her brother's upper lip curled, but no sound came out. "Queller bitch," he murmured. Every other male in the room growled a warning and the younger man, realizing he couldn't win against them all, dropped his head.

"First off, suck a lemon. My house, my rules. And what the holy hay are you going on about? That's the second time you called me something. Queller. Kerr, you called me that too. What is that?"

Her brother raised his eyes in surprise. She couldn't recall ever standing up to him when he was in his semi-changed state. Or at all, really. This was the first time he'd ever broken into her home, however. She glared at him, refusing to let herself be embarrassed by being caught post coitus by her sibling. His surprise was slowly replaced by a sneer.

"He didn't tell you, did he?"

Kerr advanced fist raised to strike her brother silent. "Shut up! You're going back on the first plane to—"

"Tell me what?" Lexi blocked Kerr's advance with her bare arm. She remembered he was naked. She elbowed him, gave him a significant look and he snorted. Then gave her brother a wicked look, snatched her up and kissed her deep and with great enthusiasm. This set her brother into hysterics again. The three others held her brother back while Kerr calmly walked over, picked up his boxer briefs and put them on. Lexi watched his slow, deliberate movements, an uneasy tightness between her shoulders growing as he took on the stance she'd often seen in her stepfather when he was disciplining a lower member of the Pack.

"Lexi Coolen is mine. She is of my Pack, boy. She will not go with you. She will not leave her Pack, her lands. And you need to be disciplined for entering another territory without permission. Did you even pay the tithes to the other Packs whose territory you crossed? Shall we take their payments out of your hide for them? The Fundy Bay Pack has made agreements with our neighbors for just such an occurrence."

Her brother wasn't afraid and the sneer never left his face. "Did she submit to you?"

"Take a sniff, boy. You know what we just finished doing before you burst in here. Look at her. Think she was taken by force? Or is that how you get your females and assume every other Pack does the same?"

Her brother wasn't fazed. "Did she say she was yours? Did she give in to your leadership? Did she acknowledge you as dominant? *Did she say the words?*"

The tightness between her shoulders traveled up the back of her neck to blossom as a headache in the base of her skull. Stupid, how could she have been so stupid? They were in a pissing contest and she was the measuring stick. And she'd slept with Kerr. Talk about sending the wrong message. The blood pounded hard in her ears. He'd claimed her. But he never said he loved her. Just that she belonged to him. Her breath wouldn't come in anything but short little spurts. A possession. That's what he saw her as. An object. Objects got put in their places and weren't generally allowed to move on their own. Or make their own decisions. Or be free. He'd trapped her and she'd let him. Pain shattered her vision and she sucked in breath. The cold seeped in through the afghan and cut against her skin. But she wouldn't cry. Wouldn't let him see how deeply she was wounded. She felt heavy, her body bruised and slow.

Lexi tried hard to be angry at Kerr for the mess she was in, but she had no one but herself to blame. Her stupid hormones, making her confuse lust with love. She should have bought a vibrator or something. Gotten a friend with benefits or anything to avoid this mess. Two things wolves could never be trusted with. Your heart or your freedom.

She turned from the whole display going on and slowly started up the stairs to take another shower and wash him off her. She felt dirty. Used. Tired and defeated. Kerr had said this was her Pack. Ha. One Pack emergency to talk to a younger member while Kerr was doing some Pack mojo. To make her feel important and useful. Some chores done for her around the house, a dinner and dancing date and the gift of a leather brief case. That's what her price had been. That's how easy she'd given up everything for which she'd fought. He hadn't even had to work for the sex. Not really, anyway. She was utterly disgusted with herself. She would not say she was broken hearted. But no one was ever going to do this to her again. She wasn't letting anyone else get this close, ever.

"Whoa, Professor. Where are you going?" Kerr snatched her hand and tugged her back to him, ignoring her struggles and pressing her against his chest. He bent his head close to her, giving her the illusion of a private conversation on the stairs in plain view of the other Shifters in her house. But she knew they could hear every word. Her brother had a look of triumph. And she was suddenly furious at him. The ragewave inside her abruptly reappeared, just under the surface. She let the sting of it seep out, just a bit, in her words.

"No! You don't get to look at me like you're going to cart me off to Mum. I'm staying here. I'm living here. No matter what he says about owning me, this is my life! You don't get a say, you gave up that right when you changed and became Mum's lap dog. Gave up your ability to choose for yourself. You have to do what Mum and Sunny say. I don't."

Her brother bellowed at her, probably not used to a simple human female telling him off, being his equal. She had a say in her own home. Had power here. Had a right to be safe and by heavens and all that was holy, she was going to exercise it. He wasn't going to make her feel weak or guilt her into going with him. He was his own man, made his own decisions. He'd proved that long ago. She was her own woman. It was high time her brother, and by extension her mother and Sunny, acknowledged that fact.

Kerr's smile split his face as he gazed down at her. Possession. Wolf males thought they owned their females. They had in her stepfather's Pack. Only her mother had had any type of freedom. Every other female had been under their males' proprietary rights. That's what he thought of her, she could see it. The gleam that said 'mine' was practically a neon sign. She had to nip this in the bud too. He wasn't going to drag her back into the hell of being less than human again. She didn't owe him anything.

"Same for you, hot shot. You're a good lay, but I'm not going all butterflies-in-the-tummy, bowing before you because you know what to do with your dingy. Still horny? Get one of these guys to hit their knees for you. Because that was the first and last time we'll ever be having sex. Separate rooms, separate lives, buddy. I'm not a threat to the locals, but I'm not part of your Pack, either. I'll expect rent, half utilities, some chores from you as long as you continue to live here. That's it. Clear?"

Kerr's jaw hung open and the rest of his Pack hid snickers and smiles behind their hands while her brother glared angrily, unable to respond to her the way he wanted because the others were in the room, and they'd kill him for it. She pushed away from Kerr, pulled the afghan tighter around her and marched up the stairs, hoping the tears stayed away long enough for her to lock her bedroom door. She didn't know if she was crying because the thought of losing Kerr scorched her heart or because of the headache that had started throbbing behind her eyes the second she'd seen her brother. She couldn't avoid the wave of anger rising in her and she was tempted to scald everyone in the room as badly as she'd just been burned, but didn't. She just couldn't bring herself to injure anyone, no matter how corroded they had made her life.

***

Kerr watched his mate walk up and close the door on him. In front of his packmates. No matter what she said, his scent was all over her. And hers was all over him. She'd claimed him on a public dance floor. His friends here wouldn't try to take Lexi away from him. Couldn't. She'd asked for tonight, for him inside her. She had to know what that meant. Didn't she? For fuck's sake, what was wrong with the woman? What had he done to piss her off now? If she thought she was going to throw what was between them away, she had another think coming. The anger at the territorial breach he'd managed to stuff down for Lexi's sake threatened to break free.

She is terrified, his wolf side told him. *My mate is angry, yes, but this cub makes her fear rise. This is not good.*

Kerr sucked in a breath. Why hadn't he seen that? For the first time in decades, he was glad he had his wolf inside him. Fear made you do strange things, like yell at the man you'd just made love to. He turned to the strange wolf—her brother. Whatever had Lexi upset was this wolf's fault. He was going to find out what had happened if it killed him.

"Taskill? Get a piece of plywood from the shed I'm building out back. It'll do as a door for now." He reached into the Pack bonds and pulled a blanket of silence down on the house, focusing on the basement. It wouldn't block all the sounds, but the neighbors would think they were much farther away. He turned his finger into a claw and hooked it under the stranger's chin, forced him to look at Kerr.

"What's your name?" Kerr's voice was soft and Taskill leaped to complete his task. The others, if they hadn't been holding the wolf between them, would have left too. Kerr hadn't used his dark voice for a long time, too lost in his own sorrows for too long. Lexi had done away with a lot of them just by being her. It was his chance to give back to Pack and mate equally.

The wolf cub before him obviously didn't know Kerr's reputation or else chose to ignore it.

"You're not the Alpha. You can't make me do anything." Contempt etched his face, made it ugly. How the two of them could be brother and sister, Kerr didn't know. But this boy wasn't anywhere near as kind and loving as his mate.

"No," Kerr agreed. "I'm the Beta. Kerr MacDonald."

The boy didn't blink. Hadn't heard of him. And there was a time every wolf worth his salt knew the Alpha and Beta of Fundy Bay Pack. Kerr tsked several times. Let the claw slide into the flesh, up and quick enough to hook the young one's tongue through the chin. Lexi's brother registered surprise and the first inklings of fear. Kerr wondered if the boy, being the Alpha's stepson, had been indulged, rather than educated about their world. Kerr would fix that.

"The Beta's role in every Pack is much the same as the Alpha's. Protect your mate—mine happens to be your sister—protect your Alpha, and protect your

Pack. You represent a threat to both my mate and my Pack." Kerr gave a tug on the male's jaw, who yelped in pain.

"Kerr. She can hear this." Dax's eyes were on the door at the top of the stairs.

"True. Why don't you and I get to know each other, shall we, Lexi's brother? Oh, I'm sorry." Mock concern had the boy eyeing Kerr warily and he withdrew his claw. "I don't even know your name."

"Rafe Coolen, Denver Pack. I've come to take my sister home."

"She is home," Taskill said as he returned with the plywood and a hammer.

"She's welcomed here," Wallace said, walking around Kerr and blocking the boy's access to Lexi.

"We're honored to have her for as long as she wishes to stay, Queller or no." Dax opened the door to the basement. Kerr was proud of his Pack. They hadn't even been properly introduced to Lexi, but they could smell the way she'd been treated on the little pup in front of him and were just as determined to protect her as he was. No one was ever going to harm his mate again, certainly not this whelp.

"Obviously, she's under Pack protection. All the humans in the Annapolis Valley are, you know. We take our duties seriously. Now," Kerr threw his arm over the boy's shoulder as Taskill joined them, "let's see why your sister is so afraid of wolves, shall we? I have a feeling you're going to be telling all kinds of stories tonight, little Alpha-wannabe."

CHAPTER SIXTEEN

Lexi pulled on her one dress, a ratty sundress her father had said was a pretty color on her but her mother said made her look matronly. *Oh God, Daddy, I wish you were here. I need someone I can talk to about anything.* If she went to Hannah, she'd put her friend in danger. Dr. Engles had a child who was a Shifter. Talking to him would be asking him to choose between his family and their Pack and her. She couldn't put him in that position. Her mother was out, for obvious reasons. Kerr was someone she might have turned to, but he was the reason she felt like she was suffocating and broken. She couldn't talk to him. But he would probably get how she was feeling. Which made her feel even lower.

She petted what her mother had called her ugly dress. She'd always been reluctant to wear it before, but here, her home, she could wear it anytime she wanted. It came out of the closet most every weekend. The material was soft and she was comfortable in it. And she didn't think it was ugly at all. She took out one of her books, curled up on the window seat in the corner and put in her headphones. Maybe they couldn't block out noises the Shifters were making downstairs, but she could try. Sometimes she used classical music to soothe her headaches away too, getting lost in the rhythm and beauty. Lose herself. And right now she didn't want to be Lexi Coolen. She wanted to be her father's daughter. She wanted someone to tell her it was going to be OK and hug her close and want to be with her, simply because they liked her. She felt absolutely miserable. Even her window seat, made from scratch in the place she'd proudly made her own, didn't help. It felt like she was breathing ash.

She felt the elastic snap of Pack magic hug around her, and her headache doubled in intensity. Great. What were they doing down there while she was having a pity party up here? Forget it.

Worry ate at any calm she had left. What was he doing with her brother? He'd promised he wasn't going to hurt him. But would he keep that promise? What had Rafe been thinking, just wandering into someone else's territory without so much as a by-your-leave? She was merely human and she knew better than that. She went to the medicine cabinet and dry swallowed some liquid ibuprofen gels so relief would hit fast. She rubbed her temples.

She cracked open the door. All was quiet. She peeked down the stairs. No one in sight. Her skin crawled. Something wasn't right. Being quiet in a house full of Shifters was difficult, unless they were focused on something else entirely. No one in the living room. She picked up the remnants of clothes scattered about, tidied up as best she could and tried to ignore the skittering fingers of magic that were trickling down her back. They got worse the closer to her basement door she went. And her damned head wouldn't let up.

Her basement. Her home. And they were using it like some extension of Pack property. Her gut clenched from the impact of a fist of emotion. Kerr had taken advantage of her. Tricked her. Tried to take her home away from her. No. No way, no how. This place was hers. She might have fallen for Kerr's tricks, but she was going to re-establish boundaries and this was a prime opportunity. They could have their little meeting somewhere else. They could tell her where her brother was so she could phone her mother and tell her. They could get the hell out.

"Kerr!" she palmed open the door and started stomping down, even though she felt like crawling up into bed and crying. *Get angry, Lexi. It's better than being pathetic and heart-broken.*

"Not now, sweetheart." Kerr mumbled a few other words and the kind, blond man came part way up the stairs.

"Yes now," she shouted around the blond man.

"My name's Taskill. Now's not really a good time for you to be—"

"For me to be in my own basement in the house I bought using my inheritance money from my father's death?" She pushed passed the man.

The sight when she reached the bottom of her steps knocked the breath out of her. Her brother was tied with his arms spread, cuts closing as all the men turned to her simultaneously.

"What are you doing?" Her limbs were cold and icy agony stabbed up her legs, doubling her over. Kerr was beside her then, tried to put her hair behind her ears and she couldn't bear to let him touch her. Her head was just about ready to explode. She batted his hand away and waited for her eyes to focus again.

"Lexi, I don't pretend to know everything you went through in Denver. But I do know that seeing your brother shouldn't make you afraid. The kind of fear I smelled off you, that only comes from pain. They hurt you, Lexi. I know it. They don't ever get to do that again. Not while I'm alive." His voice held steel and pain of his own and the thought of losing him forever made her more than afraid. Panicked. Hopeless. She wanted him to be true, but was petrified that he was lying to her, seducing her, using her as a trophy for a Pack she didn't belong in, for a world that had rejected her long ago as being worthless. She was even more scared that everything that had happened between them, the caring, sharing her body, letting him in, it was all a fiction that any Shifter used with their human playthings. The fear that she hadn't caught on to what Kerr was doing with her, that her own instincts had been so wrong, terrified her more than anything. She had to get that back, or she was done. She wasn't ever going to let them make her afraid again. Not now, not ever.

"No." She straightened up and walked to her brother. No one stopped her, though they could. She grabbed one of the knives she saw sitting on a trunk. She would not throw up, despite her head. Despite what she thought she had to do now. Methodically, she cut her brother's bonds on the right.

"Lexi. They say they have claim on you. I won't let them take you," Kerr pleaded.

He tried to take the knife from Lexi's hand, but her grip tightened. Wolves could snap a human's arm bone easy. He couldn't get the knife free unless he wanted to hurt her and that, he wouldn't do. She hoped.

***

The brother had talked. Just a little. Kerr knew there was more, but what he'd heard had made his blood boil. And everyone's in the room. The nights of terror they'd put her through, all shifting in front of her then snapping and growling and *hunting* her, as if she were worthless, as if she were an enemy of the Pack, as if she were prey. That was unacceptable. It was also taboo. There was no hunting humans. The Wardens had decreed that there was one exception: if a human had become a direct threat to Shifters. There was a part of him that was human. A part that would always remain human, no matter what, but he still had a predator inside of him. He'd learned to accept that long before his brother had facilitated his change. He controlled his monster, not the other way around. Never again. Chaining it up behind his fears was the worst thing he could do. His brother, Tam, had told him that over and over again. He hadn't listened back then. Now, with Lexi, he finally got it. His brother had had the right of it.

Lexi had been Sunny and Thea's daughter, Rafe's sister, a member of the Denver Pack and they had thrown that away. Because she couldn't access her abilities then? Had they even known she had them? Not that it mattered. She was family. They had let her go. By Pack Law, they had thrown her away and now that she was developing her abilities, now that she was useful, now that she could be used as a bargaining chip by them, they were willing to have her? No. Hell no. Kerr wouldn't let any wolf of his go because they weren't *useful*. He wouldn't respect Denver's claim. Not at all.

But how did they know to make one? Kerr needed to find out how they knew about the Queller abilities Lexi was developing. How they had got their information. Who was in Lexi's life that she couldn't trust? The phone call from her car when he was going to shift didn't prove anything. Her abilities had just barely started to surface. And according to Rafe, they'd put her in worse situations, without any Queller abilities coming to the fore. He needed more time with the boy, needed to find out who was selling the Pack secrets. Then he'd eliminate them. He looked at his mate, who was shaking like a leaf in the wind. She wouldn't look at him. That was when her scent really hit him. She was scared, yes, but there was the undeniable trace of mourning, like she had lost someone important in her life; the most important thing in her life.

***

Lexi tried to keep all the emotions in check. To bottle them up until she was somewhere she could let them out safely. Her head throbbed with every heartbeat so she knew it was faster than normal. She needed to keep the fear down in a room full of wolves if nothing else. "Rafe. Rafe, can you hear me?"

"Sure, Sis." His answer was fainter than she might have liked, but it sounded much more like the little brother she remembered, less like the wolf-y jack hole that had replaced him. She sawed at the bonds, conscious that the others in the room only watched. Except Kerr. He paced behind her, but didn't stop her.

"He's dangerous, Lexi." Kerr raked his hand through his hair.

She paused in her endeavor. "Rafe, are you going to hurt me if I cut you down?"

If looks were as sharp as claws, Rafe was shredding the men behind her. But the blades were gone when he looked at her. "No."

She whirled, started to make eye contact with Kerr but couldn't. The kind, blond man stepped forward. She looked him in the eye instead. "Is he lying? Shifters can smell lies, after all." Her mocking tone wasn't like her, but pain was making her careless.

"Again, I'm Taskill. And no, your brother isn't lying—"

"But he might not be telling you all there is to that statement," the long haired man said. He bowed to her quickly. "I'm Wallace, by the way."

She nodded. Turned slowly back to her brother. "Rafe, are you going to try to take me back to your home, away from my home? I don't want to go. You know that. You know I've made a life for myself here. I've got things to finish up, my degree for starters. I've made non-Shifter friends here. So tell me, are you going to try to take me back?"

Rafe's eyes blazed. He tried to stare her down, but started shaking. Couldn't hold it. "Yes."

She felt the word like a blow. "Why?"

Rafe angled toward her. "They want you back, Lexi. Mum and Sunny. They want you. Sunny *finally* wants you." He pleaded with his eyes, big and green, just like Mum's. "Please, Sis. Come back."

"No." The word was quiet, but heartfelt.

Rafe jumped and strained against his restraints. "You've got to come back, Lexi! You *have* to come back."

"Because they want to use me? I've already spent Dad's money, so there won't be any financial gain. Or will I be sport for the Pack again? Why do you want me to go back, little brother? Didn't I suffer enough?" Her eyes blurred from the tears. Her brother was one of them now. It was all they cared about. Control and appearances and how her leaving made the Alpha and his mate look weak instead of strong.

"It's not up to your brother, Lexi. He's been ordered to bring you back by the Alphas. He has no choice, unless another, stronger wolf changes the order. It isn't entirely his fault, Lexi." Wallace stepped up to her, hesitantly extended his hand, as if to touch her shoulder. It hovered just above her skin. She could feel the warmth from it, but not the physical connection. She looked up at him. Understanding dawned.

"You've been in the same situation."

He didn't respond. He'd stopped just short of skin contact to let her move to complete the touch, if she wanted. He'd given her choice. This one understood. She felt more kindly toward him, though she didn't let her guard down.

"Sis?" Her brother's timid reminder of his presence was unnecessary. She could never betray him the way he'd done to her. It just wasn't in her.

"I can't let you hurt him." She looked up at the man in front of her. Wallace looked over her shoulder. Kerr's voice answered.

"We have to question him, Lexi."

She refused to turn around. "And you can't do that without hurting him? I hate it. I hate Pack Law so much right now. And Shifters. Magic. All of it. What you are, it took my father away from me. What you are took my brother from me. And I can't even talk to my mother anymore." *Or you,* she added silently. Kerr took a sharp breath and held it. No one spoke for a long moment. If she believed the act he was putting on, she'd feel guilty for the glisten of moisture in his eyes right now. If she felt guilty, she'd cave. So she held onto her anger, to make her stronger.

"That's a lot to lose, Lexi." Kerr's voice was soft, a caress against her senses and she wanted to sink into it, wanted to believe that this was who he was, a kind man. A good man.

"We never left you, Lexi. You left us," her brother croaked.

She whirled. "How can you say that? Mum put me in a room with twenty men about to shift, some of them for the first time. Naked. You think that was a loving thing to do to an eighteen-year-old girl, Rafe?" She took a step toward her brother, who had the decency to flinch. But the flood gates had been opened.

"How about when she left me in the mountains without food or water and let a bunch of wolves track and herd me for three days. Is *that* something a mother would do?" Rafe was shaking his head from side to side as she spoke, trying to throw off the words. But she wouldn't let him hide from what they'd done to her any more.

"And what about Mum standing there while Sunny ordered three of his wolves to fight to the death, winner got to take my virginity? You think I should have stayed for more of that? Are they planning on selling me off again, Rafe? The poor human girl who wouldn't turn? Who wouldn't become what they wanted so they beat me every mooncall? You think that's right, Rafe? That's a life I should return to?"

"It would be different, Lexi. I'd protect you. I'm higher in the Pack now. I can keep you safe." Rafe was crying. Lexi knew then. Rafe had known. Had always known what was going on. But he'd been powerless to do anything about it as a human. He must have reasoned that a Shifter could protect her better, but he'd been even more helpless because of the structure of the Pack. Newbies entered on the bottom rung of dominance until they proved themselves.

"Did you let them change you, take away your humanity, for me, Rafe?"

Rafe looked up at her in confusion. "What do you mean?"

"Did you become a Shifter to try to protect me?"

"Lexi, you're *born* a Shifter. You *can't* be turned. And you're not a Shifter. You'll never run with us. But you can protect us. You're a—"

***

"Enough!" Kerr smacked Lexi's brother across the face, knocking his head backward. "You think you have the right to explain Quellers and Shifters to her, after what you did?"

They had made his mate see only monsters when she saw wolves. He wanted to howl his pain to the top of the North Mountain. His mate hated what he was, and the acid of that thought burned through him. Had he lost her so soon? But nothing could compare to the way she'd hate herself once she admitted the truth of what she was. And that he could not allow. There was beauty in their world. There was wonder. Nights spent running the forest. The feel of fur against skin. Cuddling together under the moon while her magic sang through the blood. The song of your Pack, together, knowing that no matter what, you would never be alone again. There were things ordinary humans would never know. Lexi might not ever grow fur or fangs, but the best part, the Pack song, that gift he could give her, could share with her forever. And through the mating bond, she would feel what he felt on the night of the Moon Gathering.

To protect such beauty from mortals' prejudices and panics beget the harshest of punishments, sometimes. Sometimes the monsters were necessary to fight the other monsters.

"I had no choice—"

"Because you were low in the Pack? You know enough of the Law. You could have asked one of the Little Alphas to take up your cause. Or gone to another Pack and asked for that Alpha to help your sister. Hell, you could have gone to your Warden for help. You had a choice, boy. You were just too weak to make it. Or worse, she just wasn't worth it to you."

The boy flinched and he knew that was what had happened. The boy didn't believe his own sister was worth losing face with his Pack. Or going up against his mother and Alpha for. Kerr was glad he lived in Forbes's Pack. Was glad that each member was valued, cherished, saw themselves as protectors of the humans in a valley full of magic, mayhem and witches. Was glad, above all else, that here was a Pack where he could champion members like Ellar against more established members like Wallace. That he could help balance things. Keep things safe. Here was a Pack that was worthy of Lexi, once he showed her the joys of what they were.

"Boy." His tone made promises as he re-tied Lexi's brother to the posts in the basement. "You are going to tell me everything I want to know. I advise you to do it quick, for Lexi's sake. She hates to hear anyone in pain. Taskill, be a good man and escort Lexi upstairs. Lexi, I'll be up to talk to you after I've finished here. Wallace, call the Warriors. We've got a threat to the Pack."

***

Taskill had gently laid a hand on her elbow, but he firmly steered her up the basement steps and then up to her own room. Then he positioned himself right outside her doorway. There was no hope of escape for her. She could hear other people coming and going. It was exactly what she'd feared. They were taking over. It should have kept her up. Should have made her squirm and fight and try to think of a way out for her and her brother. Instead, she felt drained. The constant barrage of emotion piled up and short-circuited her coping mechanisms. Everything went numb and then everything went blank. She fell asleep.

Her next conscious thought was when the sunlight streamed in and someone was knocking. She was hugging her knees, curled up not on the bed, but on the window seat. She grimaced.

She wiped the spit from her lips. Great, to top it all off, she'd drooled over herself. God knew how many strangers had been coming and going from her house. And she'd worked so hard at reassuring her neighbors she was going to be a quiet, considerate member of the community. The knocking came again and she glared at the door, scratched her head. But the knocking wasn't right, the door seemed too far away and the knocking too close. She rubbed her eyes, turned to the window, and fell off the seat. Kerr was hanging on the side of the house, his eyes bright but his lips in a straight line. She frowned and struggled upright, then threw open the window.

"What do you want?"

"Good morning to you too, Professor. The Alpha's back. He wants to meet with you."

"My brother?" She couldn't keep the note of hope out of her voice, but what exactly she was hoping for she had no idea. That her brother was all right? Definitely. That he'd escaped? Since he wanted to kidnap her, no, she didn't want that. Most of all, she hoped that Kerr wasn't going to turn out to be the bad guy. She had a confused jumble of feelings and thoughts. She understood what her brother had done was wrong. That he needed to be punished for it. But a punishment that was both severe enough that Rafe, who could heal a knife wound in a day, would be cowed into never doing it again and yet was gentle and fair enough for her sensibilities? Someone was going to have to compromise on their values and she was in no doubt of whom that someone might be. She hated this world, God how she hated this world.

Lexi poked her head out the window. Kerr had climbed up the lattice she had for her rose bushes and swung over to the narrow sill. His fingers were claw tipped and she narrowed her gaze at the holes he was leaving in the frame. He followed her line of sight and shrugged.

"You wouldn't answer when I knocked at the bedroom door."

She pointed down. He raised his chin.

"Can I have a kiss? I did climb up to your balcony, after all. That deserves some reward for effort, right?"

"Get down." She slammed the window shut in his face. Had a thought, turned and threw it open again. He was still there, looking hopeful.

"Is there coffee?" she asked him. She was not going to be able to handle the stresses of this day without bolstering her defenses.

"I made a pot of Chai tea…"

She shut the window and locked it this time for good measure. She raced for the door before he knew what was happening. The first test today would bring was getting all these wolves out of her house. Now.

CHAPTER SEVENTEEN

She raced down to the kitchen, but he still beat her there. He was standing next to the pot, holding out her favorite mug. Her favorite tea and mug? He knew she was upset and was trying to charm his way out. She grimaced and grabbed another from the cupboard, just to be contrary. Filled it up slowly, enjoying the aroma and the heat as it seeped into her hand through the porcelain of the cup. She trundled over to the table and took a banana out of the fruit bowl for breakfast. He was unperturbed by her actions, or he was trying to be, and he pushed the tab on the waiting toaster for a bagel, taking the cream cheese from the fridge and setting it in front of her. He sat in the opposite seat until the bagel popped and he quickly retrieved it, sliding it in front of her. Then he put his chin in his hands and stared without blinking. He was being helpful and endearing, so of course it got on her nerves.

"Do you have any idea how unnerving it is to have someone stare at you like that when you know they can turn into a wolf and tear your throat out?"

He grinned. "I was going for cute. And I do, actually. My brother shifted way before me. Used to do it to me over the breakfast table all the time too. I never really knew how fun it was."

She snorted. "Great, we're really bonding over cream cheese and bananas."

"Don't forget the Chai."

She nodded. "We'll always have Chai." It slipped out before she could stop herself. She didn't want to banter with him. She wanted to be tough and establish boundaries.

He leaned across the table and caught a strand of her hair, let it slide between his fingers and sat back before she could protest his intrusion.

"You just can't leave it alone, can you?" She grimaced into her cup. She had to deal with it sooner or later. It might as well be now. "Look, the sex was good—"

"The sex was fantastic and I can't wait until we do it again."

She took a sip of tea. He knew he was in trouble, just not how much. "You're going to go blue with waiting."

He shrugged. "I can be patient."

She sighed. "It was a mistake. I shouldn't have let it happen. I'm sorry."

He blinked. Took a sip of his own tea and curled his lip up at the taste. "I can't believe you drink this stuff."

"There are monstrosities that brew single servings for heathens like you who only drink a cup of something. You want something else, buy one of those. But we are not a 'we', do you understand?"

He took another sip and locked gazes with her over the rim. She counted the seconds. He was trying to get her to break first. But she'd played this game before and knew how to wait it out. He smiled and set his cup down.

"You're right; this is a good time to set some things straight. Number one, you're stuck with me. Whether you treat me as just a roommate or a mate, it's up to you. But you're it for me."

She swallowed a mouthful of tea, even though it was too hot for so big a gulp. He held up his hand before she could start her end of the conversation.

"I claimed you, in front of a rival Pack member. He could scent the proof in the room. Hell, he probably heard us. My side of things is undeniably there. You're brother's been sent back home, by the way. With a list of reparations he has to pay to us, and our allies. I didn't kill him. Or even hurt him all that much, if what he was saying last night was true. He's a tough kid and he's hurting over what he's had to do as a wolf. Sunny's not a good Alpha. Your mother's nuts for staying with him."

"Tell me something I don't know."

She slumped in the chair. Relief coursed through her. She felt he was telling her the truth. Wanted to trust him. But there were too many things between them. She had issues to iron out.

"The second thing you have to accept is that the Alpha is coming to meet you. He's going to offer you a place in the Pack."

Lexi frowned. "What do you mean, offer me a place in the Pack? If you've claimed me, don't I have one as your property, anyway?"

Kerr's hand tightened on the mug, so much so that it cracked. He leaped up and grabbed the dish cloth before much of his tea could spill. Lexi spread cream cheese on her bagel and watched him clean up the mess. It gave her time to think. Her heart and her head were telling her two different stories this morning and she had to sort it out. Now. Kerr swiped at the table, jabbed his hand under the fruit bowl all the while grumbling under his breath.

"I said it before, you will never have to worry about your safety here. Even if you don't accept a place with us, we'd never allow harm to come to a Queller."

She remembered what her brother had yelled at her last night. It wasn't a made-up word? He'd never been able to think up insults fast enough. "What's a Queller?"

"Ask the Alpha when he gets here. I wasn't supposed to say anything."

"You also weren't supposed to use her abilities without me being present, but you went ahead and did that while I was gone too." A tall, lanky man stood in the back doorway, but he hadn't crossed the threshold yet. He wore a red plaid shirt with roughly patched elbows and jeans with worn knees, as if his clothing wore away at his sharp corners. His work boots had seen better days and his smile was faint but genuine, his brown eyes crinkled in the corners. His brown hair was flat to his head and needed a bit of a trim, but was shiny like a shampoo commercial. Overall, the man gave the impression of being a farmer or a carpenter, someone who worked with his hands all day and was out doors most of it as well, not of the most powerful being in the Pack. She instinctively trusted him and forced herself to quash the feeling. She crossed her arms and glared, waiting for him to barge into her life.

"As Alpha, I have the right to enter the house of anyone aware of us. But I prefer to ask permission to come in."

That was…unsettling. She took a bite of breakfast to cover her surprise. Examined him again. She waved her bageled hand in his general direction and he bowed, low, and came into her kitchen. She eyed the boots and he immediately bent to untie and deposit them on the mat under the coats.

"Do you ask permission to come into everyone's house?"

He paused in the act of rising, met her eyes so she would see the seriousness as well as hear it. "No." His gaze slid to Kerr, who sat and glared back like a child. One who was definitely in trouble. That kicked her right in her protective instincts. Dear Lord, she still had it bad for him.

"We haven't officially met. I'm Lexi Coolen." She stood and held out her hand. It conveniently blocked his line of sight to Kerr. She did not want the second of the Pack arguing with the Alpha in her kitchen. The remodeling from that fight would send her into bankruptcy.

The Alpha's brows rose. She'd done something surprising, and from Kerr's chuckle behind her, something funny."Did I do something wrong?"

Kerr wrapped his arms around her waist. "Nope." He kissed the back of her neck and then started rubbing it with his thumbs. She should have told him to stop, but found she didn't want to. She liked his touch, and wasn't that an inconvenient truth. He was excessively chipper about whatever she'd done. She thought about it for a minute. She'd stood between them and protected Kerr, her "mate", from the Alpha's reprimand. Darn it. So much for establishing her boundaries. The Alpha took her hand in his cool grasp and shook.

"I am Forbes MacIvor, Alpha of the Fundy Bay Pack. Welcome to the Annapolis Valley, Alexandria Coolen. And thank you for welcoming me into your home.

I hear from Kerr that probably wasn't easy for you to do." He bowed over their joined hands, kissed her knuckles and let her go abruptly.

She swallowed and looked up at him. She was in her pajamas. Her hair was probably a frightful mess and he was shaking her hand and treating her as if she were dressed for a formal dinner. She looked back at Kerr for guidance. He had on his Cheshire grin; no help there. She opened her mouth to say something, realized she didn't have anything to say and shut it again. Forbes seemed to understand her dilemma.

"Perhaps Kerr will make himself useful and bring me a cup of that tea while we sit and you can finish your breakfast while I explain a few things?"

Lexi nodded and trundled back to her spot, put her foot on her seat and leaned her elbow on her knee as she stuffed her bagel into her mouth before she said something stupid. Only then did she stop and wonder.

"Did you just do some sort of Pack mojo on me?" she accused around her mouthful of food.

Forbes shook his head. "Did I use Argot against you? No. You're a bit off-balance is all. I don't tend to use that particular skill on my wolves. We're better behaved than that."

Kerr snorted as he returned with a cup of milky tea. Forbes gave him a dark look but the corners of his mouth were turned up. They had genuine affection between them, Lexi realized.

"As for my Pack, I've asked that they refrain from using your home as a train station from now on. You'll only have guests that you invite here. I am here to formally offer you, Alexandria Coolen, daughter to and former Pack member of the Denver Pack, a place with the Fundy Bay Pack for as long as you wish to remain among us."

Lexi took a sip of her tea and hurled her ace at him. "Because I'm a Queller?"

Despite her mixed up feelings about Kerr, despite the fact that her brother had used her as a pawn just like her mother and Sunny, she wasn't about to just roll over and become the whipping girl for the Fundy Bay Pack. Especially not without finding out what the hell a Queller really was. And how she was one.

Forbes seemed unperturbed by her slings and arrows. "Because you are the mate to one of my oldest friends. Because you have been abused by other wolves and need the protection and shelter a Pack can offer you. Because you are a smart and sweet and caring person. Because you are you, Lexi. There are so many reasons a Pack would be honored by your presence."

She was suddenly and very thoroughly angry at Forbes MacIvor. "And because I'm a Queller," she ground out again. How dare he. How dare he try to hide his motivations behind the mask of being kind. Of charity. Of being decent. That was the last straw.

Forbes held up one long finger. "You are not a Queller yet. Your abilities haven't fully manifested. If it eases your conscience, you may never become a Queller, though I seriously doubt it. Knowing this, I still offer you a place in our Pack. One of standing and safety, Alexandria Coolen."

"And if I refuse, I have to leave town, right?" Yeah, she knew all about being offered something from the Alpha that sounded too good to be true.

"No."

She stopped short. "What? Why? And aren't I already technically part of your Pack as his mate?" She jabbed a finger in Kerr's direction. The fool hadn't stopped grinning. "We'll be dealing with that mating thing in a minute, pal."

"No, you're not a part of the Pack because of your mating status with Kerr. You're part of the Pack's responsibility, but so is everyone in this territory. I asked you because I like you. It's true that you could be a powerful addition to my Pack. It's true that many Packs would fight over such a resource as you are likely to become. But I have governed this Pack for centuries in a place that both strengthens our abilities and threatens our control of those abilities, without a Queller at all. The truth is, I don't need you. I have to want you to become part of my family. And I decided that I liked you the night you brought my best friend to me rather than run away screaming. I admired your courage in the face of a stronger, unknown Alpha.

I admired that even though you had hidden from us, you didn't betray us. You could have. You could have been a great threat, revealed everything about Shifters long ago. From Kerr's interview of your brother, you certainly had motives aplenty. But you protected us when you had no reason to anticipate kindness from us."

He took a sip of tea, blinked at the cup and smiled, seemingly genuinely pleased by the flavor, before continuing. "Then I found out how Sunny does things. Trust me when I say that there is no comparison between the way your stepfather runs his Pack and the way I run mine, Lexi. It took great courage to let us, any of us, in." He accepted a bagel from Kerr and spread cream cheese on it, as if they were old friends discussing the weather. He was comfortable here and rather than making her angry, it made her comfortable too.

"I want someone with that courage around me. Around my family. You are welcome to stay or go as you please. But I would consider it a great honor if you would be willing to join my wolves with the status of Queller, whether your abilities surface or not."

"But what *is* a Queller?"

Forbes's gaze cut to Kerr, then raised his eyebrow in question. Kerr shrugged.

"It seems my second didn't explain things at all, did he?"

"Did you expect him to?" Lexi asked, annoyed that she felt like an outsider in her own kitchen.

"I thought he might have. The connection is powerful between you. But to answer your first question, what does the word suggest to you?"

"Well, quell means to suppress. So Quellers are capable of suppressing what, exactly?"

Forbes shook his head. "It's not just suppress. Quell can also mean to defeat, conquer, repress, mollify and mitigate. Quellers are capable of many things. Most of it involves being able to either calm or overwhelm Shifters' supernatural abilities. You can, with training, stop us from accessing our wolf selves. Or you can moderate meetings and keep magics contained from both parties. You can help us hide from humans. You can stop wars."

Lexi's mouth went dry. "Whoa."

The corner of Forbes's mouth quirked but he stopped short of a full smile. "Yes. So, do you accept our offer of Pack?"

Lexi took a gulp that echoed in her kitchen. "You're gonna make me choose right now?" Her cup sloshed when she slammed it down on the table.

Forbes's eyes crinkled as he regarded her over the rim of his mug, mirroring her earlier actions. "I figure you'll have other things to clear up after I'm gone."

"Boss!" Ellar Engles burst into her kitchen. Lexi reminded herself that this kid was a wolf. Elyse's brother was a wolf and she needed to be careful around him. Except she felt calm when he came in. Well, not calm, exactly. She felt safe. Yeah, that was the word. Safe. He wasn't going to attack her or hurt her or do anything that might in any way make her feel uncomfortable. He was safe. She was safe with him. Was that because of Forbes's offer, Kerr's mating her, or because she was a Queller?

"Yes, Ellar?" Forbes didn't seem upset, but he put his cup down and his body tensed. He was ready to deal with whatever had happened. The perfect leader. So it seemed to Lexi. Even Ellar, whose cheeks were flushed and his eyes bright, responded to it. His breathing slowed and he rolled back on his heels. He flicked his eyes toward Lexi, then back to Forbes.

"Sampson 'Sunny' Gallow's private plane just landed at the Waterville airport. He's here. And he didn't come alone."

Chapter Eighteen

Lexi's backside left the chair so fast it fell over. She forced herself to stop running up the stairs to hide and managed to stand still.

"I do not want to go back with him. No way, no how. I don't care what I have to do, I'm not going back."

Forbes held out a hand to her and she took it without thinking. Kerr looked like he wanted to say something, but wisely held his tongue. Forbes stroked the back of her hand absently, offering comfort like he would one of his wolves. She blinked back tears.

"You won't go anywhere you do not want to," Forbes told her. Ellar gave a fierce nod of agreement and Kerr crossed his arms, as if whoever it might be would have to go through the wall that was him.

"OK." Lexi's voice sounded small in her ears. Her stomach roiled. The wave was back, pain swelled behind her closed eyelids. Her pulse pounded, drowning out what the others might have been discussing. She took several deep breaths and managed to make it tolerable again. When she opened her eyes, they all were looking at her and she realized they were waiting for a response.

"Sorry, I missed that. What?"

"We're going to have to go and meet them. This is not a good thing to have happen and I won't let them just waltz into my territory unchallenged. Your brother was obviously the first option and he failed. Miserably."

Her brother. "Did anyone actually *see* my brother get on the plane? Watch the plane go?"

Three sets of male eyes blinked. They all reached the same conclusion at once.

"Son of a bitch!" Ellar exclaimed.

"That asshole," Kerr growled.

"How very clever," Forbes mused. Everyone turned to him.

"Sunny will claim Rafe was supposed to offer me tithe, since an Alpha arrives by plane. Rafe's actions will be dismissed as an isolated incidence of insubordination. He'll claim he has come to take his stepdaughter home, that Lexi requested it."

"I didn't. I swear. I've always been clear—"

"Hush, Lexi. I know you didn't. He must have landed in Halifax first and when his minion didn't retrieve what he wanted, he had no choice but to come get it himself. Sunny has been very vocal of his opinion that any Alpha who remained in wolf form as long as I did must be weak. A flaw in character. I've never disputed his public silliness because he's never challenged me face to face and anything else is just words. I don't play on the North American scale and have no ambitions to, but Sunny obviously does. Perhaps he thinks this coup will put him in the running for a much greater prize. Hmm."

"Boss, that's the longest speech I think I've ever heard you make." Ellar stood with a slack jaw. Kerr elbowed him. Forbes looked at Lexi and rolled his eyes.

"Gather the Warriors, Kerr. We're going hunting." Forbes turned to Ellar. "How many came off the plane, did you find out from your source at the airport?"

"Not many, Boss. It's not that big. Not even enough to match the sitting families."

"That's it, then. He's going to claim kinship over you, Lexi. In front of some of his wolves. Will you come with us, to formally dispute his claims?"

Lexi didn't have to think about that. "Absolutely."

The Warriors who had come to Kerr's call unfolded themselves from the vehicles that they had driven to Promontory House. Lexi watched them from the kitchen window. The stone house layout resembled a farmhouse on first glance, but was massive inside. It had to be, to accommodate the homing not only of Pack members but other Shifters visiting, tithing, or asking for sanctuary. As the biggest organized Pack in the area, protection and loose governance of all Shifters in the vicinity fell to the Fundy Bay Pack.

It had been decided, since Sunny and his crew had waited to be met at the local airport as tradition dictated, that confronting her stepfather would be done in one of the rooms downstairs designed for fighting. Lexi wanted to call it a dojo, but Kerr had called it some sort of Greek name. Argos, maybe. The men and women filed inside, each one giving her a brief nod or full-out bow before descending a set of stairs hidden behind the refrigerator, which swung out on cleverly hidden hinges.

"That was Forbes's own design," a voice said behind her. Kerr nuzzled the back of her hair. She turned to face him.

"Smart idea." She took a step away, to keep a bit of distance.

"He's a clever guy. Keeping up with the times and all that." Kerr leaned on the counter next to her. Not close enough to touch, but making it clear he wasn't going anywhere any time soon.

"Mm-hm. Is he the only wolf who does that?"

Kerr tapped his chest and smiled. "I'm very modern, Lexi. Up on all the bedroom trends. You just let me know when the Professor wants a lesson."

Lexi leveled an iron glare at him. This was something that had been eating at her. It probably wasn't the best time to air the issue out, but she wasn't sure if she was going to survive this encounter with her stepfather. "You lied to me. About wanting to mate. We're going to have to deal with that, you know."

Kerr's blue eyes widened. "I never lied. My man-bits, as you called them, didn't want a mate at all. It's my wolf that said you were my mate and I wasn't allowed to touch anyone else."

Ouch. Could he be more callous? His wolf would mourn her, and she knew it. How much would the man? Lexi shook her head. Probably, he didn't realize that Sunny could call for her death tonight. Either that or he wasn't admitting it. "That makes it all better."

To give Kerr credit, he must have realized some of what he'd said. He straightened. "I didn't mean that like it came out."

"It's fine, Kerr." Her head started aching. The wave was building again.

"No, really, Lexi. My wolf side has more sense than I do. It saw you for what you are right away."

Lexi rubbed her temples, only half listening. "And what's that?"

"Perfect for me."

Lexi grunted, unconvinced.

"No, really. You belong with me. Give me a chance after this, Lexi, and I'll prove it. Our house is going to be lots of fun, I'll cook every day. You need to eat more good food. And I work from home, remember? I have plenty of money saved up, but I can hunt for a job to help you if need be. I'll be the perfect house husband—"

"Who says we'll be in the same house?" She wanted to shake him. Wanted to hurt him the way he was hurting her, and most of all she wanted to hold him close and never let go. But she couldn't. She had to be cruel to be kind right now. "You broke the deal. After this, you're moving out."

Ellar, who'd come up behind Kerr to watch out the window, snickered.

"Nothing from the peanut gallery, young 'un," Kerr snapped over his shoulder. "What do you mean, I broke the deal?" Both wolves stood absolutely stock still. A car door slammed outside and Lexi was suddenly behind both men.

"I take it my stepfather just showed up?"

The door to the kitchen swung open and a female form launched itself at Lexi.

"Oh darling! I'm so glad you're safe! Let me look at you. I've missed you so much."

Lexi swallowed hard.

"Hi Mum."

The men eventually got Lexi's mother off her, after she cursed them and called them "traitorous wolves" and a hundred other names that didn't make a lick of sense. She shook her head at Thea Gallows. She'd been beaten for even trying to call her mother by anything other Mum. One of many reasons she'd made her choice. Her mother had asked Lexi to leave in the ultimatum she'd issued twelve years ago—marry a wolf of her mother's choosing or leave. She'd left.

As a group, they moved down to the Argos, where the gathered Warriors waited, most with their shirts off and skin glistening with sweat. They'd either been warming up human muscles or practicing their shifting. And they weren't alone. Though the center of the room was empty, the crowd on the sides was at least four people thick and the aisle was long. Being in a room with this many wolves made the hair on the back of her neck stand on end and her stomach ache redoubled its efforts at making her incapable of standing upright.

The Argos had a sandy floor and a high ceiling. It looked as if they had carved out a huge cavern inside the South Mountain walls. It would have taken forever, as the stone wasn't limestone, but granite, possibly part of the Canadian Shield. Immediately in front of the door that Lexi had entered with Kerr was a dais. On the dais sat a…throne? A wooden masterpiece, it looked as though it had been carved from one piece of wood wide enough for two men to sit on it. None of the local trees were anywhere near that wide, so it had to have been joined together. But Lexi couldn't see where. And that wasn't the only sign of superb craftsmanship. It had lupine, deer and forestry images running throughout and the back ended with twelve wolf heads howling to a central moon. It gleamed in the muted light. Lexi was impressed with what she could only describe as Forbes's chair of state.

Sunny, her mother and six other wolves, including Wessel and her brother Rafe, had been shown in through another door at the very end of the chamber. They were forced to walk in front of the entire Fundy Bay Pack and their extended families. Sunny had his head held high, no doubt trying to impress on everyone how imposing he thought he was and how important they should think he was. He was a regal wolf. His black hair was slicked back and brushed his collar. He had a crooked nose that hadn't healed straight before he turned, but it added character to his face rather than detracted from it. He had warm, amber eyes that glinted in the dark with a fire that could be infectious if you didn't know him well. His frame was lean and long, like a swimmer's. And his hands had long fingers that were currently wrapped around her mother's hand.

Her mother was a head shorter than Sunny, but the difference did nothing to lessen the impact of her personality. Her mother had bright green eyes and orange hair. Every inch of her was dusted with freckles. Her musculature was more evident than her husband's. She looked like a fighter. The fierceness of her gaze dared every wolf in attendance to challenge her and see what they got. She'd always been a force of nature, pounding against her children like the surf until their resistance crumbled and cracked. Lexi felt the force of her glare from here, the anger blistering her skin. She waited for the guilt from her disobedience to hit her, but her conscience stayed silent. Kerr put his hand on her shoulder and any residual shame of being less than the perfect daughter withered and died away completely. Her mother looked…less intimidating. It was as if a spell had been broken and Lexi wondered if that was the truth of it. If her mother had woven some sort of mystical influence over her and she'd somehow resisted all these years. And whether her brother hadn't been capable of it.

The other wolves, apart from Rafe and Wessel, she didn't recognize. For that, she was grateful. They were all good looking wolves, but they were quite obviously Sunny's creatures, looking to him for their lead. Lexi tried hard not to feel sorry for them and failed. They looked so young. This could have been a trick of the blood. Kerr didn't look much older than thirty, though he was at least a century older. They all came to stand in front of the Warriors, spread out at the foot of the dais.

"I, Sampson Gallows, have come to retrieve my daughter, Alexandria Coolen-Gallows—"

"It's Coolen. Always has been and always will be. And I'm your *step*daughter, Sunny." She crossed her arms.

Sunny gave her a cool look while her mother glared daggers. Sunny continued as if she hadn't interrupted.

"I am the Alpha of the Denver Pack. Alexandria is a member of my Pack and—"

"Lexi, if you please. Unless you prefer for your stepfather to refer to you by your full name?" Forbes didn't turn to her, but his body leaned a little toward her, waiting for her answer.

"Lexi's fine. It's what I call myself."

"Your father's ridiculous nickname for you. You should be ashamed of yourself. Stop this foolishness at once and come home." Her mother pointed to her feet, which pretty much described where she thought Lexi ought to be in the scheme of things. Lexi's smile was grim and her hands tightened. She felt the wave behind her eyes again. It was starting to burn. Sunny gave his wife's other hand a not-so-gentle squeeze and bones cracked audibly.

"Control your mate, Sampson Gallows. I would not have Lexi's first act as our Pack Queller be to tamper the bloodlust your murders would cause." Forbes's voice gave her chills and Lexi stepped back a hair. Kerr's arms came up around her, and pried her fingers from her biceps. The returned blood flow helped with her temperature problems.

"I'm her mother, you monster."

"We're all monsters here, Mrs. Gallows. You would do well to remember your place among us. It is not one of power. You have come to beg me for someone you threw away. Someone you should have valued above your Pack. Above even your mate."

"She wasn't a Queller when she was with us." Her mother pouted. Lexi's stomach plummeted. This was the only reason a Pack would value her, despite what Forbes had said in her kitchen. Fear crept up her throat and she fought to keep her airways clear. Kerr growled.

"I was referring to the fact that Lexi is your daughter."

The impact of that statement hit Lexi a split second before her mother. She took her first clear breath in a long while. Her mother had made a grave error. Every man, woman and child present now had gleaming eyes. They were all ready to defend her. Because they agreed with Forbes. You didn't throw your children away. No matter what.

Sunny cleared his throat. "Lexi was not an obedient child."

Behind her, Kerr snorted. Some of the Warriors snickered and spared a moment to eye their own offspring. Forbes sat on his throne and waited for Sunny to continue.

"She's ours, despite how her mother may have treated her. *I* never approved of her leaving."

"I've been gone for *twelve years—*"

Forbes held up his hand and Lexi stopped. She shivered. Forbes wasn't going to make her go, was he? A grin crept up Sunny's face as he delivered what he obviously considered his *coup de gras.*

"And she hasn't been formally accepted into your Pack, has she?"

CHAPTER NINETEEN

"You are mine. I own you. Come here, Alexandria."

"I don't belong to you, Sunny. You're not my Alpha. You're not my Pack. You certainly never treated me like I was family. I am the constant reminder that another man met, married and mated your wife before you ever got there. I'm surprised you didn't kill me the first time we met."

Sunny stayed silent, but the gleam in his eyes was deadly. If he somehow managed to get her out of here, she was in for the beating of her life. She stepped out of the protective circle of Kerr's arms, down off the dais toward Sunny. Sunny's gleam turned triumphant. His mouth straightened in grim satisfaction. He was misinterpreting her actions.

"Oh no. I'm going to say this once. I am not going with you. This is my home. These are my friends. This is where I stay. Sunny, go home. You don't belong here. I don't want you for my Pack. I don't want you for an Alpha."

Sunny let a small smile slide over his face. It didn't reach his eyes. "You admit that you're my stepdaughter?"

She blew a raspberry. She couldn't deny the truth of the statement. But she could make him wait for it. Kerr gave her a warning look, but she ignored it.

"Yes."

Sunny's smile grew. He turned to Forbes. "She is family. She does not have the scent of your Pack on her. I will accept her mate in my Pack, for her sake. But she is mine."

"No. I'm not."

"You should have studied our ways, little one. You belong to me. To do whatever I wish. Just as your mother does. Just as your brother does. You are mine. Unless you wish to challenge—"

"I challenge it. I'm free of you, Sunny. Have been for a long time."

Behind her, Kerr gasped and from the corner of her eye she glimpsed the Warrior Taskill's expression. It could have been the angle, but it looked as if he were going to cry. Sunny rolled up his sleeves.

"Fine with me, little one. It's time I gave you a proper beating. So that you learn respect."

Lexi turned back to Forbes, who was glaring Kerr into silence. He looked as though he were carved of ice. She caught his gaze and quirked an eyebrow.

"You are not my Pack, Lexi. He is within his rights."

"If I win, what happens?"

Sunny barked a laugh. Lexi's eyes watered a bit from the bright lights and Forbes's face softened.

"You would be Alpha of the Denver Pack until someone took it from you." Forbes's voice was the saddest Lexi had ever heard. For her? For the death sentence that being Alpha would become? Was that truly her only option? Live as Sunny's pet or die in bloody battle? Well. The last few years of freedom had been the best in her life. Lonely, yes. She'd instinctively muzzled herself. She didn't want Hunters killing her mother and brother. She did love them. Sometimes you couldn't help but love your family, she realized, even if they didn't love you back. But here, with her friends, with her job, her own house, things had been different. Wonderful. Her own. She was valued.

Going back, living under Sunny's rule? No. She couldn't do it even if she wanted to. She'd seen what she'd be missing and wasn't willing to give up without a fight.

Then there was Kerr, who didn't try to change her. Didn't push her to do things she wasn't ready to do. Who tried to make life somewhat easier. Dare she consider him a partner? Not quite yet. He was high handed. He was arrogant. He drove her nuts. And he'd lied to her because of Pack Law.

But he cooked her dinner every night. He vacuumed the hallway just to wake her up because he missed her. He danced with her and made her laugh. He made sure she saw him as soon as she got home. He did the grocery shopping. He got her favorites and he experimented, asking her opinion. He valued her opinion. He talked with her. He wanted to be with her.

And he understood about family betrayal. He listened to her and he made her feel safe without boxing her in. She wanted him in her life. Not that he'd get off easy. She wanted to be mad at him. If she survived the night, a massive argument brewed. But they'd get through it and make up. That's what couples did. That's what she wanted. She wanted to try. She needed to try.

"Or, could I stay where I was if I wished?"

Forbes pursed his lips in mock thought. "You could return the title of Alpha to Sunny. He'd have to fight any usurpers, and there would be many, given that a non-wolf like you would have been the one to defeat him. You'd then be accepted into my territory."

"As a Pack member, under your rule? Or could I have some autonomy?"

Forbes didn't fake considering that. Looked her up and down. His wolf glowed softly from his eyes for a brief moment. Gave its judgment. Slowly he shook his head. "As a Queller, affiliated with the Pack, but not under my direct rule. I could accept that, given what I know about the person that you are, Lexi. I would accept you here in my territory and mate to my second. You would have our protection in exchange for access to your services as Queller."

Lexi turned back to her stepfather. "OK, then."

Sunny doubled over laughing. "I can see why you're not on the list to become Warden, old man. Weak as you are."

Lexi ignored the exchange and moved to the center of the circle. Sunny wiped his eyes. Lexi felt tears slide down her cheeks. Some were from fear. Some were from the pain of the wave building in her. Of the rage finally breaking the bottle she'd locked it up in. There were more words said, not that she paid attention. Rules stated, something about not interfering until the whole thing was over. She ignored it. Her skull was starting to ache. She needed to focus. She stretched. The others closed ranks and the loose ring became an impenetrable barricade to keep the combat contained.

Lexi had never been in a fight before. She had muscles, knew how to run and how to swim and how to do a few yoga stretches. But how did you actually fight? She was suddenly envious of her younger brother. Boys seemed to learn naturally. Or at least they weren't muzzled.

"Raise your hands, little one. Like this." Sunny curled his fists and put them at his chin level. Lexi grimaced. She had a punching bag in her basement; she knew how to make a proper fist. He was mocking her, that much was clear. But Kerr was suddenly behind him, nodding. He carefully mimed curling his fingers with the thumb on the outside.

Lexi glared at him. *Tell me something I don't know,* she mouthed. Kerr put his fists up around his cheekbones. OK, she should have known that. Protect your face. Made sense. Kerr dipped his chin toward his chest and Lexi did the same. Yeah, that she hadn't known. Boxing lessons were definitely on the list of things to do after she survived tonight.

Sunny laughed and the sound echoed. The man had a lovely laugh. She could see why her mother had been attracted to him. Too bad he was a bastard.

"Very good! That might protect you against a human, little one. Perhaps when we're done, I'll give you some proper training."

Sunny started bouncing on his feet, making a show like a boxer. Lexi tracked him, but didn't copy. She didn't know if she could do that for long, so best to conserve her energy. That and the sand underfoot wasn't the steadiest of footing. She nearly went down on her knee when she closed the distance between them in rush and took her first swing. She panted. The blow bounced off Sunny's chest, doing no damage whatsoever.

Delighted, Sunny cackled as he danced away. "Excellent! Now try again, girlie. I'll even let you get one in for free." He leaned forward and down so she could reach. Which pissed her off, but she wasn't stupid enough to waste the opportunity. She lashed out and connected the flat of her hand with his nose. The satisfying crunch of it was clearly audible. A coppery scent filled the air. Blood dribbled down Sunny's chin and he howled, dancing away.

There were a few coughs around the room and one bark of laughter. Sunny glared at the one person who dared laugh at his folly, then turned the look on Lexi. Shivers ran down her back and her stomach dropped. *Dear God, he's going to kill me.* The impact of the thought sent lightning bolts down her spine. Adrenaline kicked into her system, let her see the blow coming at her in slow motion. Not that it did her any good. The jolt to her muscles effectively froze them for the split second it took Sunny to dance in and dance out. Pain raced up her right arm. The one she'd hit Sunny with. He'd hit her inner elbow and she stumbled awkwardly out of the way a second after Sunny had left. He was laughing now, daring his audience to doubt the foregone conclusion of this fight. And his nose seemed to be completely healed. Oh shit. How could she beat an opponent who instantly healed all his injuries when he could inflict maximum damage on her and flit away?

Kerr, I'm so sorry.

The wall of people shifted, ready to push her back into the fray, except she wasn't trying to run. She'd made the challenge, she'd suffer the consequences. Before she could plan her next move, Sunny was there again, this time with a shot to her liver. She couldn't breathe. The pain wasn't so unexpected. Debilitating, yes, but she found the immediate dizziness more disconcerting. Could sounds spin? It seemed like they were spinning. Difficult to stop. She needed to, though. That and trying to make her lungs work right again.

She staggered away. Again. They must all see a drunk. She couldn't walk right in this damn sand.

Kerr. I don't want to leave you. Think. Think. Think. How do I win?

The sand shifted under foot and she went down. Her heartbeat tripled. This was bad, a bad spot to be in. She twisted and slipped again. Her very position saved her. She'd accidently ducked under Sunny's latest lazy swing and came down with her left elbow on his inner thigh. All of her weight, too. Like it was planned. Good. Maybe she'd done to his leg what he'd done to her right arm, which was still almost useless.

"You little fucking bitch!"

Get up! He's coming again! Hit him!

She could almost hear Kerr's voice in her head, urging her on. Reacting to her body's command, she hurled her left fist into Sunny's cranium, connecting just above his ear. Fire laced itself through her knuckles. Both hands, she'd just lost the use of both hands. Fear turned her stomach and her headache became a tattoo in her skull. She couldn't believe it when Sunny actually reeled a bit, and retreated to his corner. She took the first proper breath she'd managed since Sunny's hit. She couldn't believe it. Did she stand a chance?

"Enough playing, little one." Sunny stood and let his flesh pop, his claws unsheathe from his fingertips. His teeth became fangs. He snarled and shifted, became the monster she'd always feared. The one she'd always seen below the surface. Terror gave her mouth a bitter taste. She let him come at her, dancing back in the sandy circle that the gathered Warriors made around them in the center of the Argos. This was it. He was going to kill her right now.

Kerr howled in frustration, Forbes himself holding back the man she'd come to adore despite herself. The one stubborn enough to love her. The one she loved too, damn it all. She was worthy in his eyes. Equal. Loved. And he was *hers*. Nobody else better go near her mate. Not while she was around. She was here to stay. But in order to stay, she had to win this fight. Enough running away. She faced the demon.

She blocked out everything but the creature in front of her. The one that had counted on using her for the rest of her foreseeable life. He toyed with her, sending a slash of his fangs her way, making her flinch. He knew the damage her arms had received. Then he feinted with his claws again, making her back up into a brawny chest of one of the Warriors. She recognized Wessel's chuckle. Damn it, the last man she'd wanted to touch. She moved to the left, around, out of Sunny's reach, fully aware he was letting her go.

The wave of rage built inside her. Throbbed against the walls of her skull. Behind the wall she'd built year after year to hold it back crumbled as Sunny turned to the crowd, smiling, raising his arms in triumph. He was enjoying this. Hatred slipped into her voice.

"Sunny. You're a son of a bitch."

He chuffed, a sound that passed as a laugh in his half-altered state. He turned to her and she saw an unfamiliar expression slide over his face. Uncertainty. He saw something dangerous in her expression. It was quickly replaced with delight as she nearly doubled over from the pain in her skull. She crossed her arms to keep it together. The simple movement took a great deal of effort, but the fire from her head burned through her muscles, turning them liquid and movable.

Sunny crowed to the ceiling, recognizing that she wouldn't run any more. That she was injured. That he was winning. Kerr roared and she knew he'd challenge Sunny as soon as she was dead, if this didn't work. And from the look in Sunny's eyes, that wouldn't be too long.

He charged her and she threw open her arms. The wave crashing against the inside of her forehead broke through, exploded from her. Her ability manifested as a color-shifting, cresting ocean-breaker. Like the Fundy's high tide rushing at him. The force of her wave hit Sunny in mid-air like he'd been thrown into a mountain wall. In fact, he had. The swell had pinned him against the stone wall of the cavern.

She sent another breaker of power from her hands, letting his form slide slowly down the rough rocks. She flicked her fingers and his body contorted back into human form. She'd forced him to change. Something that only an Alpha should have been able to do. She hadn't been gentle about it either. He screeched. Sunny finally hit the sand with a dull thud. His retinue gasped. Only Forbes seemed unsurprised. There was no more groundswell of power at her disposal. She had flooded her circuits, maybe. Didn't mean she wasn't done yet. Lexi leaped on her stepfather's chest.

"Asshole!" She swung her arms like clubs. She didn't even care where they connected.

"You fucker!" Thud, thud.

"You took my mother!" Thud, thud, thud.

Lexi didn't have any experience fighting. All she had was the rage in her. She let it fly to her fists, which seemed to be working now, and slammed them into Sunny's face. She felt his nose break again, but it didn't start knitting together immediately. Instead, it stayed broken, gushing blood. In the back of her mind she thought that was strange. But she kept pounding. Felt his face rip, bleed, and break. Then his shoulders. Ribs. Things got squishy. Then she rose and started kicking, any part of his body she could. Her legs were strong from running. Powerful. And this was the man who'd made her run. Sweat dripped from her forehead into her eyes.

Some part of her whispered *enough*, that Sunny was unconscious. She stopped and surveyed her work. Bloody, pulpy, and gore smattered, Sunny was broken. She was alive and he was broken. The thought stunned her. He was defeated. She should be doing something, but she couldn't get her mind to function. Couldn't get past that fact. She'd won. She wasn't elated. Shouldn't she be elated? But she wasn't. Exhausted, yes. Sore and bruised, check. But how did she feel? Empty? Hollow? A part of her just a little bit horrified. A little bit terrified of what she'd done. Of her own monster. Jesus Christ.

"Kneel before the new Alpha." Wessel's sibilant command brought her out of her stupor. She dragged her gaze up from the ruin of the man who'd been the terror in her night to his army. The six of them dropped to their knees in front of her. Her mother's mouth hung open. Her brother looked totally lost. The others glared. She was Alpha of the Denver Pack. She was their leader. She held all the power.

She fell in the sands and puked.

CHAPTER TWENTY

Kerr watched Lexi fall forward on her hands and knees, retching. He wanted to go to her, but didn't dare. The fight hadn't been declared over, even with the other Pack showing their subservience. She was alive. By all that was holy, she was alive. He tried to let it be enough, but his wolf side wouldn't stop insisting he retrieve his mate. She had seen what she was capable of and it terrified her, as he knew it would. But she was safe. She was alive. She had won. She needed him.

He compromised and moved into her line of sight, squatted down, and waited. She sat back on her haunches and wiped her mouth with the back of her hand. He watched and waited for her to realize she was still human inside, even if there was *something other* living in there with her. Quellers were different, but they could relate to living with two different, for lack of a better word, spirits inside one body.

No one else moved. Forbes slowly rose from his throne and moved into the circle, effectively breaking it. A visceral symbol of his authority. He put a hand on Lexi's shoulder.

"I declare this challenge over. Do any here dispute the end of the conflict?"

Forbes waited until the echo's death was old before he turned to Lexi to speak again. Kerr held his breath.

"You have a decision to make, Alpha."

Lexi recoiled from Forbes's touch.

"I'm no Alpha," she exclaimed. Her regard cooled as she examined those on their knees. By the time she got to her mother, Lexi's face was devoid of any emotion.

"Pick Sunny up. Take him back to Denver. Tell him I'm not property. Never was." Lexi levered herself up from the ground, swaying. Every instinct Kerr had, both man and wolf, screamed at him to go to her, but the power of his own Alpha held him still. This wasn't finished. Not quite yet.

"Lexi, honey, don't you know what you're throwing—" Her mother, sensing her position may be in more danger than she'd ever realized, reached out to her daughter. Lexi brushed away the outstretched hand.

"I'm not throwing anything away. I earned my place, mother. It's just not the one that you had picked out for me. It's mine. Here. I built it by myself for myself."

Lexi turned to those assembled. "I'm Lexi Coolen, Queller for the Fundy Basin, girlfriend to Kerr MacDonald. I'm not owned by any Pack, but I'll work with the Shifters of the Fundy Bay Pack and Forbes. If I can help someone here, ask. If someone comes to the territory for me to help them, come get me." She turned to Forbes. "I'm not doing any enforcing of territories or any of that crap."

The corner of Forbes's mouth quirked upward. "You wouldn't be expected to."

Lexi swayed, caught her balance on her own and nodded. "Good. You'll help me figure this…" she waved a hand down at herself and looked back up to Forbes, "…out?"

"Of course. I'll expect you to stay in territory while we train."

Lexi's eyes narrowed suspiciously. "And after?"

Forbes opened his arms. "You'll be free to go where ever you desire. You'll be free to stop training with me at any time and leave, should you wish. I cannot foresee any territory refusing entry to so powerful a Queller, even an untrained one. Though, for the sake of my Pack, I do hope you choose to stay here. I just got my Beta to smarten up. Hate to lose him to globe-hopping while he courts his mate."

Kerr gave his Alpha a look filled with affection, gratitude, and a little bit of chagrin. While Forbes had saved him the trouble of seeking the sanction of the Alpha in front of the next Moon Gathering, he hadn't quite declared their courting finished. Still, he'd declared her off limits. She was Kerr's mate. But did Lexi understand what Forbes had just done by declaring them a couple?

Her next words were as if she'd read his mind. "It's girlfriend for now. I'm gonna deal with the mate thing later, if you don't mind." Several of those assembled snickered at the look of relief Kerr knew was all over his face. She hadn't denied him in front of the Pack, which would have made courting her soul-breaking. Lexi swiveled to face her mother again, but spoke to Forbes. "She's gotta leave and take tha…Sun…*him* with her, right?"

Forbes's body was very relaxed. "You are certain you do not want to be the Alpha of the Denver—"

"Hell yes. No Alpha status for me."

Forbes made a few quick movements and every member of her mother's party now had two powerful escorts. Sunny, still unconscious from what she'd done to him, was hefted unceremoniously over her brother's shoulder. Lexi swallowed. Kerr badly wanted to wrap his arms around her, but he couldn't go to her yet. She was standing on her own, in front of the Pack. To go to her now would be like taking away her independence, making her a prisoner. He'd never cage his Lexi.

"Sir."

Every eye turned to Rafe. Some hostile, some with a measure of sympathy, but none were what you might call welcoming. It took guts for the boy to even open his mouth. Kerr wondered what the little bastard was up to.

"I would like permission to enter your territory, to apply to be a member of your Pack, after I drop my mother and stepfather off, that is."

The balls on the kid. Kerr's jaw worked as he chewed back his words. Her brother, he reminded himself. This was Lexi's brother. She might think she needed her family. She definitely wanted one of them close. Forbes pursed his lips. There were mutters among those assembled. The Alpha waited for them to die down. He turned to Lexi.

"Do you have any objections to him entering the territory as a new member of my Pack?"

Lexi shrugged, but hope shone in her eyes. "I have no power over what you do with your people. Or who you let in."

Forbes inclined his head. "True, but you do have a say in whether you want to see your brother on a regular basis again. I value you, Lexi. Your brother has yet to prove his worth to me. As a wolf or a man. I will be honest. I don't feel inclined to give him permission to stay. The tests he would be put through would not be kind, and that would jeopardize my relationship with you. Something I do not want to do."

The boy came to his senses. Realized that he was in danger of not getting what he wanted and turned to the one person who could help.

"Please. I…need to fix… Please. Please? Let me come back?" He stretched out his hand toward his sister. What was this little prick doing? Kerr paced a little as he watched the attempt to manipulate his mate one last time.

"You don't need her, Rafe. We'll be fine." Her mother's words were brave, but her voice was hollow. She was in trouble and she knew it.

Rafe's eyes never left his sister's. "What can I do to make this right?"

"I don't know. I love you. I will always love you. But I don't know if I can trust you. You'd have to prove it to me."

"How?"

Lexi shrugged. "I don't know."

Forbes's voice boomed through the chamber. "Your actions will have to speak for you, young one."

The boy drew in a deep breath and stretched to every inch of his height. He puffed up his chest. He gave Forbes an even gaze, even if his chin wobbled a bit.

"As will yours, if you betray my sister." The gesture was not unimpressive as a show of courage, but it couldn't hope to match Lexi's or intimidate Forbes. Even the boy knew it. Still, he tried. That was not nothing.

"So now blood is thicker than water? Because I'm an Alpha. Nice." Lexi glared at him, swaying on her feet.

Rafe smiled at her, their stepfather still dangling over his shoulder. "Blood was always thicker, sis. I just didn't pay attention to all of my blood."

Lexi stared, not sure what to say.

"You're gonna see me again, sis. And next time, you'll be happy to see me. Promise." She blinked. Rafe turned and carried his burden out the door. The other Denver Pack members followed him.

"Hmm. There's hope for that one yet," Forbes mumbled. All eyes turned to her and Lexi's legs finally gave out on her. She fell to the sands.

"Please let me help her now?" Kerr chafed at the invisible barrier that all the other wolves stood behind.

Forbes regarded Lexi regally. Then he grinned, and broke the distance between them. Kerr vibrated while he waited.

"What about it, Queller? Need help out of here or do you want to stumble out yourself no matter how long it takes?"

Lexi frowned. "I could use a hand," she admitted. Kerr scooped her up in the next second. He held her close for a moment, taking deep breaths and nuzzling her neck. His wolf quieted, now that his mate was safe and he could take care of her. But he payed attention to her body. She was just shy of feeling claustrophobic when he let up and gave her space. Well, as much space as he could while she was in his arms.

"I've got a room upstairs. You're staying here for the night," he informed her. He couldn't stop the command from coming out. He was too used to being in charge. It was something he'd have to change if he wanted to keep the woman in his arms. And he intended to keep her forever. She glared up at him. He could feel a stupid grin peeking out.

"Have you learned nothing, my friend?" Forbes's voice sounded amused. Kerr took a deep breath and fixed his expression. Lexi wouldn't appreciate his enthusiasm just now.

"Lexi, you look exhausted and we can help you contain any residual outbursts of your power up here so much easier. Would you stay?" There, that was better.

Lexi, looking drunk-tired, leaned up and kissed Kerr's cheek. "Good boy. You can teach an old dog new tricks."

The grin sneaked out again. Lexi's head lolled to one side and her breathing softened. She was falling asleep in his arms.

"Lexi?"

She flinched awake, her eyes rolling wildly around until they lighted on his face and she relaxed again, a lopsided smile appearing.

"Is there a bath in my future?"

Kerr's grin turned sly. "Can I join you?"

Lexi snorted. "How else am I gonna keep my head above the water?"

EPILOGUE

Kerr adjusted the framed print Lexi had given him. It hung over his bed at Promontory House. He'd moved back with his Alpha for a bit, until Lexi accepted his marriage proposal. He'd given her a promise ring the day after the events in the Argos. A blue sapphire she thought was fake because she couldn't handle the thought of being taken care of fiscally, yet. Kerr smiled at his mate's proclivities. Wait until she saw the princess cut, platinum engagement ring he'd picked out for her. He didn't really understand the princess part of the description, but Lexi deserved to be treated like one, so the saleswoman hadn't really had to work very hard.

Lexi didn't really want to know much about what happened to the Denver Pack, but Forbes and Kerr had kept up on events. Thea had lost her place as queen-bitch because Sunny was nowhere to be seen, having been ousted in a challenge two days after returning to Denver. That worried Kerr. But there were a lot of Shifters between Denver and here, and Forbes had put them all on alert for the power-hungry former Alpha.

The new Alpha, one of Forbes's friends from the "old days" as he put it, was just what that Pack needed. Since he was happily mated, Thea Gallows was out of luck. Lexi's brother would learn the proper way of the wolves from a proper Alpha. Forbes had seen something in the kid that day. Something that deserved a second chance. Kerr had a hard time with that, but he trusted Forbes. It wasn't like they were accepting the kid tomorrow.

Mrs. Faye was very disappointed with Lexi's appointment as assistant professor. She'd given the dean a list of dire possibilities, but rumor had it he'd laughed in Mrs. Faye's presence. The town was counting the days until the man moved. Lexi was thrilled with the assignment of mostly first years. Gleeful, if he told the truth.

He stepped back and examined his handy work. He hoped that Lexi would see how close he kept her gift when she came over tonight—if he could convince her to come over. She was taking their relationship s-l-o-w. There was no rush, but he was having a hard time waiting to take her to bed again. Then he'd take things really slow, and make her scream his name over and over… He rubbed his hands together in anticipation. They were going to have dinner at one of the fancy bed and breakfasts before coming, hopefully, here for some alone time in his rooms. He grabbed his jacket, swung out into the hall and whistled a happy tune.

The End

Coming Soon…Dark Moon Thunder

Excerpt from Dark Moon Thunder

His instinct was to shift and run to the cove Kassia had told him about. The wolf always wanted out. But he took the truck, a beat up wreck he kept running. It wasn't that he couldn't keep up with the times; it was simply difficult to remember to do it. Things worked until they didn't and then you fixed them. Too much throwing away these days. He crossed the bridge into Port Williams and turned down Starr's Point road. The barely two-lane roadway wound around, climbed sharply, then dipped just as fast. Houses hugged the broken painted lines closer to town. The farther away he got, the farther back the drives went, and farther apart. He smelled the sea long before he came up to the dirt road nearly hidden between two willow trees. This was a beach only locals could find. The truck bounced and gravel flew as he finally parked behind a green Camry.

"You drive like a maniac." A rail-thin figure appeared out of the woods, well out of reach of any stray rocks that might have flown from his tires. She had pink skin from the incessant wind, and her warm brown hair had escaped the severe bun she'd tied it up in to float around her face. She had on olive green cargo pants, a surplus army jacket over a black-and-flower blouse, and combat boots. A leather purse sat at her hip, a flashlight hooked to the strap crossing her chest. She might have come up to his chest if she stood on tiptoe.

"You're young." He slammed the truck door and cursed himself. He was hundreds of years old. Everyone looked young to him. And she was a Priestess. She'd take offense and there'd be hell to pay.

Rather than snipe at him, she snorted, pulled a cap from her back pocket and tucked it onto her head. "This way." She didn't turn to see if he followed. Used to authority, was she? Probably inherited her title then. Hmm.

The trek through the woods was short and uphill. Neither of them left much in the way of tracks, nor did either of them have any trouble with the shrubbery. He couldn't smell anything from her but a faint odor of roses and cardamom.

"Baking before you came here?"

She stopped short and turned to him. "No, why…ah, you can smell it. No, the spice isn't me."

He frowned. "What about the roses?"

She blushed a little. "That's me. I was in the greenhouse when they called."

"They?" He stayed put. More than one witch was here? "You didn't say anything about there being more witches on the phone."

She smirked and his estimation of her age edged upwards. "There's just me, unless you count the dead. I sent the others home with Maverick. Now, unless you're afraid…" It was his turn to snort. "Lead on, little Priestess."

She grunted, piqued by his 'little' comment, and hiked up the hillside double time. When he came up beside her in the little clearing at the top, she was huffing from the exertion while he didn't feel a thing. She motioned to the two older women lying in what had to be an unnatural clearing this close to the ocean.

"What do you think?" she puffed, hands on knees while she watched him closely. He turned to the scene.

The elderly ladies were in their nightgowns, the material flowered, faded and thin. That alone would have killed them last night, given the frost. Their lips were blue, their hands clasped in front of them. Their hair was unbound, silky and spread out like a halo around both their heads. The wind didn't touch it, though the leaves of the trampled bushes and saplings of the man-made clearing wavered. They both smelled like cardamom.

"There's no death scent," he whispered. He squatted down, tilting his head as he let the wolf out a little. The Priestess let a little gasp out and swallowed.

Good, witchling. See the hunter I am and do not forget my claws.

Forbes snorted at his wolf side. The witch waited patiently while he slunk around the circle, trying to pick up a scent other than cardamom. Not even the broken plants and trees gave off a distressed odor, almost as if they'd been lulled into death peacefully. He came up to the Priestess again and just to tease her, leaned in close to her ear and took a deep breath. She didn't move. It almost impressed him. He sniffed her shoulder, her bag, her hip and started to lean in close to her bottom.

"Aaand that'll do." She danced a few feet away from him, swatting the air just above where his nose had been headed. "You have my scent, wolf-king. Tell me what you can about my witches."

He chuckled and straightened. He liked her title for him. "They aren't exactly dead, are they?"

She frowned at him. "What do you mean?"

"When a body dies, their bowels and bladder let loose. These two don't give off a hint of it. There's no mess under them. Every once in a while I hear a heartbeat that isn't mine and isn't yours. Somehow, they aren't dead. How'd you do it and why show me?"

She picked at her lip. Walked the circle until she was directly across from him. She knelt and muttered a few words. The hair on the back of his neck stood up, but nothing else happened. If she'd just cast a spell against him, it had failed. She stood and stared at him for a long moment. He waited patiently. He was a hunter, after all. Finally, she came to some decision, and gave him a terse nod.

"It wasn't us, wolf-king."

His smile didn't reach his eyes. He knew they were still yellowed from the wolf and often chilled those not used to his stare. The witch stood her ground, nothing but the fists at her side showed her discomfort.

"It wasn't one of us that did this, wolf-king," she repeated. He could hear and smell the truth in her statement.

"Shifters don't possess this type of magic." Was she trying to accuse him or one of his wolves of this?

She held up her hands. "I'm not saying it wasn't a witch," she amended. "Just that it wasn't one of *my* witches."

He stroked his chin, thoughtfully. He didn't think witches fought over territory the way wolves did, but he'd never dealt with many witches. Unless you counted killing them. Could this be some sort of declaration against the Burntcoat Coven? If so, why involve the Fundy Bay Pack? Was she going to ask for his help in her business? That would be a first. And not something he was inclined to give at the moment. Let the witches figure out their own problems.

"Do you know what this is?" He waved a hand at the prone women.

"They're sway-locked."

Forbes glanced up in surprise. He'd heard of the condition but never before witnessed it. Witches tended to hide their weak and sick, like a wolf Pack. A thought struck him. She nodded before he could speak.

"That's right, wolf-king. They're not the only ones. The twins two moons ago, plus we found two children last month, and now these two. Someone, or something, is attacking my Coven."

"And what has that to do with me or my Pack?" he crossed his arms and gave the little witchling a glare that had cowered many a wolf cub in his time.

"Because the last time someone went after witches like this around here, they went after the Pack next. Help me find who's doing this now or face it *after* they've collected enough power to put even you down, wolf-king. What do you say?"

ABOUT THE AUTHOR

Taryn Blackthorne was born in Nova Scotia. She learned how to read before she started school, often making up stories to entertain her friends. In fifth grade, she was sent back to her desk to write instead of doing her math…because her teacher wanted to see what happened next. Since then, Taryn hasn't stopped. She divides her time between her family (including fur babies), her keyboard, and her teaching.

DEAR READER,

Thank you for reading *High Tide at Harvest Moon*! I hope you enjoyed it. If you did, please help other readers find this book by lending it to a friend or writing a review. Every review helps a reader decide whether a book is right for them. I love to hear from readers, and I look forward to connecting with you on Twitter (@ tarynblackthorn), Facebook (www.facebook.com/paranormalauthortarynblack-thorne/) and my website (www.tarynblackthorne.com)

For exclusive content and information about the Pack members, settings around town and tidbits from the next Fundy book, join the Facebook group Fundy Bay Pack .

Hope to see you soon!
Taryn